Highest Bidder

DAWN ANDERSON

AUTHOR'S NOTE

Highest Bidder is intended for mature audiences only. This book contains on page intimate scenes and flashbacks from an abusive relationship (not between the two main characters).

PLAYLIST
SPOTIFY: HIGHEST BIDDER

Walls - Emery
Just The Way You Are - Bruno Mars
You Belong With Me - Taylor Swift
Someone Like You - Adele
Party Rock Anthem - LMFAO
Tonight Tonight - Hot Chelle Rae
We Found Love - Rihanna
Somebody that I used to Know - Gotye
One Thing - One Direction
A Thousand Years - Christina Perri
Without You - David Guetta
Just A Kiss - Lady Antebellum
Love You Like A Love Song - Selena Gomez
Give Me Everything - Pitbull
Pumped Up Kicks - Foster The People

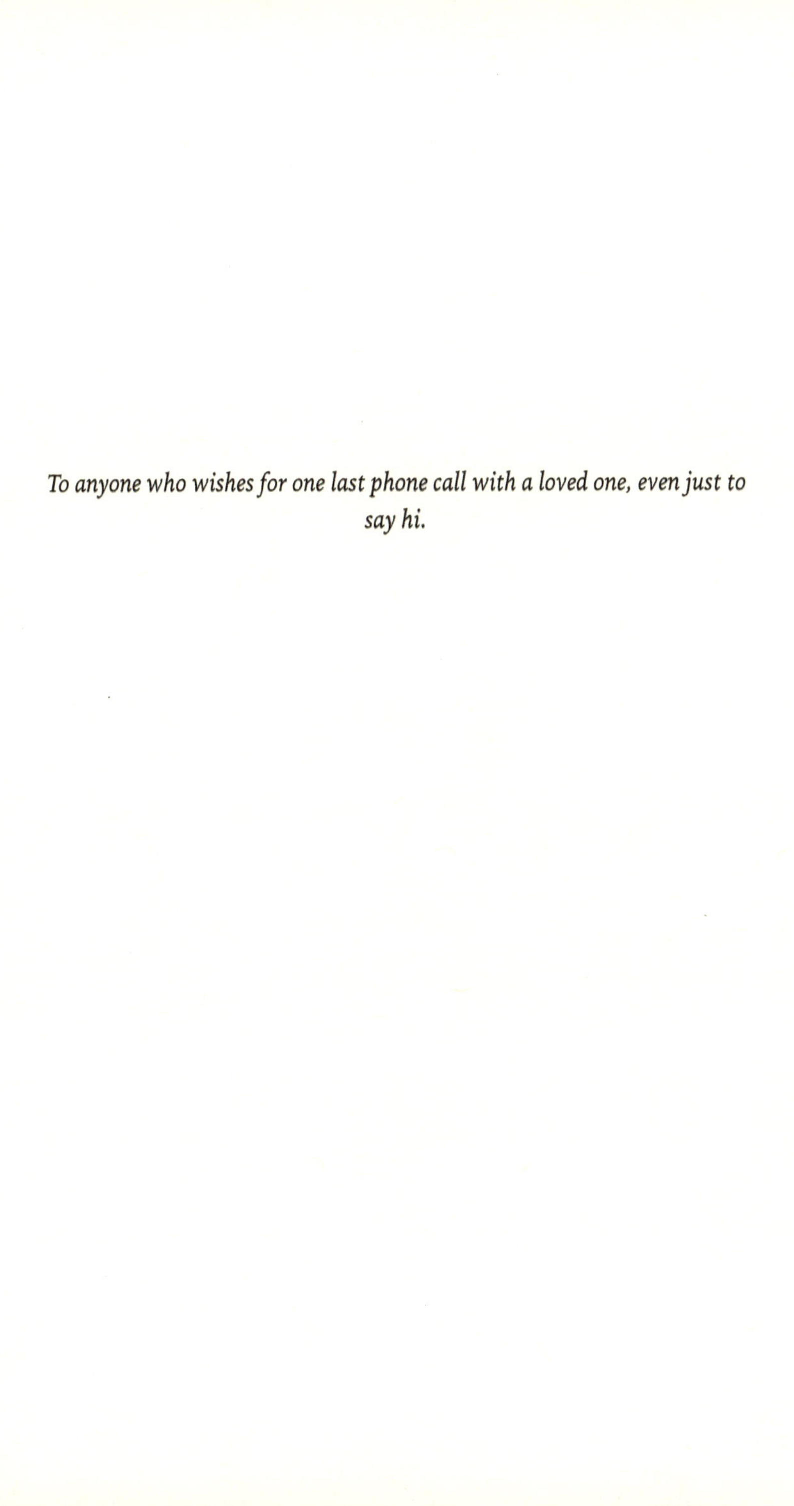

To anyone who wishes for one last phone call with a loved one, even just to say hi.

1

MYLES

Gʀᴀᴠᴇʟ ᴄʀᴜɴᴄʜᴇs under my truck's tires as I pull into work. I hope today is the day I get the opportunity to prove myself. It's past time, and I've paid my dues. My first break in the auction industry came fresh out of high school. I worked hard and soaked in everything I could, refusing to take the opportunity for granted. Then two years later, Manheim gave me a shot. It's been eight long years of slowly rising through the ranks ever since. I started on the worst lanes, but now I'm only one step away from reaching my goal.

Manheim has auto auctions all over the country—five within driving distance of central Florida. For an auction to be successful, it has to run like a well-oiled machine. Everyone has an important role to play, but no one is more important than the auctioneer.

My boots scuff the pavement as I walk into the large white building, and drivers jump into cars to park in position. Gusts of cold air hit my face when I pull open the front door. I nod at the clerks behind the front desk while dealers impatiently wait their turn.

I've been a ringman, basically an auctioneer's right-hand man, for close to a decade now, and I'm a damn good one. It's my job to yip back and forth between bids to try to get the dealers to write the biggest check, and I never miss a bid. But even though I love my job, adrenaline pumps through my veins at the thought of finally standing behind that podium and being the person *actually* responsible for selling the cars. I get a taste of this each week when I fill in for the auctioneers during their breaks, but it just isn't enough.

Give me a mic. I can sell some cars. But auctioneers rarely retire or get fired, which means there are limited lanes available and claiming one of them can be difficult. A promotion is hard to come by. But by some miracle, an auctioneer retired last week, and I know this is my chance to run my own lane.

"Good morning, Ann," I say, passing by a woman with blonde hair, wearing a pantsuit. She's our General Manager's secretary, and nothing happens at this auction that she doesn't know about. Ann is always friendly, but by the way she's grinning at me, I think she knows it's my turn too.

The office is filled with the rowdy commotion of voices talking over each other as the office workers try to help as many dealers as possible. It won't be long before the sale starts, and dealers run around bidding on cars. I love the chaos of it all. Walking through the office, a dealer bumps into me and, not even bothering to say sorry, he scurries away to get to a counter. I watch as he demands the office clerk to give him a bidder number. He slaps the sticker across his chest. Turning, I see another dealer put one on the back of their clipboard.

I wave at a few people walking by as I enter the large meeting room. I haven't seen JT yet. He normally strolls in right as it's time for the meeting to start, while I'm always at least five minutes early. Griffin, the general manager, comes walking in. He stands in front of us, his deep voice echoing around the room. "Alright! Today isn't just another Tuesday. We all know the second Tuesday of every month has a shitload of cars. So we need everyone to be on their game today. There will be twenty-five lanes running. Check the schedule, get to your lanes, and let's sell some cars." He rubs his hands together. "Oh, one last thing. We have a new auctioneer joining our team straight from Oklahoma. We all know Conrad Smith."

Holy Shit! Of course, we all know him. He's the best cattle auctioneer in Oklahoma. He sometimes makes guest appearances at other auctions and always blows everyone out of the water. He's been my idol my entire career. He prefers to sell cattle, but that man can sell anything.

I look around for him. I'm a big guy at six foot two inches, easily towering over a crowd of people. The only person who seems out of place is standing toward the front. I can only make out the top of their head because of how short they are, but it's clear it's a woman. Who is that? There are never any women in these meetings. Not because women can't be auctioneers, but because not very many are. I keep trying to peer around people to get a better look and try to catch a glimpse of Conrad at the same time.

"This is Hunter Smith." Griffin motions toward the woman. "Come on over here. She is Conrad's daughter. So it's like having him here since she learned from the best."

Whoa. I feel my eyes double in size before I blink, making sure the woman standing in front of us isn't a mirage. I've seen beautiful women before, but I've never been struck speechless by one. She's gorgeous, with unruly brown curly hair, and a big, bright smile that has me forgetting how to breathe.

"Let's welcome Hunter as our newest auctioneer. Be sure to say hello. She'll be starting on lane eighteen." Griffin turns, meeting my gaze. "Myles, help her out and show her around. You'll be her ringman. Make sure she has a good first day." Griffin gives me a slight nod, then turns his attention back toward the room. I open my mouth to speak, but nothing comes out. They gave the open position to this woman. My heart races inside my chest. I can't seem to focus enough to acknowledge him. "Okay everyone, let's go to work."

Everyone files out, but I'm frozen in the same spot, wondering what just happened. At first, I was excited to meet a legend's daughter. Now I'm purely pissed. They had an opening, and instead of giving it to someone like me or even JT, who are here every week working our asses off, they give it to this out-of-towner. I have no doubt she's good. How can you not be when you have Conrad Smith giving you a leg up in this industry?

I'm jostled out of my spiral when JT barrels over and slings his arm around my neck. "Hey! What did I miss? Anything new?" he asks, looking around the room. I know the moment he spots Hunter because he perks up. "Wait a second. Who is that pretty little thing?"

I roll my eyes. Of course, he was late today and missed the announcement that this *pretty little thing* took my dream job. Unlike JT, I'm not happy about being a ringman. I'm ready to run the lane, sell cars, and make more money. My mama hasn't said it, but I know money is tight. I want to be able to take care of her like she always took care of me. I'd like to pay for her house and her bills, so she never has to work again. After my deadbeat father left her high and dry, she worked enough to provide for me growing up. I had thought today could be the start of repaying that debt. Griffin lets me fill in whenever there's an opening, and the auctioneers have me take over while they take their breaks. I don't just let the cars roll through the lanes, I get a lot of them sold. Dealers take notice when I step up. A few have even mentioned that I'm made for the role and request I be the one to sell their cars. I felt like I was right there, so close to getting the job I've always wanted. Fuck. I need to get some air.

I shouldn't be completely shocked. Auctions are filled with liars and managers who cut corners just to spend less. Dealers are always trying to pull one over on you and kiss your ass to get a better deal on a car. Since they're independent contractors, auctioneers are only looking out for themselves. Ringmen are also independent contractors, but most are only doing it until they get promoted to auctioneer. It's a stepping stone to the next promotion.

"Hello. Are you Myles?" a sweet voice pulls me from the chaos in my head. I turn and meet the most beautiful eyes I've ever seen. Ones as green as I imagine the hills of Ireland to be. When it's obvious I'm not going to answer–not because I don't want to, but because I've been struck mute–she continues, "Griffin said you could show me around. I'm Hunter. It's nice to meet you." She sticks out her hand and gives me an award-winning smile. My eyes slowly fall to the hand hovering in front of me. I'm torn. This gorgeous woman stands in front of me, smiling as if we were friends. I so badly want to take her hand in mine, but knowing she's the reason I'm not getting a promotion grates on me. My blood boils at the realization that loyalty means nothing to Griffin. I clench my fists to keep them from shaking before I do something stupid—like storming out of here and quitting without looking back.

Knowing I need to get away from her to calm down, I jab my finger at the doors across the hall. "Bathrooms are there. Lanes are through the double doors on the left"—my hand sweeps in that general direction—"we're lane eighteen where all the Toyotas are sold." Gesturing in the other direction, I say, "Cafeteria is around the corner to the right." I bring my gaze back to her and find a perplexed look on her face as her eyes shoot from one direction to the next. I clear my throat to get her attention back on me. "The lane will start at 9 a.m. sharp." Once her head bobs into a nod, I turn and hightail it out of there, never bothering to shake her hand. When JT calls after me, I ignore him, leaving him with her, and keep walking. I've got to get some air.

2

———

HUNTER

THE EXIT DOOR of the building slams, distancing myself from this jerk of a man as frustration vibrates through me. *Some welcome.* When Griffin brought me up in front of a room full of men, my sights zeroed in on Myles. I didn't know who he was, but he stood out. He towered over everyone and pierced me with those eyes. I couldn't stop myself from looking him over. His defined muscles in his arms and shoulders were pronounced in his long sleeve button-up shirt. Wearing a worn hat on top of his short brown hair, his chiseled jaw dusted with facial hair. I thought it was my lucky day when Griffin introduced him as my ringman. But then he opened his big mouth, proving not all men are gentlemen. It's too much to hope for the whole package— someone good-looking *and* nice. Now I want to smack his attractive face. It probably wouldn't be the best move on my first day. But seriously? What kind of welcome was that?

I came here knowing I would have assholes to deal with. It comes with the job, but that was ridiculous. Just because my dad is the best doesn't mean everyone is nice to me. They're usually only nice when he is within sight, but I can handle myself. I came because I was tired of living in my dad's shadow. I wanted to make him proud and make a name for myself without his help. But once I said I was leaving, Dad was already talking to someone about a job for me before our conversation ended. I told him I wanted to do it myself, but he's so protective. He also knew I needed to get out of a bad situation with my ex-boyfriend. He's always been on my side. So when the job offers started rolling in, I knew it was all because of him. The first one came from an auction in New York. I didn't hesitate turning it down, knowing it would be too cold for me. When Manheim Orlando called however, it was impossible to say no. I know not everyone has this opportunity or the connections, so I'm determined to be something.

I realize I'm still staring after Myles when I hear someone clear their throat. It startles me, bringing me back to the present. "Hi. I'm JT Moore. Sorry about that guy." He juts his chin toward where Myles disappeared. "His pet frog bit him this morning."

I look at him, shocked. Then we burst out laughing. I hardly noticed the man standing next to Myles until he stormed off. Now that he has my attention, I see JT is a tall, hunky man. He has the type of body you get by working hard. There's no way he got all those muscles from the gym alone. He has sandy brown hair that ends right above his shoulders. Half of his hair is up in a small man bun. I have never seen someone pull off the look, but he definitely can. There's a fun type of twinkle in his eyes, like he doesn't like to take things too seriously. He stands there casually, thumbs laced in his belt loops, and acts like he has nowhere else to be.

"Hey, JT. I'm used to it, although I was hoping I'd get lucky and have a decent ringman." I pause, looking in the direction Myles fled, then back to JT. "I don't need him, though." That's an understatement. I don't. I was thrown to the wolves—the dealers, ringmen, and other auctioneers—on a regular basis to see if *I had what it takes to make it.* They aren't known for pleasantries.

"Oh, you're the new auctioneer." He nods, understanding

written across his face as his gaze flashes to the doors then back to me. "Myles will be on the lane. You can count on that. He's a damn good ringman too. He just"—JT pauses, pressing his lips into a straight line—"Well, I'm going to give it to you straight. He thinks you took his job. So he's a little sore."

Did I take his job? I guess most ringmen are waiting for their chance, but they're usually a little more professional, unlike the guy I just saw. He could still surprise me though.

"Well, if he's so good, why would they allow a woman to come in and take a spot that should've been his? Sure, I have my dad's last name, but it means nothing at all to the car auction world." I lightly poke his chest a couple of times and add, "But in a male-dominated industry, it doesn't seem likely." I stare at him. These men will walk all over me unless I stand my ground and make my confidence clear. Yes, a phone call got me in the door, but I'm the one who makes sure they keep calling me back because I'm damn good at what I do.

He blinks a few times, then smirks. "I guess you're right." Rubbing his chin, he chuckles. "I like you." He returns the gesture with a poke to my shoulder. "Alright, do you want me to *actually* show you around?"

I like JT, but I don't need anyone's help.

"No thanks. I can handle it. Thanks, though." I have plenty of time to get my bearings. I'd rather just take a look at the lane I'm running and then grab food in the cafeteria. I smile at him and walk out the door.

I push on the heavy glass door that leads outside to the lanes. The large ceiling fans whip my hair around my face, forcing me to capture it between my hands until I'm past the force of the draft. I breathe in the strong car exhaust and rubber smells as I walk down the row of lanes. Massive garage doors are on either side so cars can pass straight through as they are slowly shown. Looking toward an auction block on the left side, I see an auctioneer standing behind a counter a few feet above the main floor. A low rumble turns into a piercing screech as he tests the microphone. The block clerk next to him clicks a few buttons as the TV screens flicker to life, ready to display the prices for each car.

The hot Florida air surrounds me as I continue down the lanes. Many pairs of eyes shoot in my direction, flipping my stomach with unease at the unwanted attention. What I'm not used to is the absence of my dad. I pause once I get to my lane and let it all sink in. This is my chance. I can do this. There's no doubt in my mind. The only issue rests with the men staring at me. If I don't at least get a few of them on my side, then it won't matter how good I am. I'll be gone before I even get a chance. I walk toward the auction block to where I'll sit. Someone comes barreling around the corner and plows me over, causing me to fall hard on my ass. *Fuck! That hurt!*

"Oh shit! I'm so sorry! Are you okay?"

I got knocked to the ground pretty hard. Thankfully, I'm wearing jeans, so I didn't flash anyone in the fall. I start to get up and blink a few times out of shock. I brush my hands across my butt and legs to get any dirt off. That's going to leave a bruise.

"Yeah. I'm okay." Readjusting my white blouse and jeans, I look up at the girl who whacked me with her enormous purse. "Hello. I'm Hunter," I say, reaching out my hand, but she grabs me by the shoulders and squeezes me tight. Okay, what is happening right now?

"Oh, my god! When they said someone named Hunter was our new auctioneer, I assumed it would be a man. I can't believe it! I came here right away to get everything set up for the new *man* whose ass I was going to have to kiss. But you're a girl! I'm excited! Who knew these people had the balls to go against the grain and hire a female auctioneer? Oh God. I'm talking too much." The girl covers her face with her hands. "I get this way when I'm nervous. I guess even though you aren't a guy, I still might need to kiss your ass, so you don't bury me today. Oh!"—

she sticks her hand out— "I'm Jess, by the way." She finally stops speaking and gives a small smile.

I blink a few times. I don't think I saw her take a breath in the whole spiel, but who am I to judge? She must keep the money I say on the screen, so the dealers know exactly what I'm selling and can see the latest bid amount. So she's sort of like an auctioneer's scribe.

I shake her hand. "Um, no, please don't *kiss my ass*. But I'm assuming you're my block clerk?" She nods. "Okay, have you worked this lane before? Anything I should know? I'm not sure my ringman will be much help." Again, that's an understatement. I'm not even sure if the asshole will show up.

"Oh, you met Myles!" I swear I see stars in her eyes, and I fight the urge to roll mine. "He is so great! Kind of a loner, but he's close with a few other auctioneers and ringmen. Um, the lane is pretty much standard. We start at 9 a.m., and it's usually finished by noon, if not sooner. Depending on how quickly you want it to go. There's usually a lot of action on both the floor and online. So the screen up there will show when I have an internet bidder."

She gestures to a TV screen hung on a lane divider. I imagine all the microphones blaring to life as the auctioneers begin their chat. The noise roars from the speakers, bouncing off the walls. I can picture the lane across from me trying to compete with how fast we go. I'll send my car out first, but they may sell their vehicle before I can say, "sold." The lane dividers stretch toward the ground to help keep the sound on the appropriate lane. Though it won't completely block out neighboring lane commo-tion. I can still yell to the auctioneer across from me as we chal-lenge each other.

Jess continues, "I'll also point it out if you don't see it. The toyota seller"—she points to an older man with a clipboard and a furrowed brow, standing right outside the door—"will stand next to you and show you the amount they need to sell the car."

Not all cars sell, unfortunately. You need a dealer or auction rep standing with you to show how much they can sell the car for. On this lane, the auction rep will point to the number on the run list that I have to get to sell.

I admire her long rainbow-striped maxi skirt. It takes guts to wear such a bold look. Her blonde hair is wrapped in a messy bun on top of her head. She has large, brown eyes with long eyelashes. "Of course, you know all this." Jess fidgets with her large purse. She's gorgeous with a good amount of quirky. Her energy level is unmatched. Maybe I'll have at least one friend here. Other block clerks I've worked with are usually not very happy that I'm a woman, or that I don't like to slow down. I'm not a jerk to them if they miss a bidder number, but I do expect them to keep up. My dad taught me if you don't keep your lane moving, then the seller isn't happy. If your seller isn't happy, then you shouldn't be happy. Since I don't have a reputation here yet, I want to start on the right foot with my team. So far it hasn't panned out with my ringman. But I'm hoping my block clerk and I will be able to flow.

Block clerks are used to auctioneers, ringmen, and dealers not being the friendliest to them. Since auctioneers are the ones responsible for selling the dealer's inventory, and block clerks just process the sale, they don't see any reason to give a shit about the clerk sitting on the auction block. That's not always the case, but I know they always have their walls up just in case.

"Thank you for the tips. I won't keep you. I'll see you back here when the lane is about to start." Giving her a friendly smile, I go up the stairs. Scanning the lanes, the calm before the storm finally gives me a moment to take a breath and be thankful for making it this far. Soon, dealers will be running from lane to lane to bid on different cars. The speakers will blare so loud that your head will ache when it's quiet. Then the cars will drive through, and I will attempt to sell over three hundred of them in three hours.

I've been doing this since I learned how to talk, so I rarely get nervous. But this is my first job away from my dad, and the butterflies have made a home in my stomach. I still remember my dad teaching me how to sell a teddy bear or candy to anyone who would listen. He always said, "It doesn't matter what you sell, auctioneers should be able to sell anything." He used to sneak me into his jobs, and I would watch him, amazed.

My mom never wanted this life for me. In fact, if she had it her way, I would be married off by now. She still thinks I should have stayed with my ex, Steve. He was always a kiss-ass and didn't care about me other than how he could use me to get to my dad. Steve's the main reason my dad didn't hesitate to help me leave. My mom doesn't know what he's actually like, doesn't believe me is more like it. He was always the perfect gentleman, until he had a few drinks in him. Then everyone needed to steer clear.

He showed me his true colors one night, and I got the heck out of there. I just packed my things and left. I wanted to get out of Oklahoma City anyway and this auction position was the perfect opportunity. I know my dad was sad about me leaving. Also, he doesn't care as much for car auctions; his heart is with cattle auctions. But we looked before coming, and there weren't many around. Car auctions are way more common than cattle auctions though. And if I want to make a living doing this, I can't be picky starting out. But I'm going to try to find a cattle auction myself. He would be excited if I were selling cattle. It would be like a little piece of home.

3

MYLES

THE MIDDLE of August is smoldering hot, and the Florida humidity is suffocating as always. The lane starts in five minutes. Looking around, I see dealers running from lane to lane, often running into people, and dealers looking at the cars that are waiting to come in. I get a feeling today is going to be a different kind of sale. I've already seen men whisper while they point at Hunter with a scowl on their faces. Whenever I've worked with or seen a female auctioneer, I've noticed they can get harassed a bit by the dealers. I may not like her being here, but I won't tolerate anything unprofessional. Maybe one day, I'll get my shot, but today it's my job to work with her.

I walk toward the lane outside, passing cars when I spot Hunter standing on the auction block. She seems deep in thought with her nose scrunched and brows pulled together over eyes so intense I can't help but be drawn to her. God, she's beautiful. And that hair. It seems to have a mind of its own, the way it tumbles around her shoulders and down her back. Because my eyes are on her and not paying attention to those around me, I stumble when JT bumps into me. Our lanes face each other, so we usually have a little bit of fun messing around throughout the sale.

"Are you ready for this?" JT asks, slugging my shoulder as he grins in the direction of the auction block Hunter stands on.

JT has been my best friend for eleven years. He transferred to my high school during our senior year. I wasn't a social person, and he seemed to think I was someone who needed a friend. He couldn't fathom someone actually enjoying being alone. I've been stuck with him ever since. Not that I'm complaining. He always has my back, and I don't know what I would do without him. He's become more like a brother to me than anything else. So he knows when something is off.

"Want to talk about what happened after the meeting?" he asks another question without waiting for me to answer the first.

I cast my eyes in Hunter's direction and hold back a curse as her eyes meet mine, catching me staring. I allow her to get too far into my head and not in a good way. I second guess if the dream I have will ever be a reality. My pride has taken a pretty hard blow today.

"Nope," I bite out.

He nods. "Well, I'm going to enjoy my view." He looks over at Hunter, giving her a wink.

He can never keep it in his pants. I risk taking a glance over my shoulder and see her giving him a bright smile. As soon as she notices me looking, her expression morphs into a scowl. She turns back to JT, and he chuckles.

"Think you can do your job without drooling?" he asks.

He has no idea how hard today is going to be. "What? Seems to me you are the one who might have a problem doing your job. I'll just be here when she screws up, and they need me to take over." I say it like it's a fact that is bound to happen, although I'm not naive enough to believe that based on where she got her training. JT's eyes widen and flit to something over my shoulder.

"Oh, is that why you're here? To save the day?" Hunter's warm and intoxicating voice fills my ears, and I slowly turn around, cringing inwardly at what she just heard.

Where the hell did she come from? Had I known she was standing behind me, I wouldn't have said something so arrogant. But in reality, was anything I said untrue? She may not like it, but there's a good chance of it happening. Nerves are a bitch, especially when you're starting a new job. I stand by what I said, even though I didn't mean to say it to her face.

I take a step back and look into her eyes. "Look, that wasn't meant for your ears." I stuff my hands in my pockets and shrug. "But, yeah—if I'm being honest—I don't think you're going to be able to hack it. It's a lot harder than you think. Not sure even the great Conrad Smith could keep you from sinking."

"Hmm." She taps her finger against her chin in mock deliberation. "Okay. Well, I was going to try to be nice and let you know you need to bring the cars in. But since you're too busy gossiping out here like a little schoolgirl. . . I'll do your job for you. Mike was it?" she taunts.

"Myles," I say through gritted teeth. "I'll get the cars, sweetheart." I taunt right back, glaring so hard I see red. This wildhaired beauty is going to be the death of me. I want her gone. Why the hell would Griffin hire this girl? What could he possibly gain from getting on her daddy's good side?

She swings around, her hair flying every which way as I turn back toward JT, whose mouth is pinched into a smirk. A telltale sign he's about to burst out laughing. I send him a glare while I follow the little miss back inside the lane. He's enjoying this too much, the asshole. I watch as her hips turn toward the stairs to go up the auction block. I look over and see JT walking down his lane to get his cars, too. Why am I the one getting stuck with the newbie princess? Why didn't she just stay where her daddy can give her a leg up?

This is going to be a long ass day. I take a look at the run list. We have over three hundred cars to get through. On a good day, Dave, the auctioneer usually assigned to Toyota, could get through three hundred in three and a half hours. I have another auction to get to. Auctioneers, ringmen, and a lot of the block clerks drive from auction to auction to run the sales. We drive all over Florida. I don't have time to go at a slow pace for this woman, even if she is auction royalty. Whatever, I was probably right. They will end up having me take over for her. I usually get to fill in when my lane gets done or if Dave ever wants a break. So even though I think they should have given me the job straight, I know it'll be mine soon. I knock on the hood of the first car to let the driver know we are ready. He pulls forward and follows me back down the lane. Other lanes are starting up, too. It's the quiet rumble before the storm. With this many lanes and this many cars, I know it's about to get loud. I look directly into Hunter's deep eyes. My heart skips a beat, as if she's looking into my soul. She goes to open her mouth but gives me a wink first, then starts rattling off, leaving me standing here shocked.

"Lane eighteen, let's have a good day, and let's roll. Number one, do I hear twenty-five thousand dollar bid, twenty-five dollar bid, twenty-five thousand, twenty-six thousand dollar bid, twenty-six dollar bid, twenty-six, twenty-five thousand five-dollar bid, twenty-five five, twenty-five dollar bid, twenty-five thousand two dollar bid, four, six, eight...."

She keeps going while I'm standing here gaping after her. I was not expecting that. She's got the smoothest chant. The dealers are all bidding. Jess is clicking away with the online bids. "Twenty-seven, two, four, six...send it out, eight." It's then I quickly bring myself out of whatever mind-altering trance she has me under, realizing she's telling me or the driver to get the car out of here. I jump into action, knocking on the hood to signal the car out before she can finish selling the car.

"Sold," she calls out, as the next car rolls into its place. "Twenty-nine thousand one hundred dollars to bidder number thirteen-seventy four. Number two, do I hear thirty thousand, thirty-dollar bid, twenty-eight thousand dollar bid, twenty-eight, two, four, six, eight, twenty-nine thousand, two, four—"

Before she can say anything else, I send out the car and start taking bids. "YUP!" I yell, pointing at one bidder. "YUP!" Pointing at another. I point back to the first one when he nods. "YUP!" Hunter and I get into a steady rhythm. If I missed a bid, she got it. If she missed a bid, I would point out who the new bidder was. I've been on this lane for over three years, and I've never seen this many cars sold and so many bidders bidding on the same cars. Don't get me wrong, this is usually a very good lane to be on. We always sell over fifty percent of the cars, but this is something completely different. It's like the bidders are drawn to her, and Hunter knows how to suck them in. The next thing I know, the last car pulls into the lane.

"Alright everyone, here's our final beauty." Hunter motions toward a top of the line, 2011 silver Toyota Avalon. She looks back out at the audience walking around the lane and places a hand on her hip. "Now, I have a rule on my lane. I always sell my last car. I like to end the day right. You all have been amazing, so please don't let me down." Taking a breath, she brings the microphone back to her mouth and begins her chant. "Car, three hundred and thirty. Twenty-nine thousand dollar bid, twenty-nine dollar bid, twenty-nine, two, four, six..."

Hunter keeps going, and I send out the last car, pointing out each bid. Usually, the last car of the day is a little harder to sell since dealers usually head into the office to pay for their cars. They could also have too many already. But this one seems to want to sell, or maybe the bidders don't want to let the beautiful auctioneer down.

"Sold. Thirty-one thousand one hundred to bidder number twelve-eighty-one. Thank you everyone. Enjoy the rest of your day." With an enormous smile, she turns off her microphone and turns to talk to Jess.

I look over, and JT's lane is still running. He jerks his head, trying to get me to join him on his side. I head on over to see what he wants.

"Hey, give Aaron a break." JT points over his shoulder to his auctioneer. "He said he needs a breather."

I give him a little glare because he usually gives his auctioneer a break, but I'm not going to pass up getting up there. I go over and tap Aaron on the shoulder, letting him know I'm here when he finishes the car. He sells it, unhooks his mic, and lets me plug in the one I always keep in my back pocket. I turn my hat around backward and begin with the next car.

"Alright. Two hundred and seventy-nine. Twenty-six thousand bid, twenty-six, now two, now four, now six, now eight, eight, eight bid. Sold twenty-six thousand six hundred, bidder thirteen-fifty-six." I open my mouth to start on the next car, but something catches my eye. I look up and see Hunter is watching me from the floor. She looks small compared to all the people around her. I shake my head to get my focus back and continue my chant. After about twenty more cars, Aaron comes back, and I hand his lane back over. When I get to the floor near JT, Hunter has disappeared. JT gives me a smirk when he sees me looking around. Rather than trying to talk to him over all the noise, I lightly punch his arm and walk away. I'm still blown away by how well she did today. It was not at all how I thought it would go, although that doesn't change my disdain for her being here in the first place. Maybe this will be the only auction to hire her, and I can get the position at the other sales. I'll just keep telling myself that, but I have a feeling I'm going to be seeing her again real soon. That thought alone annoys and excites me at the same time. Whatever the fuck that means.

4

HUNTER

LISTENING to Myles on the auction block, I understand it. He's good. He knows what he's doing, and seeing him run that lane probably could have made me weak in the knees if he wasn't such an ass.

Yes, my dad taught me everything I know, but I still had to fight to get where I am. I'm a lot better than most men, yet more times than not, they get the positions over me. Even with my dad calling around, if I suck, it wouldn't matter what my last name is. I'm thankful the GM, Griffin, has given me a shot. I need to find him before I head out. The biggest thing I need to do is find a place to live because I don't want to stay in the hotel for much longer. However, I know better than to buy a house before getting several jobs lined up. I'm hoping I proved myself today, and Griffin will put in a good word for me at other Manheim auctions around the state. Usually, other auctioneers can give you some leads on where to go, but so far, none of them are talking to me. That's fine, I'll let my work speak for itself. The auction rep for Toyota said it was their best sale to date. I sold over eighty percent of the cars that ran through my lane. Not too bad, if I do say so myself.

"Hey!" a booming voice behind me carries over the speakers.

Looking over my shoulder, I see a man jogging up to me. I smile. "Hello!" I recognize him from my lane. He bought about a quarter of the cars that ran through. "You're bidder thirteen-seventy-four, right?" After saying the bidder number so many times, it tends to stick in your brain. Also, since most dealers are middle-age, the younger ones always stand out, especially this guy, with his shaggy blonde hair, brown eyes, and megawatt smile. The fact that he's wearing a white T-shirt that stretches over well-defined biceps and has long tan legs extending from black tailored shorts doesn't hurt either. The guy is damn hot. I definitely didn't mind the sight of him as he bid on and won a good amount of those cars.

Nodding, he grins back at me. "Yeah. I'm James with Carmax." He puts his hand out as he steps up beside me. "You did amazing today," he says, raising his voice to be heard over the speakers.

"Thanks," I say as we head toward the office.

"Seriously," James continues. "When I heard we had a new auctioneer, I didn't know what to expect. One thing is for sure, I had to stay on my toes the whole time or you'd sell a car before I even got a chance to bid on it. I wasn't expecting that, but it kind of made the sale more exciting." Smiling at me over his shoulder, he opens the door to the office for me.

"Oh, you had more than enough time, and you bought plenty. Need to spread around the deals." I laugh because that isn't the first time I've heard that type of thing from dealers. I don't like lazy dealers who want to wait till the end to bid. Or who try slowing me down to give them more of a chance to look at their phones or whatever else they are doing. I won't beg for a bid, and I won't wait for a dealer either. When we are in the lanes with one make of car, the rep has his numbers in front of us when we need them, so there is no reason to take it slow. I don't have to wait for the different dealers to get on and off the block then wait for them to show me the number they need. These sales are my favorite. You can fly, and as long as the reps are getting their cars for the right prices, they are happy.

James chuckles. "True. Well, I wanted to introduce myself to the beautiful new auctioneer. I'm usually assigned to the Toyota lane, so I'll be seeing you again." He gives me a big smile and runs back out the doors into the lanes. I can't help but watch as he jogs away. It's hard not to notice the way his muscles roll and flex beneath his T-shirt.

Finally prying my eyes away, I turn and head toward the GM's office. I don't need to be caught drooling over a dealer on my first day. Plus, dealers have a way of being friendly face to face, but they all have their cliques behind the scenes. So I don't give anyone special treatment when I'm selling cars.

I take a deep breath because now the nerves are creeping in. *You nailed it out there. You got this! He's going to be happy with the way you handled your lane today and help you get more jobs.* After giving myself a little pep talk, I reach for the door that has Griffin's name on it and knock.

"Come in," his loud voice booms.

I push open the door, and my eyes land on a desk stacked high with papers. "Hey, Griffin. My lane finished about fifteen minutes ago. I was hoping to talk to you for a few minutes before I leave."

Griffin looks up from his computer screen. "Hunter, yes, come in. The Toyota rep already called me, and they were pleased with how many you sold."

Thank god! My shoulders immediately relax.

"I have to say," he adds. "I was pleasantly surprised. I looked at past sales and lane eighteen has never sold so many. You also had a good amount of online sales. Good job today. I know it's not going to be easy for you, but we would love to keep you around."

Giving him a huge smile, I open my mouth to speak, but he puts his hand up to stop me.

"Also, I took the liberty of calling around to other Manheim auctions. I know you didn't ask me to, but I figured you would want to get a few more sales."

YESSS!

"Oh, my god! Thank you." I beam at him. My face might freeze this way. "That's why I was coming to talk to you. I would love to keep coming back, and I really appreciate you putting in a good word for me at other auctions." I can't believe I didn't even have to ask. He's already made calls for me. I must be dreaming.

"There's another sale today if you want to head over there. It's in Orlando, at Manheim Central. They said they may be able to get you a lane but aren't completely sure. They also lost Dave as an auctioneer when he retired last week. It might be good for you to show your face so they know you're interested. Not guaranteeing anything," he says with a shrug. "I'll have the other auctions give you a call if they're interested, too. But you blew me away today. I figured being taught by your dad would give you an advantage, but I didn't expect what you did out there," he praises. "I even came out and watched a little of your lane. I'm very happy we were able to add you to the team. I know it's not easy, but I'm on your side. So let me know if anyone is giving you a hard time."

He gives me a warm smile, and it's then I realize he reminds me a little of my dad. They both have a commanding presence but also will do what they can to make sure those who need help are taken care of.

"I know how hard it is to get started at new locations. My son got some help from your dad years ago. I don't think your dad knows it was my son, but if I can repay the favor, I'm going to."

"Thank you so much, Griffin!" I reach over and shake his hand. "It means a lot to me. I'll see you next week. I'm going to run over to the other auction now." When he nods, I smile and wave goodbye, shutting his door behind me. Hopefully, I'll be able to make a life here after all.

I'm loving everything so far. I wasn't sure how much I'd like Florida. Everyone says it's so flat, but compared to Oklahoma, it's a nice change of pace. It is humid, so I know my already wild hair is even bigger than normal. I've always embraced my unmanageable hair, and it makes me stand out. I have never wanted to blend in, so I let my hair do its thing, much to my mother's dismay. I walk outside toward my one true love, my 1968 blacked-out Ford Bronco. I named him Westley from The Princess Bride. It's my favorite movie, and he always wears black. I got it completely refurbished, and now he's the most important thing in my life. He has always been reliable and takes me to all my different sales. Yeah, the gas is expensive, but it's worth it. I climb in and crank the engine to hear "Somebody That I Used to Know" by Gotye, blasting through the speakers. Singing loud and proud all the way to the next sale and picking up Chipotle on the way, I find out the sale doesn't start until three at the earliest.

It's only two when I pull up. I know I need to at least show my face and make a good impression. Marcella's the GM here, so now I need to track her down and see if she will give me a shot. I walk through the double doors to the office and begin looking around. I don't completely know where to go, but I'm sure someone will point me in the right direction.

"Hunter!" I turn and see Jess standing behind the counter.

Wow, I didn't realize how anxious I was until I saw her. I give her a huge smile. "Jess! Thank god, a friendly face!" I had fun with her on my lane, and we meshed well together. We also kept talking for a bit after the lane.

"I didn't know I'd be seeing you here. Guess I shouldn't be shocked, though." Jess smiles, and it's a warm smile that lets me know she's genuinely happy to see me.

"Do you know where I could find the GM, Marcella? Griffin told me to head over here, and she might be able to fit me in."

"That's awesome! Yeah, her office is around the corner on the right. It's before the cafeteria." She points me in the right direction.

"Thanks, Jess! Wish me luck."

"You don't need luck. You're a rockstar. They'd be stupid not to give you a shot." Her eyes widen as she looks around. Lowering her voice, she says, "Just don't tell anyone I said that. I mean, I kinda need this job."

I laugh. It feels like auctions here aren't much different from the ones back home. One day you're in, but if you say the wrong thing, you'll be out so fast your head might spin.

"Don't worry, I got you." Winking at her, I take the route she pointed out. When I turn the corner, I get knocked on my ass. "What the fuck! That's the second time today." I grumble and start to get up when a pair of large muscular hands grab mine and yank me up so fast I smack right into a solid body. I know I'm petite, but damn, that made me feel like a rag doll. I slowly look up and get lost in deep blue eyes that are staring down at me.

"Didn't think I'd be running into you here." His familiar voice sends chills down my arms. He's got me tight in his grip, but then shakes his head and steps back. His body was so warm I still feel the faint memory of it against mine. It makes me want to be pressed up against him again, but then I remember who it is standing in front of me. *No way in hell*. Keep this one away from me.

"Myles. I figured I'd see you, but I didn't expect you to try to take me out." I glare up at him and cross my arms over my chest. His body is still too close for me to think clearly.

He smirks. "You know, I just had to get my *hands* on the new girl."

His eyes rake down my body before meeting my eyes again. It sends my blood boiling. I don't know what it is about this guy, but he's so frustrating. Especially that stupid little smirk. Crap, don't look at his lips. I quickly flick my eyes up to meet his, and his deep blues draw me in. Forcing myself to look down, my eyes zero in on his lips when his tongue slips out to wet them, and I can't seem to pry them away.

Remember. Him: asshole. Me: not interested.

I leer up at him. "You couldn't *handle* this new girl even if you tried."

He encroaches toward me, making us less than an inch apart. He leans down so we are sharing the same air. "Just let me know when, *sweetheart.*" Is he flirting with me? It feels like his eyes are drawing me in, but it ends too quickly when Myles straightens and clears his throat. Making me question whether it happened at all. He steps back. "So you're here to steal my job again?" I give him a puzzling look. "Do you think the great Conrad Smith will be able to continue getting you jobs?"

Unfolding my arms and clenching my fists at my sides, my mouth falls open, "Excuse me?" I swear steam is going to come out of my ears.

"When someone like myself has been working hard, proving themselves for years for a position only to have it ripped out from beneath them after one phone call from Daddy? Yeah, I have a hard time respecting what wasn't earned," he says, towering over me.

Wow, low blow.

Standing at his full height, he continues, "Now, I don't want you calling dear old dad, trying to get me fired, so"—he sticks his hand out—"since it looks like we're going to be seeing a lot of each other, why don't we play nice and get along?"

As he takes his hand back, the scowl he was wearing slowly melts from his face, and a fake-ass smile takes its place. "Fake it 'til we make it, right? Have a great day." He tips his hat, then swings his arms toward the lanes, dismissing me.

This guy is unbelievable. I roll my eyes, but before I can make it past him, he steps back in front of me and lowers his lips until they're hovering above my face. My eyes go wide. *What the hell?*

He pauses and moves his mouth to the side of my head. When

his lips brush the shell of my ear, I stop breathing as my eyes flutter shut.

"Good luck out there, *sweetheart*."

When his condescending tone rumbles through my ear, my elbow is moving before I can stop it, landing directly in his stomach.

"Umph." He lets out a few coughs.

Jerk.

"Oh, sorry. I tripped," I say, giving him a smirk as I walk on by. Should I have elbowed him? No, but man, he irks me. Now I gotta get into the right headspace to talk to the GM. Ugh, that man. How can someone annoy me so much, but draw me in so fast? I don't even want to think about how hard his stomach was when I elbowed him. *Focus, Hunter.*

5

MYLES

STANDING HERE SLACK JAWED, I can't believe that girl elbowed me. I know I wasn't exactly friendly, but I also couldn't stop myself from getting closer to her. She's like a damn magnet. I could have sworn her breathing hitched when I grazed her ear. But then out of left field, right in the stomach. Damn, she smelled good, like flowers and vanilla. It's like the scent was designed to put me under a damn spell so I don't try to get her fired.

I don't necessarily want her to lose the job. I just don't want her taking *mine*. I can't wait any more years to take over my mama's bills. I make decent money, but I can't send her as much as I would like. My phone vibrates in my pocket, and I pull it out to look at the screen. Speaking of the angel.

Unable to stop the smile from taking over my face, I answer. "Hey, Mama! You okay?"

"Miney, I'm sorry to call you between your jobs."

I inwardly groan at the nickname she gave me when I was little. My father left us before I was born. I have never met or heard from him. I think she was afraid I would feel unloved or unwanted. So every day before leaving for work, she would wrap me up in a tight hug and say, "I love you. You are mine, Myles. You'll always be all Mine-y." She would wake me up after she would get home from her second job at night, saying the same thing. I haven't been able to get her to stop calling me Miney since. She uses it more than my real name, which only falls from her mouth when I'm in trouble.

"Mama, you know I don't like you calling me that," I grumble. "What's going on?"

"Myles Alexander Johnson." *Here we go.* "I brought you into this world after twenty-five hours of labor because your big head decided to block the path out. I'll call you whatever I want." I can only imagine the glare she is giving the phone.

"Okay, okay, Mama." I sigh, rubbing the back of my neck. "Is everything okay?" We could go round and round all day, but I have a lane that starts in a little less than an hour. She would have no problem explaining to me for hours all the reasons she has for calling me Miney, and I don't have time for that.

"Oh yes, right. My faucet in the kitchen is leaking under the sink. I put a bowl down and dried out the cabinet, but I'm not sure what to do. You told me I'm not allowed to call any fixer people. So do you want to call a fixer person, or can I do something to make it stop?"

I swear she can be madder than a wet hen and the next second, sweet as a Georgia peach. I shake my head and let out a small laugh. I became pretty efficient at fixing things growing up. Picking up stuff from our neighbor, Mr. Arnold, who took me under his wing and taught me all there was to know about tools. He stepped into a grandfather role when he didn't have to. He died when I was a teen, but I wear his hat everyday, a constant reminder to be more like him and nothing like my dad.

"I'll be there after my lane ends, okay? Don't touch anything." Knowing her, she would try to fix it and break the whole damn sink.

"Okay, okay. I won't touch it. I'll have lasagna for you when you come. Gotta put some fat on those bones." I roll my eyes. She's always making comments that I need to fatten up. There's no way I want that to happen. When I'm not at the auctions, I'm at the gym or out at JT's house. He lives on a farm, and I love to ride his horses. I help him with the upkeep of the farm too. "Miney, do I hear you rolling your eyes at me?"

"Mama! There's no such thing as you hearing that. I'll be over later. The lasagna sounds good. I gotta get going." This woman is my world, but she also drives me insane.

"Okay, you are welcome to bring someone along with you if you want. You know I love JT. That boy is the sweetest thing there is. Or maybe you have a lady friend you'd like to bring over. I don't know if you already had a date lined up for tonight or something."

I groan. She is relentless. "Mama, you know I don't have time to date." I pull the phone away from my ear and readjust my hat. "I'm not bringing anyone over." As the words fall from my mouth, an arm is slung around my neck.

"Is that Mama?" JT asks, leaning in to place his mouth near the phone. "Hi, Mama. I'd love to come over, especially if you're cooking."

I glare at JT and shrug his arm off. He knows damn well if he comes over, she'll flirt with him all night. I'll practically have to carry him out over my shoulder to leave. There are no boundaries for either of them.

"JT! There's my boy." she screeches, and I can hear how big her smile is over the phone. "Wonderful! I'll have plenty of lasagna for all of us! I'll see you boys once you finish your lanes. Have a good sale. Oh, and Miney, mind your manners. If you were nicer, maybe you would have a lady friend to bring over to see me."

Oh, good god.

"Okay, Mama. Love you. Bye." I hang up before she or JT can say anything more and fix him with a glare.

"Have I told you I love your mama?" he says with a broad grin. "She's the best!" I have to refrain from punching him right in the jaw.

"You bother me, you know that, right?" I growl.

"Yeah. It's great." His smile is still firmly in place. "Oh, when I was coming in, I saw the new girl, Hunter, with Marcella. I didn't realize she was coming over to this auction right away. Can't say I mind. She was mesmerizing. Did you see the way her hips swayed as she moved around on the block? I'm not sure how you stayed focused this morning." He gives me a knowing smirk. I guess he noticed how I faltered and got tripped up when she started the lane. Watching her captivated me. But there's no way I'm going to talk about that with him. He'd eat it up and act like a damn gossiping schoolgirl.

Rubbing the sudden headache forming above my eyes, I sigh. "Let's not talk about her. We literally collided when I got here, and she had the gall to elbow *me* in the stomach!"

JT's lips twitch, and I can see he finds this funny. "Why would such a sweet-looking thing do that?" he asks.

I drop my hand in frustration and scoff. "The little doll claims she tripped."

Bursting with laughter, JT wipes his hand across his mouth to try to regain his composure, then slaps a hand down on my shoulder. "Oh, my god! And I thought she couldn't get any better." He loses it again, his loud laughter blaring in my ear.

"I need new friends," I grumble over my shoulder as I walk toward the lane.

This auction isn't as nice as the one this morning. While that one had just one seller on my lane, this one has many different seller's cars on one lane, which means you have to go a lot slower. Each seller walks up and shows you the price they need to be able to sell their car. About ten lanes run every Tuesday evening. They also have a bigger sale on Wednesday mornings where they have sixteen lanes running.

I walk over to the auctioneers' meeting. I say, "meeting," loosely. We gather around lane one, and the GM gives us the rundown and the list of where everyone is going. I'm always on lane seven. It's not a bad lane. I'm usually done by five. I wonder where Hunter will end up. As if my thoughts conjured her, she suddenly appears, walking up in her tight-fitted jeans, showing off all the right curves. She may only come up to my shoulder, but damn, she has great legs. She locks eyes with mine, and I can't look away. She smirks before giving me a wink, making me think she knows something I don't.

6

HUNTER

OF COURSE, they would stick me with him. Why give me the chance to actually become friends with my ringman? Sure, give me the one who hates me for simply existing. When Marcella said they would let me have lane five, I could hardly believe my ears. I know it's not common to have an opening at an auction. But the guy who was on these lanes before me retired and got the hell out of central Florida. Good for him, better for me. But then Marcella said Myles was my ringman, and I felt like I was getting punked. *Of fucking course.*

The auctioneers and ringmen have gathered around for the meeting. Marcella introduces me similarly to how Griffin did, although I'd rather they let me do my lane and leave. No need to bring attention to me, but of course, people will cling to any reason to bring up my dad. While walking to my lane, Jess comes running over. Even though I don't know many people here, she's the closest thing I have to an ally. I can picture us having one of those close friendships you see in movies.

"Hey! So Marcella gave you the job. Congrats, rockstar! Not like I'm surprised, though," she says with a wink.

I return her smile. She is the sweetest and dang good at her job. This morning, we were rolling. We didn't have to stop for any problems. When I said the money, she'd get it on the screen so fast it was like she was reading my mind. It was easy to work with her.

"You're stuck with me again," she says, raising her arms in the air. "I hope I didn't bother you when I was eating candy or pointing to the online bidders. I wanted to make sure you saw them, and I eat while I'm working. My brain runs on high octane. Eating helps me focus on the auctioneer, so I don't miss anything. I know it seems weird, but it helps. If it bothers you, I'll stop," she says, rambling as her hands dance wildly around in front of her.

I stop walking and turn to her, placing my hands on her shoulders. "Jess! You were amazing this morning. I didn't care what you were eating. It smelled good. It made me want some." I smile, wanting her to feel comfortable around me. "I'm glad we're working together again. It means I have one less thing to worry about." With a laugh, I loop my arm through hers and continue walking toward the lane.

"So I need to find a place to rent. Do you happen to know of any places centrally located to all the auctions?" I ask. If anyone knows where to buy or rent, it would be someone who's friends with everyone. I've noticed that Jess will talk to just about anyone, and people are genuinely happy to talk to her.

"I'm actually looking for a roommate!" She looks over at me with hope in her eyes. "I know you're probably looking for your own space, but my place is a two-bedroom house, and you'd get your own bathroom. We'd share the common areas. Oh"—She turns to me and grabs my shoulders—"and there's a pool!" Jess' shoulders relax as she closes her eyes and sighs. It's easy to see she loves living there. Being around her today, I know there'd never be a dull moment if I said yes. She'd definitely be a fun roommate.

"Well, where do you live, and how much would the rent cost?" I ask.

Jess' eyes double in size. "Are you serious? You want to be my roommate?" she asks, bouncing on her toes. "Okay, so it's seven hundred a month, but we can talk about those details later."

"I'd love to be your roommate, Jess!" I give her a warm smile and put my arm around her. "I'm excited to have a girl to talk to! Come on! Let's get to our lane before Mr. Grouch steals it and holds it hostage." On our way to the lane, Jess tells me more about the house and the office gossip. When we arrive and find Myles standing there, arms crossed and eyebrows drawn together, we break out into a fit of giggles.

"You know," she says, peeking over at Myles. "You were right about Mr. Grouch," Jess whispers to me. We laugh again. I can picture making a life here. It feels good to finally feel like I've found where I belong, if only I can figure out how to get my ringman to be friendlier. One minute, he's rude and doing everything he can to get a reaction out of me. The next, he's invading my space and bringing some serious sexual tension.

"Hello, Myles." I nod toward him.

"Hey, Hunter. Not going to *trip* again, I hope?" His eyes flare.

Jess' eyes ping-pong between us.

"Nope. I never stumble on the block." I smirk right back.

He turns his eyes on Jess. I can almost see her swooning. *Give me a break.* Sure, Myles is ruggedly handsome, with his five o'clock shadow and hair the perfect length to tangle my hands into during a passionate kiss. *Oh, my god.* Where did that come from? I shake my head, trying to get the thought out of my head.

Myles slides his gaze to Jess. "Hey, Jess. How's Nickelback? Have any new photos?"

Who? I look over at Jess.

Jess looks at me, placing a hand on my arm. "Oh, I forgot to tell you, I have a dog. Are you allergic?" Without waiting for an answer, she turns back to Myles with stars in her eyes. "He's great! Always up for a game of fetch. No, I showed you all the recent pictures. I wish I could bring him with me everywhere."

I smile at her, "Aw, I love dogs! Can't wait to meet him." Turning my body fully to Jess, I add, "I'd love to join you for walks and playing fetch when I move in."

Out of my peripherals, I see Myles looking back and forth at each of us. *Ha, not getting rid of me that easily, big boy!*

"Oh, yeah!" Jess gasps. "We go in the morning and when I get home from work. I'm sure he'd love having you come along. Where are you staying right now, anyway?" she asks.

Feeling Myles' eyes on me, I keep my focus on Jess. "I've been staying at a hotel. So I'd love to get out of there as soon as possible." I smile at her. My dad will be relieved I've found a place. I can't wait to call him and tell him all about today. He's going to be thrilled to hear that auction life here is just as amazing as it was growing up. Auctions have always been our main connection. When I was younger, he allowed me to go with him to work. Everyone at the auction was like a second family to me.

A deep and sultry voice brings me out of my memories. "So you're moving in with Jess?" Just his voice makes my knees weak. But it's his eyes that hold me there.

"Yeah, she is!" Jess answers for me. "Isn't that great? We're going to have so much fun." She loops her arm with mine. "I can't believe I met you this morning and now you're going to be my roommate. We should go swimming tomorrow after the sale. I'm assuming you're working here tomorrow?"

"Yes, I'll be here bright and early." I wink at Myles, knowing he doesn't want me here. He's not going to get rid of me that easily. Turning back to Jess, I add, "Also, swimming tomorrow sounds great! I got a few new bikinis before moving here." Swimming in a pool after a long day sounds like the best way to spend an evening. When deciding to move here, I hoped that I would get the chance to go swimming more often than I did in Oklahoma.

"Yay!" Jess squeals and looks at her phone. "Ah, the lanes will be starting soon, I better go turn on the computer."

I watch Jess as she skips away and turn to see Myles watching me intently. My face falls, and I school it into a blank expression. Feeling the heat under his gaze, I force myself to walk away. "Bring in the cars, Myles." I peek over my shoulder at him. "Or do you want to sit this sale out?"

He glares, then storms away toward the cars. My eyes immediately rake over his butt and broad shoulders. I notice how well his jeans fit, hugging his ass in all the right ways. I can imagine wrapping my arms around his back and allowing my hands to drop down and grab a handful of his nice backside. Sucking in a deep breath, I quickly turn my head, averting my eyes.

My word, I need to stop. He doesn't like me, and he's such a grouch.

THE SALE GOES SMOOTHLY. I don't get to go as fast when the dealers are the sellers, but we can still cruise. I noticed Myles watching me off and on. Each time, I would raise an eyebrow at him, and he'd quickly turn around to find me more bidders. He's good at his job. Too bad he's got a stick so far up his ass. I'm amazed he can bend over.

I walk to the parking lot to rev up Westley. Blaring "One Thing" by One Direction, I drive back to the hotel for the last time. I'm looking forward to settling down in a house. The hotel has been nice, but I miss that homey feeling. Living out of suitcases is exhausting, and I've been doing it for a week now. While driving, I make a mental list of all the things I will need to order once I'm moved in. I don't doubt that Jess will let me crash on the couch until I can order a bed frame and mattress. I know it's going to take some adjusting to living with someone. I've lived by myself since moving out of my parent's house. My ex-boyfriend wanted to live together, but I kept making excuses. I feel safer with Jess than I ever did with him. I think my subconscious knew something wasn't right with him, and I never made the leap. It feels like life is finally coming together, and I can't wait.

My phone rings as I pull up to a red light. Taking a peek at who it is, my mother's name flashes across the screen. I cringe, silence it, and make my turn as soon as the light turns green.

7

MYLES

HEADING over to my mama's house to fix her faucet, JT follows in his car behind me. He can never say no to a home-cooked meal, not that I blame him. Being two bachelors who drive a ton for work, it's hard to get one. We usually eat out, so I'm grateful for my mama. She always knows what I need. But I can't say I'm looking forward to her and JT doing their harmless flirting. Hopefully, it will keep my mind off of Hunter. The whole damn sale, visions of her in a bikini kept flashing through my mind. Once she put it in my head, I imagined her diving into the pool, her body traveling beneath the clear water before slowly ascending. My imagination only got worse as I pictured her breaking through the surface, running her hands through her thick hair as water dripped down her gorgeous body. I could envision her as she climbed out of the pool and seeing her barely covered tight ass in her bikini bottoms before laying out in the sun as droplets glinted off her body.

Oh god. I need to get my act together. I have never fixated on a woman like this. I'm no prude. I like to have a good time. I hook up. Most of the time, that's all it is, though. An enjoyable night getting tangled up in the sheets. I never picture them or what they're doing when I'm not with them. I need to go home and take a cold shower. It's been such a long day, and I'm seeing her again in the morning.

Pulling into my mama's driveway, I notice there's an unfamiliar car parked out front. JT gives me a look as we're walking toward the front door. He's also curious who could be here. My mama lives about an hour away from me in Clermont. JT and I both live in Ocala, and apparently now, so does Hunter.

Mama flings the front door open before I get a chance to knock. "Now Miney, don't freak out." My eyebrows lower. "I want you on your best behavior while you are in my home." My mama has her hair pulled back into a low bun. Her face is more lined now than it was five years ago, and her thick, coffee-colored hair has turned gray around her temples, but she's still as elegantly beautiful as she was when I was younger. The way her apron hits right above her knees, accentuating her short stature, makes me smile. I definitely didn't get my height from her. She could easily hem it mid-thigh, but she's always said she has better things to do with her time. Taking a step forward, I wrap my whole world in my arms and give her a good squeeze. I would do anything for this woman.

I peer over the top of her head to see if I can sneak a peek at who might be inside. "Who's here? I told you I was coming. I hope you didn't waste your money and hire someone." I'm already annoyed. I want to be able to take care of her. I don't want her spending money when I can help.

She ignores me as she looks at JT. "I'm so happy you're here JT." She smiles at him before she faces me again, her face turning stern. "You told me not to touch the sink, and I didn't." The glint in her eye makes me nervous, but she turns too fast for me to get a good read on what she's up to. When we don't follow her, she pauses and looks over her shoulder at us. "Come inside. I want you to meet someone."

Oh, god. Is she setting me up? Forcing my suddenly heavy feet to move, I follow her into the dining room where she goes to stand next to an elderly man with gray hair and glasses.

"Miney, I want you to meet Gus." She slides her hand into his age-spotted one and beams.

My eyes dart to their entwined hands. Who is this guy, and why in the hell is he holding my mama's hand? My head hurts.

"Gus, this is my son, Myles, and his friend JT." Gus puts his hand out toward mine. I can't even bring my eyes down to look at it. I just glare at the hand that was holding my mama's.

When JT sees I'm not moving, he takes a step forward, reaching out his hand to shake it instead. "Nice to meet you, Gus. I'm JT, and this beautiful woman," he says, picking her up in his arms as he hugs her tight, "has a lot of explaining to do." He sets her back on her feet with a goofy grin plastered across his face. "Mama, I sure have missed you and your home cooking."

She swats at his chest, giggling like a little schoolgirl until her eyes fall back on me and she levels me with a stare. I don't take my eyes off the man with gray hair who looks to be a few inches shorter than me. He appears to be around my mama's age. He seems simple enough, wearing plain clothing, obviously not caring much about how fashionable he is.

"Now, Miney." She reaches up and pinches my chin to bring my eyes down to her. "No son of mine is going to be rude to my guests, especially in my home." Her eyes flare at me. "Now, are you going to say hello, or are we going to have a problem?"

I am too tired for this. I want to go home and sleep. I still have a good drive home, and I'm hungry. I was craving some lasagna, but I know she won't feed me unless I shake this guy's hand. I'm tired of meeting another guy that's going to take advantage of her. She's had enough heartbreak to last a lifetime. I don't want her to go through it again. Sighing, I reach out my hand, but only because I'm hungry.

"Hi." I see Mama's eyes narrow through my peripheral vision. She didn't say how much talking I had to do. Childish, I know.

Redirecting my gaze back to her, I say, "Can I go fix your sink now so we can eat? I've got a long drive home."

Her cheeks flush. "Um." She stutters.

"Is your sink even broken?" I slightly whine.

"Well...not exactly." She looks down at her dress and shuffles her feet.

"How is the sink not exactly broken? It either is, or it's not. Which is it?"

She squares her shoulders, looking right up at me. "Okay, well then, it's not. So let's eat." She looks over at Gus, and I see a sparkle in her eye.

It makes me want to vomit.

Why couldn't she have given me a heads-up? Of course, I want her to be happy, but she doesn't exactly have the best track record. Every guy she's been with has either stolen from her or left her for someone else.

We follow her and sit around the table before digging into the casserole dish, layers of melted cheese stringing from the dish to our plate. As I breathe in the aroma of her homemade pasta sauce, my eyes jump to Gus across the table. He better not just be in it for her great cooking. Sure, she's a great cook, but she's also kind and selfless. She has a lot to offer.

"So, Myles," Gus begins, "your mama told me you're a ring-man, but you're trying to be an auctioneer."

Mama looks at me like she is expecting me to say something she'll have to lecture me about.

"Mhm." I give back to him the least I can, and she glares at me.

"So, Mama!" JT says, probably trying to neutralize the situa-tion. "This lasagna is amazing. I was telling my mom the other day you must have a secret ingredient when you cook." He wipes his mouth with his napkin. "I'd never believe a woman could be both beautiful and a master in the kitchen, but here you are, proving me wrong."

That's one good thing about JT. He's good at reading the room and knowing exactly what to say to change the temperature. He grew up having many meals in our home, so he's used to these types of dinners. I owe him one for bailing me out. I don't enjoy disappointing my mama. I want to support her in all her choices, and I do want her to be happy. I'm here as much as I can be, but it's not the same as having a partner in life.

"Oh, JT! I need to talk to your mother." Her eyes flash to me. "She raised such a sweet, respectful boy. I need to know how she did it. Maybe she can give me her secret ingredient." Mama levels her glare at me again.

Our forks clinking against our plates is the only sound as we eat. JT glances at me, but I shovel more food into my mouth. In my peripheral vision, I see Gus rub my mama's back, and she gives him a sad smile. Minutes tick by in silence until I can't take it anymore.

"Alright, Mama. It's been a long day." I wipe my mouth with my napkin and stand. "We gotta head out. Love you. Thank you for dinner," I say, making my way around the table to kiss her on the top of her head. "Even if you conned me to get me here." I give a slight nod to Gus and hurry out the door toward my truck before Mama can stop me.

JT jogs up to my door and waits for me to roll down my window. "Want to talk?"

"Nope," I say, readjusting my hat on my head.

"Okay, so you can listen." He crosses his arms across his chest. "Your mom is just trying to live her life and be happy. So quit being a dick."

I sigh, knowing he's right. I do need to support her. "Yeah." I nod.

"Alright then." He taps his hand on my truck before backing away. "See ya in the morning. Oh, and don't forget to wear your best clothes."

Turning to face him, I arch my brow and glower at him, not getting why he'd bring up my attire.

"You're working with Hunter again." Before hopping into his truck, he snaps his fingers and points at me, as he backs away with a shit-eating grin. I flip him the bird as I crank the engine and floor it past him. I don't need to be reminded of that green-eyed devil. She's been living in my head rent-free all day.

8

———

HUNTER

"JESS, THIS HOUSE IS SO CUTE!" She showed me her room, which has colorful free spirit vibes. The room I'll be staying in has white walls. It's like a blank canvas waiting for me to make it my own. We both have en suite bathrooms. Now I'm looking through the sliding glass doors on the back wall in the living room which flows into a cute bohemian style kitchen. I can see the crystal blue water of the pool reflecting the shimmer of the afternoon sun. It calls my name after being in the heat all day, but I have a lot of unpacking to do.

Switching my gaze from the pool to the large bay windows, I take in Jess' tiny plant haven lining the window sills. "I see you're a plant lover," I say, dipping my head toward the plants as I kneel to rub Nickelback's belly.

Jess' dog has taken to me since I arrived, sniffing me and my luggage as he tried to figure out who the stranger was in his home. He's been calm the entire time, giving my fingers licks as I roam from room to room, taking in the space. Having a cuddle buddy to come home to after work will be a nice change.

Jess reaches out and gently runs her fingers across a fiddle fig, allowing her thumb to caress a leaf before looking at me with a smile. "I love plants. They bring me peace. Did you know they talk to each other?"

"I didn't," I say, walking over to join her at the window.

Nodding, Jess rotates one of the plants, giving the other side some time in the sun. "Yeah, they secrete chemicals into the soil that let other living things in its root zone know how it's doing." Peeking up at me, the corners of her lips quirk up, revealing dimples in both cheeks. "Plants are amazing things."

"Sounds like I have a lot to learn," I reply, reaching out and touching the pointy, long leaf of one before turning and taking in the entire area. "It's a nice place, Jess. I appreciate you letting me room with you."

Pressing her palms together in front of her, she squeals, "I'm glad you like it. I fell in love with this house the moment I saw it. I was happy when I got approved. I've been meaning to get a roommate to help with the costs, but I just didn't know who to ask. The pool," she says, looking out the window at the clear sparkling surface, "was definitely a major reason why I bought it. After a long day on the lanes in this Florida heat, it's nice to get in and relax in the cool water."

"I bet." My eyes take in my new home. When I look back at Jess, she has a smirk plastered across her face. "What?"

"Oh, nothing." She rocks back and forth on her feet. "You and Myles just seem to have a lot of chemistry, is all."

I glower at her. "We do not have chemistry. If anything, it's revulsion."

Jess laughs. "From what I saw, you both feel a lot of things for each other and that isn't it."

"He's awful, Jess."

She thinks about that as she walks to the fridge, grabbing two waters and tossing one to me. "I know Myles is difficult at times." She laughs when I roll my eyes at her understatement. "But,"—she puts a hand up to stop me from talking—"I've worked with him for years. He isn't a bad guy."

Opening the water, I drink half of it while I decide what to say. "I don't know. I think he showed me his true colors, and it's going to be hard for me to forget that."

She nods. "Did you ever think that maybe your first day was a bad day for him?"

"I mean, JT told me Myles thought the job should have been his. But that's not my fault."

"No, it's not. But maybe he really was blindsided. I just want you to know Myles has always been one of the good ones at work. Seeing how he acts around you though, I've never seen him like that."

Nodding a few times, I remain quiet. I trust Jess' opinion, and I'm happy she's willing to help me talk through the whole Myles issue. I'm just unable to sweep his attitude under the rug.

I look out the back door and turn back to her, grinning. "So when can we swim?"

"I think we better get you set up first. But my favorite time to swim is when we can float under the stars." She goes to the hall closet and pulls out a bag. "I have this air mattress and plenty of sheets you can use until you get a bed. Feel free to make yourself at home, and decorate your room any way you like."

I let out a relieved breath. "That sounds perfect! Thank you. I'll order everything online tonight. I'm hoping things will come in the next few days."

After Jess helps me get everything set up, we're worn out from the day and turn in for the night. As I lay down to sleep, deep blue eyes invade my thoughts long after I close mine. I came here to work. Why does this guy keep clawing his way back into my head?

My phone rings on the ground next to me, and I smile when I see my dad's name flash on the screen.

Sitting up on the air mattress, I answer. "Hey, Dad. I was just headed to bed." Tapping my palm against my forehead, I scrunch my face. I meant to call him sooner, but I got caught up unpacking and talking with Jess. It totally slipped my mind.

"Hey, baby girl." His deep voice is familiar and soothing. It makes me think back to when he would read me bedtime stories that put me right to sleep. "I wanted to make sure your first day went okay."

"Yes, it was a great day." I smile. I love how he's always made sure I feel supported by him in anything I do. "I already got hired at another auction and have a few leads on some others."

"That's my girl! Well, I know it's late, and I don't want to keep you up," he pauses before he exhales, making my heart sink. "Your mom wants to know if you'll come home for a wedding in two weeks. It's most likely one of her clubhouse friend's kids getting married. I'm not sure." I hear him let out a small groan.

I sigh. That was probably why she was calling earlier. "Tell her, no. I'm not going to travel back and forth a lot. I'm trying to make this my home now." If my mom had it her way, she would have me move home. She wants me at the wedding so I can meet a single guy and marry someone hand-picked by her. She would prefer I suck it up and marry my ex, Steve, and follow her steps into the country club world. *No, thank you.* "Dad, I'm tired. I'll talk to you another day. Love you."

He grunts. I'm sure it's because he hates being put in the middle. "Love you too, Sweetie. Goodnight."

MY ALARM BLARES, startling me awake Wednesday morning. I grumble while I reluctantly pull myself out of bed and take a quick shower, hoping it will wake me up enough to function. I slide on some jeans and a simple white tee. Then, I squirt gel into my palm, generously apply it throughout my long curls, and blow dry it so the water isn't dripping down my back. I wear simple makeup to accentuate my eyes, but I don't bother with foundation. I walk out of my room and find Jess eating cereal at the kitchen island.

Smiling, she holds up the box and shakes it. "Good morning! Want some? I know you haven't had time to get groceries, so please make yourself at home," she says, taking another bite.

"You're awfully perky at 6:15 in the morning," I grunt as I continue to walk toward the front door. "Thanks for the offer, but I'm going to go get some coffee on the way to work. I'll see you there."

"Mornings are just beautiful! We get to start a new day, and I enjoy waking up refreshed." Her eyes scan my face as she points her spoon my way. "I see you're not in the same mind frame, though. Get your coffee before someone dies from that death glare," she says with a smirk.

I roll my eyes. "It's too early for this."

"Bye!" she sings out, and her annoyingly chipper voice follows me out the door.

I head toward Orlando, but I stop at Starbucks and get a mocha frappuccino. There's a little chocolate in it, and I absolutely love it. I think chocolate should be another food group. There's something about it that makes me happy, even when I have to wake up at such an ungodly hour. I pull up to work and park next to a sleek, classic black Ford truck. Of course, *Myles freaking Johnson* sits behind the wheel. He would have one of those nice old trucks—the kind that makes you weak in the knees. I've always loved it when people make a vintage car look brand new. It's exactly what I did with my Bronco. I take another glance at Myles. His hat is on backward, and his eyes bore into mine. Something stormy crosses his expression, and I scoff, turning away from him. He doesn't deserve a truck like that. We both get out at the same time.

"Stalking me now?" he calls from the other side of his car, side-eyeing me beneath a raised brow.

"It's too early for this." I put my hand up to get him to stop talking. "So how about you shut your mouth until you have to actually be professional and pretend not to loathe me. Okay?" I raise an eyebrow at him before reaching back inside my Bronco to grab my drink and purse. When I straighten, he's still standing there. I was hoping he would stomp away while I got my stuff, but no. There he is fixing me with those hypnotic eyes. "Can I help you?"

"Just waiting to see how long it takes you to climb down from the lofty podium you've set yourself up on." He growls out at me.

"Are you kidding me? You are the one who started this. I innocently pull into a parking space, and you act as if I knew what you drove and wanted to play games with you." I walk and stand right in front of him. "How about you just go off with your little buddies and leave me alone?" I begin to walk away, but turn and poke a finger right into his chest. "Also, contrary to typical auctioneer behavior, I don't think I'm better than anyone. I've had to work my ass off in this male-dominated industry. So don't think I take this for granted. I know it can all be gone in the blink of an eye. I would like some peace this morning and drink my coffee before my ears are ringing with auction noise." I storm past him, but peer over my shoulder to find him walking right behind me. As I reach for the door to the front office, Myles' long arm snakes around me, grabbing the handle first. His body is so close to mine, I can feel his breath against my skin, and his lips ghost over my ear, causing me to hesitate with anticipation of his next move.

"Have a good day, *sweetheart,*" he says, smoothly and pulls the door open, nearly bumping into me and bringing me back to reality. I quickly walk inside and head straight toward the restroom. I need to get a grip. *That man, that very tall, strong, handsome brick wall of a man I'd love to scale—Ah! Stop it!* I have to be around him without melting under his gaze. He's mean, grumpy, and hates me. But then he towers over me surrounding me, with his woodsy scent, and he makes me feel all lightheaded. An electric thrill goes right through me. Gripping the counter in front of the sink, I lean over and try to shake the erratic feelings rushing through me. Wetting some paper towels, I wipe my neck with cold water, hoping it will help me calm down.

Once I'm feeling under control, I wad up the wet paper and throw it in the garbage, heading toward the door when Jess comes striding through it.

"Oh, hey! Get your coffee?" She smiles.

"Yes, and ran into Mr. Grouch outside. Perfect way to start my day." I grumble as she stands in front of the mirror, checking her reflection.

"Oh really? Well, by the looks of it, you felt something, and it sure wasn't irritation." Jess smirks at me while trying hard to hold in her laughter.

"What is that supposed to mean?" I put my hands on my hips. "I know you think he's swoon-worthy, but he's not nice, Jess. He's been a complete jerk."

"Come on, Hunter. I saw you watch him on the auction block. Also, did you forget I'm your block clerk, and I watched you yesterday as you majorly checked out his ass?" She chuckles. "By the way, I completely do not blame you at all. It's a nice ass." Now Jess is howling. After she washes her hands, we walk out of the bathroom.

"Okay, I admit it. Myles has a nice ass—" I say, but before I can complete my sentence, I'm interrupted by a masculine voice, causing our feet to freeze completely in their tracks.

"Oh, well thank you"—I can feel his eyes on me—"yours isn't so bad either."

Oh please, god no! This cannot be happening right now.

Jess and I slowly turn around to find Myles now leaning against the wall next to the bathroom doors.

"Were you waiting for me?" I ask while I glare at him and hope he will let me avoid all this and completely change the subject.

"Well, I wanted to give you a peace offering." He holds up a cup in his hand. "You seemed angry after I opened the door for you. So I brought you a real cup of coffee since your cup seems to be a chocolate sugar rush disguised as coffee." He smirks, holding a paper cup out to me.

I glare at him and ignore his offer. "No thanks. I love my coffee. I don't need anything from *you*," I growl back at him.

"Oh, no?" he chuckles.

Jess is soaking up our entire exchange and can't seem to get enough, judging by the glee in her eyes.

"No," I grit out between clenched teeth.

"Well, from the way you seem to enjoy my ass, it sounds like you might need more than just coffee. But, I, uh, cut you off," he says, rubbing the day-old scruff on his chin. "Did you want to add something else? Possibly about my arms? Chest? Abs?" he says smoothly.

Oh, for the love of all things holy. The last thing I need is for him to point out his body parts.

I sneak a peek at Jess, and her eyes are as large as golf balls now. I turn back to Myles and level him with a look. "I was going to say your ass may be nice, but your ego is so big you have a hard time fitting your head through the door. Also, you need a new hat. That one is old and grimy." I say, scrunching up my nose.

"Hm," he says as he takes off the dingy hat, examining it closely. "Well, there is no way I'm getting rid of this hat, but if you keep looking at my butt, you won't even notice it," he says with a small laugh. Then he pats me on top of the head with his nasty hat and walks past us toward the lanes. "I'll even walk away first, so you can have a better view, Hershey," he adds over his shoulder.

GAH! That man infuriates me to no end! I look over and see Jess smiling. "What?" I snap while rolling my eyes.

"We could have cut the tension in here with a knife. That was amazing!" Jess says, all perky. "And he gave you a nickname that fits you perfectly. You do love your chocolate."

"Come on, we need to get out there. Our meetings are about to start." I pull her toward the auction lanes outside.

"Okay, but you have to admit it, that banter with Myles was fun!" She loops her arm with mine.

"I will admit that he's annoying, and I'm here to work. He's also the one who's trying to take my job. I can't let myself get distracted." Yes, stay focused. I will concentrate and not think about *him*, or the fact that I want to grab him around the neck and kiss him while snaking my fingers through his hair. No, I will most definitely not think about that. Not at all, because I will stay focused. *Laser* focused.

Jess gives me a knowing look.

"What? I'm just here to work. It's almost Thursday, and I have to figure out how to get hired at the two auctions running tomorrow." I nod my head, trying to think about how I will make it happen. Forcing my thoughts in that direction, I hope it helps distract me from that unpleasant encounter. Manheim has two sales each Thursday, the morning one is in Tampa, and the other is in the evening in St. Petersburg.

"Right. It's good you're not going to let anything distract you," Jess says.

We walk out into the lanes and see the auctioneers gathered around to start the meeting on lane one. The block clerks are down on lane ten.

Jess leans over and whispers, "Remember, you don't want any

distractions. Especially not from the man who is simultaneously undressing you with his eyes while planning your demise."

I look over and catch Myles staring right at me. His eyes are darker, the knuckles on his balled up fists white, and his jaw flexes. It looks as if he's struggling to keep his composure. *Oh, Lord, help me. It's going to be a long sale.*

9

———

MYLES

WHY IS this girl getting under my skin? Sure, it's fun messing with her, but I can't let her distract me. I want the GMs to hire me, and they won't if I'm not on top of my game. Watching her hips move in those jeans has been torture. Marcella needs to put me on a different lane. I could use a little space to get some clarity.

Marcella clears her throat, getting everyone's attention for the meeting. "I'm sure most of you saw Hunter Smith at the sales yesterday. She will be on lane five with JT." Marcella turns to Hunter, shooting her a megawatt smile.

"Alright, Fun-Size!" JT cheers. "Let's do this." He reaches over to give Hunter a high five.

My head whips around when Hunter gives a boisterous laugh. Her face lights up with amusement, and I suddenly want to hear that beautiful sound again. She radiates happiness.

"This is going to be fun!" Hunter exclaims.

JT looks at me and winks. He says something to make her laugh again, and she puts her hand on his forearm, making me want nothing more than to be on the lane with her and get her away from that incessant flirt. This is ridiculous. Why does she make me feel like I'm losing my mind? I want nothing to do with her, but then I want to be around her all the time. She's fun, sassy, beautiful, and doesn't put up with my shit.

Fuck, I need some air.

As luck would have it, the schedule says I'm on lane four, which is the one directly facing JT and Hunter. So I get to watch them the entire sale. *Perfect.*

I walk behind them, and her giggles ring through me like a cowbell. What is he saying that is so funny? I don't think he's that funny.

"Hey, JT."

He mumbles something to Hunter before walking over to me and nods. "What's up?"

"Are you still going out with the guys after this evening's sale?" We go to another auction in Lakeland after this one and usually several of the guys go out to a bar close by after work.

"Heck, yeah." JT smacks me on the back. "I'm always trying to get you to come out with us. You always say no." Raising his eyebrows for emphasis. "I'm pretty sure there's already five of us going." He rubs his hands together. He loves going out and shooting pool after work. "What makes you want to go tonight?"

"Can't I just want to have a good time?"

"Well, considering you never like to go out—no." JT smirks, glancing in Hunter's direction. She's standing on the auction block, doing a sound check. "It seems like a certain someone is getting under your skin, Johnson."

Shaking my head, I shove his shoulder. "I don't know what you're talking about," I say, rolling my eyes and walking away. If I encourage him, he will be impossible to be around. He's like a dog with a bone. Once he gets an idea, he runs with it. I don't need someone else bringing up Hunter. I think of her too much as it is.

I WISH I spent the sale focused on my lane and not looking across to the one opposite me. But, of course, a certain female auctioneer invaded my thoughts. The woman who commanded the attention of everyone had most of my focus too. Hunter and JT worked well together, and they seemed to even have fun. I would look over and see them constantly laughing over who knows what. Aaron, my auctioneer, got irritated with me because I was distracted. After the sale, I saw a CarMax dealer talking to her. What's that guy's name? Jake? Jeremy? No. I don't know or care, but why did she look happy talking to him?

Readjusting my hat, I yell over to JT before he walks off. "Hey, JT! You ready?"

Jogging over to me, JT nods. "Yeah. Did you want to get some lunch before? I'm thinking of going to Chick-fil-A."

"Yup, sounds good to me. I'll meet you there." I need to get out of here. I can't watch Hunter talk to *what's his name,* for another minute.

After getting some food, we drive over to Manheim Lakeland. The sale starts at 3 p.m., and it's almost 2:30 p.m. "We better get inside. Don't want them thinking we aren't going to show up and give our jobs away," I say with a little attitude.

"Dude, why are you such a grouch?" He stops walking to level me with a look. "Since Hunter got here, you've been extra moody. You've always acted like you wanted to be there and you've always been professional. What is your deal? Seriously, man." He shakes his head. "Nothing has changed other than the GMs bringing on a new auctioneer without offering you the promotion."

He says it sarcastically like it isn't some huge thing, but it is.

"I'm sorry, man." I take my hat off and run my fingers through my hair. "I guess it's gotten to my head a little more than it should. I didn't think they would bring in someone from outside. I always thought if they had an opening, they'd give it to you or me. Keep it in-house." Putting my hat back on, I shake my head. "But then they bring in a girl from Oklahoma. I don't like it," I admit.

"I get it. It sucks, but we'll get our shot." JT slugs my arm and gives me a slanted smile. "Keep your head down, and work hard. I know how important it is to you. No one knows better than me how hard you've worked. Don't fuck it up and lose the chance of getting your dream job."

What am I doing? I could be jeopardizing my job. "You're right," I admit. "Damn, you got deep on me, man." I laugh. "Since when did you get all this wisdom?"

He smirks. "Yeah, don't get used to it." He stuffs his hands in his pockets as we walk. "So I heard Jess and Hunter are living together. Did you know they have a pool? Bro, you know what that means?" He looks at me and wiggles his eyebrows.

"Dude, shut up." I push him, shaking my head. "You're not helping." I don't need the distraction of thinking about that girl in a bikini.

Walking into the auction, I glance over JT's shoulder to find that damn Bronco. *Of fucking course.* I shouldn't be shocked that this auction also hired her.

"Fun-Size! You're here!" JT yells across the office, and then he glances at me and snickers.

What an asshole. He's doing this on purpose.

Hunter spins around and beams. "Hey, JT. I hope I'm with you for this one!" I roll my eyes, and Hunter turns her attention to me. She looks like she wants to say something but glares at me instead and walks away.

"Wow. You're cold, Fun-Size." JT yells loud enough to be heard over the busy office chatter. "Why did you just snub my guy?"

He always has my back.

Hunter scoffs.

I walk over to her, forcing her eyes to meet mine. Leaning down, I'm inches from her face. I swear her breath hitches. Unable to control myself, I lower my mouth to her ear. I want to be as close as I can to her, surrounded by her lavender and vanilla scent.

"Hey there, Hershey." I lean back and look her right in the eyes. Her mouth is slightly agape, and I'm entranced by the rise and fall of her chest. That's when I see it. I affect her as much as she does me. Before I can say anything else, she spins around, and her wild brown hair whips me in the face as she storms away.

JT walks over and slaps me on the back. "Well, that was fun."

I pry my eyes away from her to shoot him a look, and a guffaw bursts from his mouth.

10

HUNTER

"HEY, want to go get some drinks?" Jess asks while we're walking off the auction block. "A few of the block clerks like to go to this place close by after the sale. It's like a midweek decompression."

"That sounds like fun. I hope they don't mind me crashing the party," I say as I pull my hair into a messy bun. The humidity today is off the charts.

"Heck no, this group is the best. They'll be ecstatic to have another face joining us! Not every block clerk you meet will be so welcoming, but stick with me and you won't need to worry," she says. We both laugh, because I know what she means. I've met some nice block clerks and some really *interesting* ones. Most are only nice to your face.

I follow her to the bar, and we walk inside. There are pool tables everywhere, and I gasp, "I love playing pool!" I realize too late that I said it too loud when the bar goes silent, and almost everyone is staring at me. I give a sheepish smile and wave.

Jess snorts and pulls me over to a table where several other girls are shooting pool. "Hey, everyone." Jess motions to me.

"This is Hunter Smith. Hunter, this is Lydia, Charley, and Blake." She points to each girl as she says her name.

"Oh, hey again, Lydia," I say to the girl with red hair and a slender figure who was on my block earlier. "You did awesome today."

"Yeah, you too." Lydia smiles. "You're so smooth. I love listening to you."

"Oh, well thank you," I say, pressing my hand against my chest. "I've only been practicing my whole life." This makes everyone giggle.

"What was that like?" Charley, the girl with light brown, curly hair, asks. "Everyone knows your dad and most have seen videos of him selling things at one time or another. Has it been hard? What was it like working with him?" She's nearly out of breath from the back to back questions.

I blink a few times and give a nervous chuckle. "My dad and I are very close. He's why I chose this line of work. But he does have a huge reputation, and that's made it hard. We struggled with our relationship in the beginning, figuring out our father-daughter relationship versus our mentor-work relationship. He only wanted what was best for me, but that also meant hours of practice until any chant that wasn't flowing well was fixed. He expected a lot out of me." Becoming an auctioneer was a lot harder than I like to admit. Not only did I have to live up to my dad's expectations, my colleagues made it harder to even get a job.

"It is impressive." Blake, whose caramel-colored hair is twisted into an elegant bun, adds. "You've made your mark by getting hired at all the Manheim auctions around here. It's amazing!"

"Well, Jess is the reason the rest of the auctions hired me." I nudge Jess with my shoulder. "She called the GMs at Lakeland, Tampa, and St. Pete." The girl already has my back, and I love how close we have gotten so fast. I'm deeply indebted to her.

"Hey," Jess says. "I only told them how good you are and that everywhere was hiring you. They would be stupid not to do the same!" The other girls hoot in agreement. I already feel accepted by these girls. I'm relieved I have some friends to hang with now. I never felt like I fit into any clique before. People were either getting close to me to get close to my dad, or they were friends of Steve's. During the time we were together, he isolated me, so I didn't have many close friends to hang out with.

A loud commotion brings our attention to the other side of the bar. That's when my eyes land on a worn, tan hat, blue eyes, and an ego the size of Texas. *Oh great.* Right when I was having such a good time.

"We know them!" Charley states the obvious.

"Yeah. Let's ignore them," I mutter. They all turn to stare at me like I've grown a third head.

"Why would we do that?" Lydia asks, furrowing her eyebrows.

"Well—" Jess begins and looks at me. I give her a small smile. "Hunter and Myles kind of have some problems with each other." I'm thankful she is here to back me up.

"Why?" Charley asks while folding her arms across her chest. "He's always been nice to me, in his own kind of way," she says and looks at the other girls. "Do you guys remember when my ex-boyfriend was threatening to kick me out of my own apartment? Myles was the first one to volunteer to help move my stuff to a safer place. He also talked to my ex and basically threatened him to leave me alone. He even got JT involved. They convinced my landlord to take me off the lease, so I didn't get fined."

Charley's story has my mind muddled. Who she describes sounds nothing like the Myles I know.

"Do you remember the time my horse got injured?" Blake asks. "JT and Myles showed up to see if they could help keep him calm while the vet took care of his injuries. They came back several times to check and make sure he was okay."

All the girls are smiling while exchanging stories about Myles that paint a different picture than what I've seen. It makes me wish I knew this side of him. JT has already shown me how nice he is, but Myles has never been kind to me. Maybe we need to hang out in a non-work setting?

"We should have them join us, or we could join them," Blake says.

"Let's go!" Lydia adds.

All the girls walk over, and I reluctantly follow. The guys cheer when they catch sight of us.

"Well, hello ladies! So happy you could join us." JT's deep, velvety voice is warm and inviting. "Can we get you anything to drink?" He comes around and gives each of us a brief hug.

We all order drinks, but I've decided I'll drink one and go home. This isn't my idea of a good time. Mr. Grouch is still sending daggers my way. I'm growing tired of his moods. After hearing what the block clerks think of him, it makes me jealous that I don't have those types of encounters with him. Why can't he move past everything and be friendly to me, too?

"Hunter!" Jess wraps her arm around my shoulder. "Let's play a round of pool." She grabs a pool stick and tosses it across to me.

Catching it one-handed, I shake my head and hand it back. "No thanks. I'm going to take off soon." I'm trying to get out of here with the least amount of drama and glaring as possible.

Myles walks toward the pool table from the corner he was sulking in. Standing in front of me, he leans back, putting his weight on the pool table behind him, and crosses his arms across his chest. He's wearing worn jeans and a black T-shirt. I have to fight the urge to scan him. Did I know that he has tattoos? They are sexy as hell. I can't lie, if he wasn't such an ass and was the guy the girls talked about, I would have a very hard time not being into him. Fuck, I'm struggling even when he is an ass to me.

The muscles in his jaw flex. "What? Are you afraid you'll embarrass yourself, and we'll find out you actually suck at something?"

What the fuck is his problem? I drill him with a glare. He was giving me the evil eye earlier and then comes to intervene just when I decide to leave.

"No, I don't want to hang out with you any more than I have to." I put a hand on my hip. His eyes rake over me, and I wonder if he feels the same. Does he find me just as attractive? The heat is clearly in his eyes, and I guess there's only one way to find out. "Also, I wouldn't want to bruise your ego even more by whipping your ass in pool." It's hard not to be snarky when his whole demeanor asks for it.

His eyes flash. "Oh, it's on, Hershey." The danger in his low growl sends an unexpected thrill through me as he prowls closer with a toothpick balanced in the corner of his mouth.

Fuck, fuck, fuck. My body is screaming at me, as if it knows I'm playing with fire.

JT racks up the balls, beaming. His anticipation is palpable. I'm realizing JT loves to stir the pot. Okay, if these boys want a good time, fuck it, that's exactly what I'm going to give them. There's only one way to find out if he feels anything for me.

Squaring my shoulders, I prepare myself for what's coming. "Fine, but let's put a little wager on it. Shall we?" Looking directly at Myles, I arch an eyebrow.

His eyes darken. "Okay. Loser has to take three shots of whiskey," he challenges.

"Fine." I nod. "But then you won't be able to drive home. It'll be an expensive Uber for you." Giving him a confident wink, I chalk my stick.

His eyes flare as he rolls that damn toothpick across his bottom lip with his tongue. "Let's go."

"I'll break." I saunter around the pool table, never taking my eyes off his. Our friends stand around the high tops as they eat, drink and talk. But I don't miss the subtle glances they give each other during our exchange.

Sweeping his arm toward the pool table, he says, "By all means."

JT jumps up and yells over to the bar, "Hey, can we get another round over here and four shots of whiskey?" The bartender nods his head and gets to work on the drinks.

I aim and hit the cue ball, making all the balls scatter across the table and sinking two solids into different holes. I look up at Myles and smirk. *Take that, big boy.* "Guess I'm solids." I enjoy the devilish little smile I feel curling the corners of my lips.

Myles scoffs and fingers the rim of his hat as he adjusts it nervously. "Beginner's luck."

"I don't know, man," JT says, leaning over the table to get a better look. "Might want to change your bet."

"Yeah. I'm definitely on Hunter's team." Jess comes to stand next to JT.

Going around the table, I line up my next shot, which happens to be right in front of him. I make a show of bending over and getting into position. I make sure to give him the perfect view of my ass because I happen to know it looks good in these jeans. Giving my hips a little wiggle, I hit the white ball. I am not above using all my *assets* to my advantage. If he's thinking of my ass, he's not thinking about the game. Before standing up, I peek over my shoulder to find him biting the knuckle of his fist as an inferno burns behind his eyes.

I sink two more balls before missing the next one. "Your turn," I say in my most alluring voice. "Unless you want to give up now." I brush imaginary lint from my shoulders as I peer at him from under my lashes.

Clearing his throat, Myles squares his shoulders and stares me down. "In your dreams."

He goes around the table, looking for his best angle. Turning his hat around backward, he sinks four stripes before he misses. He walks around, leans close to my ear, and whispers, "Don't choke."

I hold back the shiver from his breath against my skin. Slowly looking up, I meet his eyes, then glance at his full lips. "I never do, *baby*."

His eyes spark with hunger as his grip tightens on his pool stick. I smirk and bump him with my hip as I walk by. *God, he's fucking hot.*

Charley leans over to Jess and JT. "Are they always like this?" she says in a low voice.

They both say in unison, "Yes." Their shoulders slump, clearly exasperated by the whole thing.

JT looks down at Jess, and she glances over at him, tucking her bottom lip beneath her teeth. When he winks at her, a huge smile begs to take over her face.

Turning my attention back to the table, I look for my next shot. There is no way I can let *him* beat me. I line up my stick and pocket another ball, immediately meeting Myles' deep, blue eyes. After sinking my last two balls, I look to see the eight ball is at a hard angle and is going to be difficult to get. I line up, but I already know I'm going to miss it. So I just try to place the cue as close to the eight ball as I can. Maybe Myles will accidentally hit it in.

Myles walks toward me. "Aw, that's too bad. I guess you do *choke*."

Blake starts fanning herself. "Is it getting hot in here?" she says to no one in particular.

I pop my hip to lean on my pool stick. "Let's see what you got, *big boy*."

Was that necessary? No. Do I care? Also, no.

Myles smirks and lands his last two balls. His last ball touches the eight ball. Oh, please let him miss. I can't let him win. He takes one more long look at me, making me squirm under his gaze, and shoots his shot. The cue ball sinks his last ball, ricocheting back and going into a hole. His shoulders slump, and he lets out a huff.

The girls and I raise our arms in the air and let out a loud scream and laughter follows. The guys laugh and each take turns smacking Myles on the back.

Picking up all three shots, I walk them over to Myles. "Better drink up."

Myles' heated gaze rakes over me slowly, and I have to stop myself from fidgeting. Picking up the first shot, he lifts it to me, holding my gaze for longer than he should before shooting it back. He does the same thing with the next one, keeping me in his sight. When he holds the last one in the air and everyone cheers, he slowly licks the rim, winks at me, and throws it back. Sliding his tongue across his lower lip, he removes all evidence of the Whiskey, then moves in closer. Someone accidentally bumps into me, causing me to fall into his arms. His strong hands grip my hips protectively. Unable to stop myself, I allow my hands to slide up to his hard abs, his eyes boring into mine intensely. Neither of us dare move. His fingers squeeze me tighter, sending a jolt of heat through my body.

Pushing up on my tippy toes, I lean forward until my lips graze the shell of his ear. He doesn't move. Doesn't breathe. "Enjoy your ride home," I whisper. Patting his firm chest, I turn to the rest of the group. "Well, I guess I'll see you all tomorrow!"

I turn to leave when a large arm snakes around my waist, pulling me back with a force that has my back smacking into his concrete chest.

"Where are you going?" The words lazily roll off his tongue, and I get a little too much enjoyment knowing the shots are already taking effect.

"It's getting late. I'm going home." I tilt my head to the side, looking up into his handsome face. "We have an early morning."

He leans into my space, sucking all the air from the room. "Fine." The pad of his thumb drags across his bottom lip, his gaze more heated than ever, making it impossible to look away. "But *this* isn't over."

11

MYLES

MY ALARM BLARES, filling my head with agony. I let out a drawn-out groan. *Why?* Why did the morning have to come so soon? Why did I make that bet with Hunter? I should have known she would win. The odds were stacked against me. Like any damn romance movie, the woman is a pool shark and the guy always loses. She seems to be my kryptonite, but flirting with her has been the best part of my days lately. I love seeing how I affect her. But mostly, I like how it isn't only me. I see the way her breathing hitches when I'm close. The way she met my challenge and kicked my ass while doing it.

Damn, it's too early. I press the pillow harder into my head, wishing it would stop the pounding. Blindly reaching for my phone, I drag it under with me. I check the time and nearly jump to my feet. I must have set the wrong alarm. Pulling myself out of bed, the room spins, making bile rise in my throat. Shit, I'm going to be late for work.

Drinking two drinks and three shots last night, I'm amazed I still remember anything. I need to take some Tylenol and head out. I throw on a pair of jeans, a black button-up shirt, and my hat, and rush out the door.

Fuck! I squint. The sun isn't even fully up yet, and it's too damn bright. I jump into my truck and pull my hat down low over my eyes. With how late I am, and the fact that the first auction today is an hour and a half away, I don't have time to go back inside for my sunglasses. "Come on, Gertrude," I say, patting her dash as if she were a living thing. "Don't fail me now." I throw the gear into reverse, back out, and speed away as I chug an old bottle of water I left in here, suffering through the warm plastic taste.

Thankfully, some of the guys we were with at the bar live close by and were able to get both me and my truck home last night. Otherwise, JT would have to haul my ass to work. But those guys weren't happy when I threw up into a bag on the way home.

Pulling into the auction ninety minutes later, I readjust my hat so the bill rides lower and rush inside. I'm late for the meeting, but thankfully the lanes haven't started. I walk up as everyone else is clearing out.

"Well, look who actually decided to show up this morning," JT teases.

I squint from the pain. "Shut up." I massage my temples to help relieve some of the aches.

"Wow." A sweet voice floats from behind my shoulder, forcing me to turn around.

Hunter stands there with one hand on her hip, the other holding a coffee. If I weren't a gentleman, I'd trip her for that cup of brown life.

"You look rough," she says, eyeing me. "Did you have a bad night, Myles?" she adds, on the verge of laughter.

This girl keeps showing up at the wrong time. A warning rumble leaves my throat. I'm in no mood today. I can barely keep my stomach from releasing its contents. I knew better than to bet against someone I've never seen play pool. There's always a chance of it biting you in the ass. I couldn't help myself. She looked carefree, shooting the balls into the pockets. I didn't want her to leave. Before I knew what I was doing, I was on my feet and challenging her.

She puts her hands up in surrender, then brings her purse to the front of her, digs around, and pulls out a bottle. "Here." I reach out tentatively and grab whatever she has. "I came with a peace offering. Here's some rapid release Tylenol, and I don't see your sunglasses. So you can borrow mine." She looks down, a little embarrassed, as if she isn't sure she did the right thing. "I know they're a bit more stylish than you're used to, but they will improve your looks by covering up half your face." She does her best to hold back her laughter before clearing her throat. "I remember coming to an auction with a hangover. They were a lifesaver for me."

Hunter's being nice, and I don't deserve it. She's showing *me* a side of her I've only seen her give to others. It hits me like a ton of bricks that I've been a total dick and not at all the man my mama raised me to be. I know it was wrong for me to blame her for not getting the promotion. It had nothing to do with her, just showed me I have to work harder and be better. I don't want the position handed to me. I want to earn it. Every day is a chance for me to get better at my craft. Each time I give an auctioneer a break, I learn just a little bit more.

I look at her, really look. Hunter seems to wear her heart on her sleeve. She's just been reacting to the hate I've thrown her way. It would be hard for someone to uproot their life and start over. There is something to be said about people like her. Her bravery shows when she speaks into that microphone like a pro, even though glares get shot her way. It spoke volumes about her work ethic and determination when all the auctions around the area picked her up. Those whose feathers seemed ruffled by her presence have thawed toward her because she's friendly to everyone.

My eyes search hers. "Thank you," I say, holding up the bottle. "Really."

She gives me a timid smile and nods. "You're welcome. I hope it helps."

"These"—I hold up her sunglasses—"are going to look *great* on me." I give her a genuine smile while I put them on, and the pressure and anger that I've been carrying around starts to dissipate.

Hunter lets out a musical laugh that makes me chuckle along with her, causing those around us to turn their heads.

"At least I'll have an amusing view while I work," Hunter says, tucking some hair behind her ear.

I look at her, confused. My brain isn't exactly firing on all cylinders at the moment.

"You're on my lane." She points behind her to the auction block. "Don't take this the wrong way, but—" Pausing, she nods and says, "try to keep up and don't break my glasses. They're my favorite." She points her finger at me and turns away, sauntering her way down the lanes.

Shaking my head, I watch her hips sway as she walks. "Looking forward to it," I say under my breath. I take a few steps backward, watching her the whole way.

One thing I quickly remember when the lanes start, is that it's hard to get rid of a headache amidst the auction noise. My head pounds the entire sale, even with the earplugs I shoved in my ears. Now and then, when a random giggle comes over the microphone, I look up at Hunter, and she quickly composes herself, getting back to selling cars. Without a doubt, I look funny sporting women's sunglasses, and as queasy as I feel, I'm sure the color of my face isn't helping either. Or maybe she's distracted by the CarMax guy who keeps giving her little signals that are unrelated to buying anything and more for getting her attention. I keep thinking he's making a bid, but every time I look, he's just waving to get her attention. Nothing is more annoying than a fake bid.

Breathing a sigh of relief, I see the last car coming through the lane. I need to get some food and take some more Tylenol before the next sale in St. Pete.

"Alright, everyone." Hunter leans over the auction block counter to look at all the dealers. "This is the last car. Let's sell this Toyota Camry. Twelve thousand dollar bid, twelve thousand, ten thousand dollar bid, ten thousand, two, four, six, six-dollar bid, six, five-dollar bid, six-dollar bid, ten thousand six hundred dollar bid." I signal to the last guy who bid, but he shakes his head no.

"Sold," Hunter says. "Ten thousand five hundred dollars to bidder eleven-thirty-four. Thanks, James." I look up and see Hunter looking at the CarMax guy, giving him a not-so-subtle wink.

What the fuck was that? Of course she's friendly with the worst guy here. I watch as he makes his way over to her. She turns and quickly says something to Blake, her block clerk, before going down to James.

I know I need to return her sunglasses. She was right. They helped, especially when the sun was streaming into the lanes and searing my eyes. I hurry over to the barista cart and point out Hunter to see if they knew her chocolatey order. Thankfully, they do, and in no time, I'm walking back to Hunter, who's still talking with James. I try to make my way a little closer without being too obvious. I want to hear what they're talking about before completely interrupting.

"I wanted to see if you were doing anything Saturday night?" James asks. "I have tickets to go see a movie. I expected my sister to be off work, but now she's telling me she has to study for a big exam." James shakes his head.

I don't believe him. His date either bailed on him, or he just got the tickets.

"Oh, that sounds like fun!" She touches him on his arm and smiles.

"I'll pick you up," James offers.

"Okay." Hunter smiles and reaches into her back pocket, pulling out her phone. "Give me your number, and I'll text you so you have mine."

I watch as she unlocks her screen and opens her contacts before handing it to James. He quickly types his number, then hands it back to her.

A grin splits his stupid face. "Text me. I can't wait."

I can't believe she's going on a date with the CarMax guy. *What the hell?* Hunter goes to open her mouth but turns and looks at me. Arching her brow, she gives me a look that says, *Do you have a problem?* I get it. I'm standing here with a chocolate whipped cream-covered cup and women's eyewear on my face. No one else is around me. There's no way to pretend I'm not looking at her, so I walk closer.

"I wanted to give you something as a thank you for letting me use your glasses." I remove them from my eyes, handing them and the coffee concoction over. "You were right, they were definitely a lifesaver."

She looks intently at the cup before trailing her eyes back to mine. The intensity of them bores into my soul. There's so much emotion held inside that it's hard to hold her gaze.

"Thank you. This is so sweet." She leans in to hug me, and I stand like a limp noodle with my arms hanging at my sides because I wasn't expecting it. When I finally bring my arms around her, she nestles into my chest, dropping a wave of surprise into my stomach. It's the most awkward hug of my life, but at the same time, I feel an immense relief. Almost like this is what my body has been craving. Someone clears their throat, and we jump apart.

I look at James, forgetting he was standing there for our exchange. "Hey, CarMax. Seems like you bought plenty of good cars today." I notice Hunter is stiff as a board standing next to me, not saying a word.

James's eyes search her face before leveling me with a glare. "Yeah. Seems like it."

Now that the noise of the auction has subsided, my headache has lessened, but I readjust my hat, hoping to get a little more relief. "Okay. Well, I'll see you two in St. Pete," I say, giving Hunter one last look before walking away. She is never that quiet, and since I haven't known her long enough to know what her silences mean, I'm not sure if I should be worried. Was that hug just as eye-opening for her as it was for me? Will she still go out on a date with CarMax? My body goes rigid as I peer over my shoulder. I can see she's still talking to him, but her body language isn't as free and bubbly as it was before. I refrain from giving myself a mental high-five.

It would be nice to get to know her, but I don't think I've earned it. One thing is for damn sure though, CarMax definitely hasn't earned it either. There are different types of dealers, and he has to be one of the worst. He hides behind his clean-cut exterior, but he's not above cutting as many corners as he can just to make a few extra bucks. Doesn't matter if he's screwing over the auction or an auctioneer. Everyone knows he's a liar, and I have no doubt it's the reason he pushed to be on Hunter's lane. She doesn't know him, so he can con her just like he has every other person he comes in contact with.

I walk through the office and JT is talking to one of the front desk girls, so I keep going. I'm almost to the front door when I hear him yell my name. I stop and look over to see him jogging toward me.

"Dude, I saw that." He folds his arms across his chest.

"Saw what?" I hope he's not talking about me wearing women's sunglasses.

He lets out a breath and shakes his head. "You weren't a total jerk to Hunter for once." He gives me a little nudge to walk out the doors.

I'm thankful because I don't want others to hear anything he says. He's always teased me, but I don't know what I'm feeling right now.

"Dude, you like her." He shoves my shoulder.

I stop dead in my tracks, looking at him with what I know is pure shock. "What?" I take my hat off, but the sun's rays cut through my eyes like a knife, so I quickly put it back on. "We just came to an understanding. That's all." There's no way he could jump to that conclusion.

"Right." He scoffs.

He always does this. He won't let it go, but if I mention the girl who broke his heart and made him into a player, he shuts down. He never wants to talk about *her*. He wants to dive into my personal life, and force me to spill all my secrets. That's the way he's always been.

JT rolls the sleeves of his button-up shirt, making me want to do the same. But I don't because I try to hide the tattoos on my arms while I work. The sun is blazing today though, so I undo the top few buttons of my shirt for some relief.

"She's going out with James."

The hard look on JT's face is everything I've been feeling. "You need to make sure that doesn't happen."

"How am I going to do that?" I look around the parking lot before looking back at my best friend.

"I don't know, man. Maybe talk to Jess?"

I nod. That's not a bad idea. I know James isn't her favorite person either. I don't know if Jess told Hunter, but he humiliated her. I heard all about how he acted like the nicest guy in the world only to screw her over for information on a car he wanted to buy. It was years ago, but I've always seen the look of disgust written across her face when he's around.

THROWING on a pair of gym shorts as soon as my eyes open, I grab my earphones and run out the door. My feet hit the pavement as Emery blasts through my ears. Running on the weekends always helps me stay in shape. By the time I get home during the week, I'm spent and a run is the last thing on my mind. But I always get up first thing on a Saturday and get a few miles in.

I tossed and turned all night thinking of Hunter going out with CarMax. I can't help but hope Jess will talk some sense into her. I don't want to step in, but she cannot be with that guy. My legs instinctively pound against the asphalt faster at the thought. It's like my world has been knocked upside down since getting my ass handed to me in pool. Images of her relaxing into my arms after I gave her the chocolate monstrosity flood my mind and make me want that feeling again.

"Walls" by Emery starts playing, and I can't fight the urge to nod my head along to the rhythmic song. I'm passing the dog park when golden fur darts in front of me, stopping me in my tracks. The fur ball sits at my feet, panting with his tongue dangling out the side of his mouth.

"Well, hello to you, too." I pet his soft hair, and he scoots his butt closer. I pick up his leash, so he doesn't bolt again. I'm sure his owner is looking for him. Pulling out my earphones, I hear a woman yell.

"Nickelback!" Her breathing is heavy. "I swear to god. I won't give you a spoon of peanut butter when we get home if you don't get your ass over here right now!"

There's something familiar about her voice. My hands pause, locked in this fur ball's hair. Hunter comes into view, and I watch her gaze all around the area. She's wearing green leggings, a black sports bra, and black tennis shoes. Her hair is haphazardly thrown into a bun on top of her head. With how much hair she has, it's amazing she can get most of it into a ponytail. She stops her search as she narrows her eyes on the dog in front of me.

Her eyes harden. "Nickelback, what the hell?" She storms over and kneels in front of us, grabbing the face of the dog and bringing it toward hers so their foreheads touch. "You can't run off like that." Placing a kiss on his head, she pets him before looking up at me. The sun blazes into her face, and she squints, having to look away. "I'm sorry about this guy. He has a mind of his own when he sees a squirrel."

"It's not a problem." I don't miss her fingers grasping the fur.

She gets to her feet, brushing off the leaves stuck to her legs. "Myles?" she asks like she was so concerned about the dog that she just realized who was in front of her.

"I'm guessing this guy belongs to Jess?" I hold my hand out with the leash. "Or do you also have a golden retriever with the same name?" I chuckle.

She shakes her head and reaches over, taking it from my hand. Her eyes meet mine as our fingers graze. "No, he's Jess' dog, but I wish he were mine." She scratches his ear. "What are you doing here?" Her head tilts slightly.

"I run here every weekend." I flex my hand, still feeling where it touched hers.

Her eyes lower and widen slightly. It looks as if she just realized I'm standing before her in nothing but shorts with sweat running down my chest. I can't help but love watching as she takes me in. Clearing my throat, her gaze jumps to meet mine, and she flushes as she looks away.

"Does he run away often?"

Shaking her head, she says, "No. He loves squirrels, and I let him chase them in the dog park area. I guess he forgot we were no longer in the fenced area." She raises her eyebrow at the dog who's looking up at her, wagging his tail. She pets his head again.

"Well, I'm sorry he stopped you. Don't let us keep you from your run."

"I don't mind. Want to run together?" I point over my shoulder to the trail.

Hunter's eyebrows furrow. "What?"

"You aren't running?" I take a small step closer.

"Well, yes." She runs the leash through her hands.

"We can run together if you want." I can't help but hold my breath hoping she'll let me be with her for a little while longer. This feels like such a simple interaction, but neither of us has been an asshole. I don't want it to end.

"No, no. It's fine." She waves me off.

My shoulders slump with the rejection, but I won't go down that easy. "Next time, then." I don't ask, and the way she looks at me tells me that she noticed it.

"Maybe."

I smirk, stepping back toward the trail. "One day soon." I turn before she can say anything and bring my run back to normal speed, popping my earbuds back in. My run is a little easier now that I have a sexy visual to focus on.

After my shower, I lounge on the couch, watching a movie when my phone rings. "Mama" flashes across the screen. I expected it to be another text from JT since I told him about my run-in with Hunter. Underneath his playboy exterior, he is a true romantic. The girl that broke his heart changed him, but I know the real him. He tries hard to shove that part of himself down.

"Hey, Mama. What's up?"

"Well, I haven't heard much from you." Her warm and comforting voice comes through the phone. "I know you're still grumpy about me and Gus, but how long did you think I'd stay single?"

I pinch the bridge of my nose. I hate talking about my mama's dating life. Doesn't help that mine is nonexistent while a beautiful brunette tortures me. I only want what is best for her, but this is a topic I'd rather avoid.

"Mama, I don't care that you're dating someone. I'm just worried about you, but I do want you to be happy. If Gus does that for you, just promise me you'll be careful."

"Oh, Miney, you worry too much." She sighs. "Gus is a great guy, and you would like him if you gave him a chance. Thanksgiving is coming up, and I want the two men in my life to get along."

Swinging my legs off the couch, I stand and pace my living room. "Mama, it's only the middle of September. We have a while before we need to worry about Turkey Day." I shake my head. This lady is going to make me gray before my time.

"Miney, I'm serious. Keep an open mind for me, please?" Her voice changes from a sweet to a more serious tone. "I want you to remember I spent twenty-five hours bringing you into this world. Myles Alexander Johnson, you owe me."

I let out a long sigh. Bringing up her long labor is her favorite ammo. "You do realize I can't owe you for the rest of my life, right?"

"Oh, no? Don't test me, son." I can picture her putting her small hand on her hip, just like she used to do when I was a child. I would do something she didn't like, and she would take her balled-up fist stance and stare me down.

"Fuck! Fine, I'll give Gus a chance."

"Hey! Mind your language! And thank you. I'll see you tonight at seven for dinner," she says a little too sweetly before hanging up.

I pull the phone away from my ear. *What the fuck?* How did I get roped into dinner without agreeing?

12

HUNTER

The past week, I've picked up seven different sales along with a sale one Saturday each month. I absolutely love it. Jess and I decided Mondays are Hallmark movie night, accompanied by a tub of ice cream. She happily joined the dark side with my love of sweets and now complains that she will have to join me on a few runs.

"So when is he picking you up?" Jess asks from the kitchen while I get ready for my date. Nickelback lounges lazily on my bed, huffing every few minutes. I never thought of myself as a dog person, but Nickelback and I mesh well. He cuddles with me in bed at night and on the sofa while I binge Netflix or read a book. He keeps me motivated to stay active by either demanding we play fetch every night or go for a walk. He's become one of my best friends, and Jess doesn't mind because I share the "dog mom" responsibilities.

I check the time on my phone. "In thirty minutes," I yell back to her.

"Where is he taking you again?"

Jess has made it clear she doesn't approve of James. She's

either making subtle comments or in overprotective mode. It's almost as if she can't decide which way is best to go about it.

"To dinner and a movie, *Mom*," I tease. Her footsteps on the hardwood floor indicate she's getting closer. I'm dressed in my purple sundress and playing with different hairstyles.

Jess places her hand on her hip. "I'm trying to look out for you. Like what if you get kidnapped? What if he takes you to his house and won't let you leave?" Taking her hand off her hip, she waves her index finger at me. "What if he takes you to another state, and I can't find you? You know that can happen!" she says while nervously biting her thumbnail, her eyes getting bigger by the second. She holds out her hand. "Give me your phone. I'm going to turn on your location, so I can find you."

"Jess, none of that is going to happen, and you have got to lay off the true crime." I glance at her reflection in the mirror as I pull a few strands of hair on the side, seeing if I want to put them in a braid.

I startle when she lets out a high-pitch gasp. My heart beats fast as I whip around to look at her. "What?"

She's still standing at my door when her hands fly over her mouth. "I'll have to call your *mother*."

I roll my eyes and turn back to my mirror. "For heaven's sake, Jess." I pull my hair back into a low bun to see how I like that. "You need to calm down. He's a nice guy. I don't understand why you don't like him. He's nice to you at work. What do you have against him?" I turn to look at her, forgoing anything I was attempting to do with my hair.

"I just don't like him *with* you." Spinning around, she goes back into the kitchen.

I still have to finish my hair and makeup, but I have to know what she means. I stand up, following her into the kitchen. "What's that supposed to mean?" I cross my arms over my chest. "Why don't you like him *with* me? He's kind, opens doors for me, and isn't bad to look at. What more could you want?" my voice elevates. Nickelback prances into the kitchen and puts his paw on my leg, his nails digging into my skin. Wincing, I hold his paw in my hand instead to relieve the sting.

She balls her hands into fists. "Didn't you notice that he only started being nice to me once he wanted to date you? Like he couldn't spend a few minutes out of his day trying to be kind until he wanted to date *my* friend."

I scoff. "What are you talking about? He's always been nice."

"No. He has not. Not to me, at least." Jess huffs and covers her face with her hands before meeting my eyes again. "Do you seriously not see it?"

My eyebrows raise while my jaw gapes. "What?"

She sighs. "I'm just saying that dealers are kind to you. Not because of who you are, but what you can do for them. I am just a block clerk, so they don't need to be kind to me unless they want something." She takes a deep breath. "Then once they get it, they toss me aside."

"Jess,"—I start to say but stop when I can't find the words.

She grabs my hand in hers. "I'm just saying that it's noticeable, and it seems really fake."

I nod, trying to understand. "I guess, but I didn't know him before. James has only been kind to me."

She sighs and turns around to get a mug out of a cabinet. "I know. I guess I was hoping he would have shown his true colors by now." She glances at the clock on the stove. "You better go finish getting ready." Putting the mug on the counter, she turns around, goes to the refrigerator, and pulls out leftovers for her dinner.

"Okay." I quickly pet Nickelback and head into my room.

"For what it's worth"—Jess peaks her head inside my door. "If you are truly happy with him, I hope he proves me wrong."

I smile, appreciating her words.

I finish my hair by putting gel in it before turning my head upside down to use the diffuser on my hair dryer. I'm almost done with my makeup when I hear the knock on the front door. *Crap.* I was hoping to be completely ready, so we could leave when he got here. But because of my little spiff with Jess, I'm running behind.

"Jess, do you mind getting the door?" *And be nice.*

"Sure," she says, and I hear her open the door. "Hi, James."

"Oh, hey, Jess. Is Hunter ready?" His calm tone comes through the house.

"No. Come in. Pretty sure she's almost done." Her voice is monotone. It doesn't sound like her at all and that bothers me. She's become such a close friend, and I want her to like who I'm dating. "Nickelback, get down. Sorry, he loves new people."

I quickly finish my makeup. It's not like I wear much of it, anyway. Usually, I prefer nothing, but I add a little around my eyes for work and dates. Taking one last look in the mirror, I wipe a little mascara off my eyelid and head out to the living room.

James stands by the door, looking a little uncomfortable with his hands in his pockets and continuous glances at my furry friend. He's wearing khaki pants with a blue polo shirt that almost looks too small, and his hair is styled a little messy.

"Wow! Hunter, you look great!" he says, looking me over before glancing at Jess and Nickelback with a grimace.

What the fuck was that?

"Thanks!" I rub my hand down my dress to smooth any left-over wrinkles. "Are you ready to go?"

"You two kids have fun!" Jess says, while holding back the dog.

"Thanks, Jess," I sarcastically say. "Bye, Nickelback. Bite her in the ass while I'm gone," I sweetly say to the dog before rubbing him on the ear. Jess gives me her fakest smile, and I stick my tongue out at her before turning toward James to leave.

His silver Toyota Camry is in the driveway, and he opens the passenger door for me. It's a sensible car with all the driving he does. Maybe that's why Jess doesn't care for him. *No, she's not shal-*

low. She doesn't care about what people drive. My quarrel with Jess will bother me all night. I don't like fighting with anyone, but especially not her. I just want to go back inside and hash it out with her, but that's not fair to James.

He waits for me to buckle before shutting my door and walking around to his side. He looks over at me and smiles. He's friendly, but I don't feel much of a spark with him yet. Maybe tonight will change that.

"Hey, pretty girl." He leans closer to me. *What is he doing?* Time feels like it slows as I watch him. My heart palpitates, and not in a good way. I don't want to hurt his feelings, but I'm not ready for this. With how I'm feeling, I'm not sure I'll ever be ready for this with him.

I turn my head and laugh nervously. "So what movie are we going to see?" I ask, trying to avoid what he apparently planned on doing. This is awkward and in my driveway, of all places.

He sits back before rubbing the back of his neck. "Um, it's called Abduction." He gives me a small smile.

He's trying to be nice, but I'll refrain from saying that I didn't like Taylor Lautner in the movies I've seen him in. I liked the Twilight books but couldn't get through the movies. Schooling my face into something neutral, he pulls onto the main highway.

Fuck. I'm terrible at this. Dating. I've had boyfriends, it's not like Steve and I didn't sleep together. But even that didn't live up to the hype. You spread your legs, and he kisses you a few times. Once he's done doing his *thing*, you go back to looking at your phone or watching a movie. I could take it or leave it, but mostly leave it. I've always wondered if there is something wrong with me. Some women say they crave sex, but I don't understand. I haven't enjoyed it enough to *want* it. Steve always initiated or begged, making me feel bad when I wasn't up for it.

"Hey, where did you go? You okay?" James touches my arm, looking at me before turning back to the road again.

"Oh, yeah," I grin. "I'm good. The movie sounds great!" I look down and watch as he reaches over to hold my hand. Stopping at a red light, I look into his brown eyes, seeing a guy who's trying to get close to me. So I hold his hand all the way to the movies and feel nothing.

"This theater has some good pizza, so I thought we could eat it while we watch the movie. Is that okay with you?" James asks. I may be crazy, but I'm not much of a pizza person. But I'd rather eat it than make it a big deal.

"Yeah. Sounds good." I turn back to looking outside.

What would it be like to want to touch someone? I mean, that has only happened once to me. It was after I'd met *Myles*, and his strong hands picked me up off the floor. He stepped away, and I had to keep myself from closing the distance.

Woah, where did that come from?

I shake my head. I don't need to be thinking about how hot and rugged he is, especially right now. Seeing him with his shirt off and his strong muscles just begging me to touch them was hard. It's like a veil has been lifted, and I'm seeing the real Myles for the first time. He gave me my favorite coffee and was friendly when he caught the furball, even asking me to run with him. It made me see the side of him that everyone else always talks about, but I can't believe he caught me checking him out. It was honestly unavoidable. His body was on complete display, and I have never been more turned on by someone in my life.

"Did you say something?" James looks over at me while pulling into the parking lot.

I whip my head to look his way, my eyes no doubt bugging out of my head. "Oh, no."

"Okay, well, we're here." He pulls his hand away to park the car. I'm relieved because as much as he seems to like holding my hand, it makes me nervous. Not because I like him, but because I'm afraid I don't like him *enough*.

My mind wanders back to Myles, and my cheeks warm at the thought of holding his hand. The way his strong hands burned their mark on my hips, or the way his lips felt as they ghosted over the shell of my ear. When he gave me the most mesmerizing smile while wearing my sunglasses. I've definitely lost sleep wondering why he acts the way he does.

James turns off the car and goes to open the door when I blurt, "Does your car have a name?"

He turns to look at me with a puzzled look. Okay, yes, it's a random question, but not unheard of. I don't know how to not be awkward on a date. Plus, I need to stop thinking of a certain ringman.

"Um, no. Why would it?"

"I mean you spend more time with your car than anyone or anything else, especially in this industry."

"It gets me from point A to point B." He shakes his head. "I've never understood people who felt the need to name their cars."

I look down at my hands folded in my lap. "Oh." I turn to open the door.

"Hey," he says, grabbing my hand. "I'm sorry. You told me you like your Bronco, and it's an awesome ride. I've never had one that was as nice as yours, I guess. I drive so much I have to buy cars pretty frequently." Giving me a reassuring smile, he squeezes my hand and gets out of the car.

I guess he has a point, but I've never understood why people don't name their cars. I spend at least twelve hours a week driving to all my different jobs. Westley and I are close, and it's not because he looks good. I spend more time with him than I do going out on dates, so of course, he should have a name.

We walk into the theater and get our food and tickets. This is the quietest date I've been on, and it's growing more uncomfortable by the minute. What do people do on dates? Steve basically dated me at work. He wanted everyone to know he was with Conrad's daughter. I tried to avoid traditional dates with him because there would be a chance he would drink. The first time he got loud and a little physical, I thought it was a fluke. But after the fifth time it happened, I realized it wasn't. I ended things and left him. I knew he wouldn't make it easy, and I didn't want to see him at work. I love being an auctioneer. I don't want to dread going to work because of who's there. Oklahoma never felt much like home, so it was easy to leave.

I follow James up the aisle to the back of the theater, passing only a few other couples on the way. It's a little eerie being in an almost empty theater, but I'm not complaining. I don't like sitting next to strangers. We both dig into our pizza before the movie starts. It's becoming obvious that we have little to talk about.

"So—" James begins after swallowing another large bite. "Now that you've been through a week at the car auctions, do you feel more at home?"

I finish my bite of pizza and wipe my mouth with my napkin. "Um. Yeah. I mean, it's still difficult sometimes, but I love it so far. I'm hoping to find a few more auctions to work at, and then I'll be good. I'm actually going for an interview tomorrow at a cattle auction." Sadly, the only thing we can talk about is work. I've tried talking to him about his hobbies and interests outside of work in passing at the sales, but he always brings the conversations back to cars. I'd like more out of a relationship than just shop talk.

I'm excited about my interview. Cattle auctions are in my blood. They feel more like home to me than the house I grew up in. It's such a different atmosphere than the car auctions. There's something about the dealers all sitting down around a pen with a cow running around that puts you more at ease.

He looks surprised. "A cattle auction? Why?" he asks and gives a disgusted face.

Well, alrighty then.

I turn to face him and cock my head. "James, I grew up around them. What do you mean, why?" It can't be that crazy. Of course, I would want to work at a cattle auction. I just had to get in at car auctions since there are many more within driving distance. I couldn't afford to only work at two cattle auctions.

"Well, yeah, but I figured you came here to get away from that." He waves his hand around in a circle in front of him. "Now, you're *in* at car auctions, and that's a better type of auction to work at." He says it like it's a fact.

Excuse me? This conversation keeps getting worse. My ears burn listening to the shit coming out of his mouth.

"Why would it be better?" I cross my arms, not hiding how annoyed I am from my tone. "I guess that's *your* opinion, but that's not true for everyone. I love cattle auctions. I was raised in them. It's where I learned to be a great auctioneer. It's more exciting too." I tuck some stray hair behind my ear before continuing. "You sound like a person who has never been to one and is judging it based on something you have no clue about. Or you can't look past the cow shit in the ring."

I turn my body completely forward, resting my cheek on my hand, so I don't catch even a glimpse of him and watch the screen as the lights lower. I'm done with this conversation. James doesn't try to say anything back. I'm pretty sure I stunned him.

He leans over, causing my body to tense, before he whispers, "Hey, I'm sorry. I shouldn't have said that." Sadness and embarrassment lace his voice.

I'm too far over this whole thing to care.

I look at him. "No, you shouldn't have." If he had taken a second to try and understand where I was coming from, it would have been different. But I refuse to give a chance to someone who bashes anything they have no knowledge about. I want to go home and not watch this movie. Maybe Jess was right. Maybe he is a dick.

13

MYLES

"Dude, I hate this store." I look at JT as he pulls in front of Target.

"You'll get over it." He opens his door and climbs out, not taking a single glance my way.

JT loves this store. I swear he's such a girl sometimes. I shake my head and get out of the truck. Whatever, as long as it has the groceries I need to make dinner, I'll let him be easily entertained.

I grab a cart once inside, and he says he'll meet me after I grab the groceries. He always bails on me in stores, probably to look at sheets or something. I shake my head as I walk to the right side where the produce is. I roam the aisles, grabbing different ingredients. We are making smash burgers with a fried egg inside. My mouth waters just thinking about the melted cheese and over easy egg oozing into the meat on the bun.

I grab lettuce, tossing it into the cart when I hear a slap next to me. I look over and a woman is bending over a watermelon, leaning her ear closer. My eyes narrow as I realize *who* is spanking the watermelons. She's wearing a loose T-shirt and jean shorts, and her brown hair is cascading around her face over top of the produce.

"You do realize that's not how you pick a watermelon, right?"

Hunter's body goes ramrod straight and whips around to face me. Her mouth parts as her eyes meet mine then looks at my cart, appraising the contents. Fucking hell, she's a Yankee fan. I stare at her navy blue with white lettering shirt. If I didn't like her before, I sure as hell do now.

"Yeah, not sure I want to take the advice of a guy who obviously mixes ketchup with his scrambled eggs."

I look into my basket and see the carton of eggs, ketchup, cheese, and bread buns. "Oh, I'd love to show you exactly what I'm cooking tonight." A smile plays at the corner of my lips.

"Maybe someday." She goes to walk away, picking up a watermelon as she passes.

My mouth is open before I can stop it. "Hunter?"

She turns to look at me after placing the melon in her cart. "Yeah?" Her face a picture of ease.

"I gotta know…"

Her eyebrows furrow, leaning her weight on her right leg. "Know what?"

I rub the back of my neck before I finally blurt out, "Did you go out with James?"

She blinks a few times. "Yeah," she answers, slowly.

My hands ball into fists at my sides. "He's not a good guy," I let slip. I have no loyalty to the guy, but it's a tight-knit industry. If someone hears you talking shit about someone else, it spreads like wildfire. Dealers definitely don't want an auctioneer who talks bad about one of their own. I sigh. "I'm just saying, I don't think he's good for you."

She lets out a humorless laugh. "And you know what is good for me?"

"Shit, this isn't coming out right." I adjust my hat on my head. "I'm only trying to say that I've heard a few things about him, and I don't want you around a guy like him."

Her jaw drops. "You don't want me around a guy like *him*?"

I rub my palms over my face. I go to say something but she holds her hand up, silencing me.

"Listen, you have no right to tell me who I can date. My love life is none of your concern. Whether or not I'm with James has *nothing* to do with you. Got it?"

I slowly nod. "I know. But…"

"Goodbye, Myles."

I watch her make a beeline to the self-checkout, quickly buying her food and storming out the door. JT walks up next to me.

He points. "Was that Hunter?"

"Yup," I growl.

Peering over at me, he says, "Do you want to talk about it?"

"Nope." I push our cart toward the checkout lanes.

SITTING ON A LARGE WOODEN STUMP, I rest my elbows on my knees, soaking up the fresh air. As I listen to the steady flow of the creek, it's the most relaxed I've felt all week. I'm at the one place that feels more like home than my own. The trails that lead into the woods from the back of JT's house can only be reached on horseback, so the area is completely secluded. I came here trying to clear my head of that wild-haired woman. But my mind continues to wander back to Hunter.

I told JT I was riding to the creek. I like to start my week decompressing out here before dinner. He told me he would try to meet me, but he got a new quarter horse after returning from the store and isn't sure he can get her settled enough to get here before dark. He always goes the extra mile for his animals. He won't leave their side till they at least drink some water and have a little hay. JT says he never sleeps well in a new location, so he wants his animals to feel comfortable before leaving them, even if that means staying in their paddock all night.

Sitting on a stump around a firepit JT and I built for colder nights, I toss a rock into the rushing water, making a rabbit dash into the woods. Cricket's song rings in my ears as birds flap their wings overhead. We spend a lot of time here sitting by the fire at night, drinking and enjoying downtime from work.

Images flood my head of what it would be like to bring Hunter here. Does she know how to ride? I could teach her, or she could ride with me. Oh, to have her sexy little ass nestled between my legs on a horse. On second thought, I don't want her to learn how to ride on her own. I immediately feel a boner growing hard under the zipper of my jeans. *Fuck.* This has been happening a lot. I can't get her out of my head. I don't even want to pick up random girls at a bar for a good time. The only interest I seem to have is picturing Hunter climbing out of her pool in a skimpy black two-piece, water gliding off every curve as I fuck my hand. It's embarrassing. It's like I'm a pimply-ass, sex-deprived virgin all over again.

Fuck, I miss sex.

I hear a snort from a horse approaching and know JT must be near. He always has perfect timing. He catches me at the worst times and loves to give me grief about it for hours. I already know this will be no exception. He'll probably take one look at me and rag on me. He's always been able to read me like a book.

"Did you get the horse settled into the paddock?" I holler, not taking my eyes off the water.

"Obviously, or I wouldn't be here, dumbass." He gets off of his horse, Sunshine, and lets her get some water before tying her up. "So what's on your mind?" He turns toward me after settling on the log next to me. "You're giving off even more broody vibes than normal. This wouldn't have anything to do with running into Hunter at the store, would it?"

I roll my eyes. "What? Do you want to go back and forth and

talk about our feelings around the fire?" I ask sarcastically. I don't have time for this tonight.

"First off," he says, holding up his index finger, "there is no fire, nor am I going to build one." He puts up another finger. "Secondly, fuck you. It's impossible to not mention your mood when it radiates off you and contaminates my air, and third"—finger number three joins the rest—"don't make me call Mama."

Fuck. That would be horrible. He knows I don't want him telling her I'm moody. JT's pushy, but good god, that woman is in a whole other category. She wouldn't leave me alone until I'd laid everything I've been feeling out on the table. I wouldn't wish that on my worst enemy…well, maybe CarMax James.

"I do *not* like you," I growl.

"Then, spill it." He motions to me with his fingers, like he's trying to drag the words out of my mouth. "We don't have all night. It'll be dark in 3 hours." He stretches out his legs to get more comfortable. "Also, I want those burgers."

I shake my head. I know if I don't at least talk to him about it, I'm going to go insane. Or I could do something stupid. Talking to him seems like the lesser of all the evils.

I rub my hands up and down my face, hoping that if I rub long enough, the thoughts will disappear. "I put my fucking foot in my mouth." I look over at him, and he just nods, permitting me to continue. I sigh. "I told her that CarMax wasn't good enough for her."

His eyebrows raise in surprise. "Okay." He knows I don't usually give a crap about what happens with a girl. But Hunter is different, and I know he understands that.

Letting out a breath, I look at the dirt between my boots. "And I kinda told her that I don't want her around a guy like him." I wince.

His eyes widen, and he drops a rock from his palm, making it land with a thump in the dirt. "Well, that was dumb."

I nod. "Yeah. I know."

"Well, what are you going to do about it?" he asks, as if I already have the answer.

I glare at him. "If I knew that, I wouldn't be sitting here trying to figure it out with your sorry ass."

"Come on," JT nudges, "it's not that hard."

I grunt, unable to shake the haze that's crept into my head.

"Dude, how did you approach women before Hunter?" he asks, picking up a stick and chopping at the dirt with it.

"It's not as easy as you think," I huff out. "I want to ask her out so we can at least get to know each other outside of the auction."

"Well, definitely don't ask her out right now. She would shoot you down faster than she can sell a car." He smirks, pulls out a pocket knife, and starts whittling notches into the stick. "You and I both know that's pretty damn fast." JT points the knife at me.

"You are absolutely no help." *Seriously, what kind of pep talk is this?*

"Bro, just say you're sorry. Be friendly. Continue to show her the real you. Then you can ask her out."

"Since when do you have all the answers for relationships?" I turn to him and grab the stick out of his hand, feeling the smooth wood against my hand before tossing it back at him. "I don't see you with a steady girlfriend."

Honestly, neither of us has had many serious relationships. I know he had one before coming to my high school, but it ended because he had to move. He doesn't talk much about it. I know it's a sore subject. But since then, we've both been single.

"Yeah. I know. It's easier said than done sometimes," he says and stares off into the distance.

"Do you ever hear from *her*?" I ask.

His head whips around in fake confusion. "Hunter? I talk to her every day at work." He gives a light laugh before going back to carving, and I know he's trying to avoid my question.

"No, not Hunter." I keep pressing.

"We aren't talking about *her*, so let's keep talking about how royally fucked up your life is." He glares at me, and I know this is as serious as he gets. He likes to keep things fun and easy, but sometimes he becomes a different person. His past changed him. Not necessarily for the worst, but not really for the better either.

"I know. I'm here if you want to talk."

He rakes his fingers through his hair. "Jesus, way to turn it around on me," he says, then nods over his shoulder. "You ready to head back, or do you want to keep talking about how you are going to fix it with Hunter? We could also paint each other's nails while we're at it."

"I'm good." I slap my knees before standing up to stretch out my back. "Let's get these horses home and fed."

We mount our horses and start our slow ride back to his house. JT and I never rush the ride back because there is nowhere else we'd rather be than on these trails listening to the crickets and frogs as they sing the world to sleep. As we make our way back, my mind wanders, and it settles back on that petite face with the button nose and sparkling eyes. I allow myself the luxury of imagining myself riding these trails, with Hunter riding behind me, her arms wrapped tightly around my waist. We are riding next to JT, with a smile on his face and a woman whose face I can't see sitting behind him on our way to the creek. We're happy.

"I guess now would be a good time to tell you I got Hunter hired at the Ocala Stockyard, and she starts tomorrow." JT's voice invades my musings and the scene I was imagining fades in the dust Sunshine kicks up in front of me.

Shaking myself to clear my mind, JT disappears through the trees. What did he just say? I thought I had till Tuesday to at least work up the nerve to talk to her. Now I'm seeing her tomorrow at my favorite auction? *Fuck me.*

14

HUNTER

I FLICK on my blinker and turn into the Ocala Stockyard. JT got me in at a cattle auction, saying they could use another auctioneer as backup. After putting out feelers trying to get hired at one, this opportunity fell into my lap. I won't be the main auctioneer, but I'm getting my foot in the door. Unlike my first day at the car auction, I don't have any nerves going into this one.

The other night's disaster can't even put a damper on my mood. I know I overreacted with James since everyone is entitled to their opinions, but it just confirmed we aren't compatible. He dropped me off at home and gave me a hug. He tried to convince me it was just a bump we could get through, but I don't think it's a hill worth climbing. I'd rather find someone who sweeps me off my feet, a man who will understand my passions and hopefully have similar ones. I had a whole movie to think about it, and I feel good about my decision. Jess was elated when I came inside and told her. I caught her spying on us through the front window.

I pull into a parking space and get out. I dressed in my favorite jeans and brown boots, finishing the look with a black tank top and green flannel button up. My sleeves are rolled right below my elbows since it's a warmer day. Peering into my side mirror, I make sure there isn't anything in my teeth. My curls twist around each other as they wind their way down my back.

The Ocala Stockyard is the closest auction to our house. I don't have to drive all over Florida to go to work, and I freaking love it. I'm one step away from skipping into the office, singing at the top of my lungs. Like that wouldn't freak them out about the woman they just hired. Instead, I casually walk inside. A blast of cold air hits my face as I walk through the front door, and it feels amazing. I'm still getting used to the Florida heat. The humidity is foreign to me, the way it causes my hair to be extra poofy, not that it ever lacked in that department.

The front desk lady looks at me. "Are you Hunter?"

I nod, smiling at her, and step forward. I open my mouth to say something, but she keeps talking.

"The boss is waiting for you in his office." She points to a door over her shoulder before going back to typing.

"Thank you," I say, walking around the large counter. I knock on the open door and peek my head inside, only to find JT, Aaron, a man who I assume is the boss - his name is Thomas - and Myles, in the corner all staring at me. Why is Myles here? He doesn't work the cattle auctions. Does he?

"Hey there, Hunter," the man says. "I'm Thomas." He gets up and shakes my hand. "I've heard a lot about you from these guys." He motions to the other three men in the room. "It's good to put a face to your name."

"It's nice to meet you too." I reach my hand out to shake his. "I can't tell you how much I appreciate you letting me help out. I love cattle auctions and can't wait to get out there," I say while also trying to rein in my excitement. I look over his shoulder at the other guys in the room and give them all a smile. But when my eyes find Myles, I pause. He's meeting my gaze, and he's giving me a look I've never seen before. Butterflies swarm in my stomach, and I quickly look away.

"The guys will show you around. I know you grew up around

cattle auctions. So do what you feel comfortable with. JT and Myles usually help wrangle the cattle while pointing out bids. We like to have extra hands, just in case. Aaron is our main auctioneer, but since the auction goes so long, we like to give him extra breaks. Today, I'd like you to shadow Myles since he's usually the one to give Aaron a break. If that's alright with you?" Thomas asks, then looks over at Myles.

Before I can reply, Myles speaks up, "Yes, sir. But I was thinking." He steps toward the boss. "Why don't we let Hunter give Aaron the breaks today? I'm sure we could learn a thing or two from her."

I have to keep my jaw locked so it doesn't hit the floor. To say I'm shocked is an understatement. I might have to look around for some hidden cameras because this must be a prank. Myles wouldn't even show me around the building on my first day. Now he's suggesting I take his job? I look over at JT to see if he'll give me any clue on what is going on, but he only gives me a wink. Alright, I guess I have to figure out what's going on by myself.

Thomas nods, looking at Myles. "Sounds good. Just be sure to show her everything and who the regular bidders are."

"Of course," Myles says. He walks toward the door and motions for me to go first through it.

I walk out of the office, pausing because I don't know where to go. Myles lightly touches my elbow to tug me in the right direction. The only problem is that his light contact sends a bolt of excitement through my body. *Seriously?* It's not like I've never been touched by a guy before.

We walk down a hall, and I can't help but glance over at Myles as he waves at a few employees. Some even ask him how his weekend was. He seems to be in his element, more so than at the car auctions.

"Why are you here?" I stop walking and fold my arms across my chest.

He pauses, looking over his shoulder, and turns to face me. His eyebrows furrow. "I work here."

I roll my eyes. "No shit. Why do you work at a cattle auction? It's not beneath you?"

"No?" he asks like it was a weird question. "Why would it be?" He takes a step toward me, putting his hands in his pockets. "This auction gave me my first shot. JT, too. It's not just a job for me here. I've worked here for a decade. These people have been my family since I was eighteen."

My mouth falls open. James thought this other world was beneath him, but Myles makes it sound as if he holds them in higher regard. I guess he doesn't expect me to respond because after a few seconds, he continues down the hall.

"You'll notice that there are men who bid on specific cattle, but I'll point them out to you. You ready for this?" Myles glances at me.

I blink a few times, still processing what he's saying. I finally nod when he stops walking and eyes me up and down. "Yeah. Definitely." I lift my chin.

He smirks. "I have no doubt."

On my first day, he was positive that he would have to bail me out and take over the lane. But now he's acting confident in my ability and suggested the boss let me take his place. It's confusing to say the least, but it's making me more attracted to him.

I see the door to the main room up ahead, and I take in as many details as I can. Cattle auctions are similar wherever you are. So I don't feel the need to look around, but I don't think I can continue to stare into his face. I still feel his gaze on me, and it's unnerving.

"You're a pro at this, aren't you?"

I look at his relaxed body. His hands rest in his pockets, and a lazy grin plasters his face. He's in his element, and it makes me relax too.

"My dad is Conrad Smith. What do you think?" I playfully arch my brow.

He stops walking as soon as we are standing in the large room where the auction is held, and leans over, pressing his body against my side. His breath tickles my ear as he says, "Alright, Hershey. Let's see what ya got." Giving me a wink, he pushes the gate open.

What has gotten into him? I'm left speechless while I watch his firm ass walk into the round pen, soon to be flooded with cows. But I try my best to push him out of my head. I want to show Thomas I have what it takes. Female auctioneers at car auctions are rare. Female auctioneers at cattle auctions are unheard of. A lot of the older men who come to the cattle auctions are firm believers that this is a man's job. I have to make sure I'm not distracted or someone will complain that I don't know what I'm doing and get me fired. And it wouldn't be the first time something like that has happened.

A cattle auction differs completely from a car auction. It's held in a large room and there is a circular pen in the middle on the ground with a gate for the cows to come and go. On one side of the room, there is a stage located above the cows for the auctioneer and block clerk. The majority of the other side of the room is all seating similar to the Coliseum. The seating gets higher the further you are from the pen so everyone can see what is being sold. It's very informal. The bidders are in casual conversation while the cows are sold. Everyone knows each other, so it's hard being a new face in the room.

There are a few ways to buy the cows. You can buy one cow or sometimes an entire herd that has several heads sold together.

I love working with JT and Myles. We all mesh well together. We rotate who lets the cows in and who helps Aaron with taking bids. It's fun, and I don't remember the last time I laughed so much while at work. Most of the cows do as they're directed. But when we get a cow that won't, we try to keep our cool while pushing until it budges.

I'm in my head about Myles, though. When JT and I are in the pen together, he keeps a wide berth when we pass each other. But when Myles passes, he always finds a reason to give me the subtlest touch. I can still feel where his hands held onto my hips longer than needed to keep a cow from pushing me over. The marks of his fingers dug into my hip bones. Now they're permanently tattooed with the heat of his skin.

It's confusing. He acted as if he was responsible for ensuring I didn't go out with James. What sucks is that he was starting to win me over. Then he went all caveman on me, and I am not okay with that.

"Hey," Myles yells, so I can hear him over the loudspeaker.

"What?" I yell back. I can feel the noise radiating through my body, down to my toes.

He motions over his shoulder to Aaron, selling the lot in the ring with us. "You're up. Remember what I told you. If there are no bidders, sell it to number five-twenty."

"Got it." I step around him, but pause when his hand firmly grasps my elbow. His smile reaches his eyes and makes them crinkle.

"Don't make me look too bad. I kinda like it here." He winks.

"Well, you should have thought of that before telling the boss to give me your job," I say before I can stop myself and grin.

His laughter is drowned out by Aaron selling the herd that JT pushed through the gate.

After the sale, we file into Thomas' office. Myles is right by my side, like he has been all day. I'm exhausted and just want to get some food in my stomach. But I had the best time. Thankfully, the men didn't haze me much, and I got to sell a good amount.

"Hey. You all did great today," Thomas says. "The sale ran smoothly, and I'll see you next week, right?" Thomas looks right at me like his question was only for me.

I nod. "I'd love to come back."

His shoulders visibility relax. "Great. I appreciate it. You make a sound addition to the team." He reaches out and shakes my hand, and then speaks to the entire team. "Have a great week, everyone."

The sale ended right after two p.m., and none of us had anything to eat except the few snacks we brought. So my stomach plays a gurgling tune as I shield my eyes from the sun. Beads of sweat break out across my body, trickling down my curves. This heat is brutal.

My body goes on high alert when I sense Myles walk by me. "Will you go to lunch with me?" Myles asks. I stop, and JT almost runs into me.

"Woah, Fun-Size. You need to lay on the horn or something before slamming on the breaks. I can't see you stopping from down there." He winks, and I fight the urge to roll my eyes.

"Ha. Ha. You're so funny." I shake my head in disbelief.

"I know. How about we ditch this one,"—he nods at Myles, who glares back at him—"and I'll take you to have some real fun?"

I laugh. "Actually, how about you join us? I have a huge craving for Mexican food." I look between the guys.

Rubbing his hands together, he licks his lips. "Oh, that does sound good." I catch his eyes flicker to Myles for a second before they land on me again. "I was just messing with Myles. I need to get home. You two have fun." He tips his imaginary hat and spins around.

Deep blues eyes meet my gaze. "Look, I've been an ass to you. If you'd give me the chance, I'd like to make it up to you. Let me buy you lunch and apologize." Myles presses his lips together and forces a crooked smile onto his face, making it easier to envision the little boy who worked hard but never got recognition for his efforts.

Why did I have to be raised with manners? It's making it hard for me to turn him down and walk away.

I look at my Bronco, wondering if I should leave, then look back at him. My rejection gets stuck in my throat. He's still watching me, waiting for an answer, apparently in no rush to go home. My stomach growls again. Okay, one lunch won't hurt, especially since there's free food involved. My shoulders drop as I give in and sigh, "Okay, but one asshole remark"—I poke him in the chest—"and I'm gone." I lift my thumb over my shoulder and gesture toward the road so he knows I'm serious.

"Yes, ma'am." He smiles, and I see a dimple I've never noticed before, peeking out from beneath some scruff that seems to have gotten longer over the weekend.

Did he just call me *ma'am?*

My shoulders slump as I sigh. "Jess will be disappointed she missed out on a chance to give you the third degree."

Myles opens the door for me to the restaurant, that grin still teasing his lips as he watches me pass, his eyes never leaving mine as I walk inside. It all feels weird, date-like even. Like both of us are feeling on edge with unfamiliarity and uncertainty about how this will pan out. Will I make it hard for him? Will he continue to be an ass? Should we both just call it quits? The hostess shows us to our table, dropping off a basket of chips and salsa. I'm freaking obsessed with chips and salsa, but my nerves have me breaking the chips into tiny pieces too small to dip, and by the time I've broken them up and popped a few in my mouth, I realize they aren't good without the salsa. This feels different. I knew I should have gone home.

Why do I put myself in these situations? First, James and now

Myles. Jess was right when she insinuated I didn't want to *be* with him. I don't want to *be* with Myles, either. Except, the big difference between James and Myles is I didn't feel anything when James touched me. But the smallest touch from Myles sends burning sensations throughout my body, making me want more. I've already imagined what it would be like to have his muscular arms wrapped around me, which is ridiculous. Except all I can think about is that they were on full display and glistening with sweat at the park.

Myles clears his throat. "I'm sorry."

I stop breaking the chips and look up. Narrowing my eyes at him, I say, "That's it?"

He sighs. "I stepped out of line. It wasn't my place to talk about whatever you have with James. I'm really sorry. It won't happen again."

I shift my legs over the leather booth, scanning over all the colorful Hispanic decor around the room, unsure where to look. He's watching me intently and seems to have no problem sitting in awkward silence, waiting for me to answer. I pause, taking in everything he said.

"You're right. It wasn't your place." I cross my arms and lean back into the booth. "I thought we were getting to a better place, and then you went and did that."

His shoulders drop as he looks down, folding his hands on the table. He looks sad, and it makes me regret how harsh my words were. "I know, Hunter. I'm sorry." He rubs the back of his neck and looks at me with the most sincere expression, and for whatever reason, I want to believe him.

His eyes are full of shame and remorse, and looking into them for too long feels like looking at the sun. It's too much, and I pinch the bridge of my nose, not prepared to have this conversation today. "Why? Why did you get weird about me going out with James, and why do you *now* want to be friends?" I ask because I can't sweep it under the rug with a single apology. I need to know his reasoning.

He takes his hat off and rakes his fingers through his hair before putting his hat on backward. "Look, I'm not proud of what I did. I got jealous, which fucked with my head because you took my job." Shaking his head, he revises, "They gave you the job I thought was supposed to be mine." He inhales through his nose and readjusts himself to sit up straighter. I open my mouth, but he puts his finger up. I look at his chiseled jaw flex a few times, looking like he's holding something in, or debating if he should let it out. "I know it wasn't your fault, but I still blamed you for it." Sighing, he rubs his hand up and down his face a few times before repositioning his hat. "It was always something. If I wasn't pissed at you for the job, I was pissed at you for making me hard every time I'm around you."

A chip falls from my hand on the way to my mouth. I can't do anything but stare at him. Did I just dream it or did those words just come out of his filthy and suddenly sexy mouth that now I can't seem to tear my eyes away from his full lips? They turn into a smirk, and I know I've been caught staring. My eyes flick up to meet his, and I furrow my eyebrows.

"What? You're hot, Hunter. Don't act like you don't know it." I continue to stare at him, unable to come up with a reply, and he holds up his hands. "I know, I was wrong."

I blink at him. *What? I'm pretty sure I misunderstood or missed something.* The waitress shows up in perfect timing, and the spell he had me under feels like it's broken, but my mind is still confused. *Did he say what I think he said?*

He just said he's attracted to me. A memory of him leaning into me and his lips ghosting against my ear flashes through my head.

"Hello, what can I get you both to drink?" our waitress asks. Myles hasn't taken his eyes off of me, and I squirm in my seat.

"Um"—I stutter and rub my forehead. "I'll um, I'll take"—I

look around, not sure what to get, and I can't seem to focus enough to decide while he's staring at me. *Crap.* "Water." I blurt. I still feel his eyes on me while I'm acting like a flailing fish. Why does this man make me nervous? I don't know what to do when he's nice to me. I'm not prepared for it. I look up and see a hint of a cocky smirk at the corner of his mouth, like he knows exactly what is going on in my head.

"Same," Myles says after what feels like several minutes of silence.

"Alright, I'll get those for you. Would you like a few more minutes to look over the menu?" she asks.

"Yes," he says, calm and collected.

The waitress turns her body toward him and flicks her hair across her shoulder before smiling at him. But his eyes never leave mine, as if he's afraid I'll bolt if he takes them off me. I don't know why though, I'm pretty much stuck here since he drove me.

"What would you like?" His voice sounds a little husky as he rubs the scruff on his chin.

I can hear the sound the friction makes, wanting nothing more than to feel it against my own hands and other places. My eyebrows shoot up, and I press my thighs together to help relieve some of the throbbing.

"Um, from you?" I couldn't be more confused right now. He just said he's attracted to me. Does that mean he wants to mend past wrongs and be friends, or maybe something more? My mind shouts to stay in the friend zone because this guy can turn on a dime, but my body screams in favor of the latter.

A playful smile crosses his lips. "To eat, Hershey."

His deep voice pierces me to the core. I have a hard time not melting. I could kick myself for looking like a fool in front of him. *Fucking hell.*

"Oh, right." Clearing my throat, I look down at my menu again. "Um. I'm not sure yet. Do you know what you want?" Is this menu in English? I can't seem to focus long enough to read one word. The Spanish names of each food aren't helping. I'm surprised he can't hear my heart pounding in my chest from across the table. I glance up at him, and he's still looking right at me. His hands folded on the table, a picture of ease. I bite my lower lip. His eyes track the movement before they slowly raise to meet my eyes. He rubs his jaw like he's thinking about what he wants to say.

"Yeah. I know what I want." Myles' eyes seem to darken, making my mouth go dry.

A hand reaches in front of me, holding water. I jump back, not noticing that the waitress had walked up. *Thank god.* I quickly send her a smile before I gulp down my drink. Water drips out of the corner of my mouth and runs down my neck. I pat myself dry with my napkin, and he chuffs out a laugh. *The waitress has the best timing so far.*

"Have you decided on your order?" she asks, taking out her pad of paper and pen.

I look at her with my eyebrows raised and mouth parted. I'm not sure what to get, and I'm the most basic food person there is. I get the same sort of thing whenever I go to a Mexican restaurant. Just don't ask me what that is right now because I don't have the slightest clue. This isn't like me. I don't lose my mind when I talk to people. What makes Myles so different? Is it that he just makes me nervous?

What's going on in his head? He has been looking at me with a stormy look in his eyes all day. I can tell there's something more he's holding back, but he just sits there completely unphased.

"Um." My eyes quickly scan the menu for anything remotely familiar. "I'll take a burrito. Just chicken, rice, beans, and cheese please," I say, looking up and relaxing a little when Myles finally looks at his menu.

"Okay, and for you?" She looks over at him, popping her hip.

"I'll take the al pastor tacos. Thanks." Instead of looking at her, his eyes immediately pin me to the spot as he passes his menu over to her.

"Okay. I'll get that all in for you." The waitress turns, walking away with our menus.

"So"—Myles starts,—"what do you like to do in your spare time?"

I blink in confusion. I thought he would continue pushing me with more uncomfortable topics. What surprises me is how upset I am that he isn't continuing the conversation.

"Really? You're going to change the subject?" Was I comfortable with the last one? No. But that doesn't mean I want to switch topics, exactly. I'm curious why he wants to change the subject. Does he regret what he said?

He nods. "Oh, okay. I was only trying to be nice and make lighter conversation." His shoulders shrug. "I don't want you to go out with James. I want you to go out with me."

My jaw drops, and I feel my eyes widen to the size of golf balls. "You what?"

"You heard me." Myles' eyebrow ticks, and he leans forward to put his elbows on the table. "Are you with James?"

"That's beside the point," I huff and wrap my hands around my hair to put it in a bun on top of my head.

"Is it?" His head tilts to the side.

"Yes." I grab a chip and dunk it into the salsa before shoving it into my mouth.

"I don't think it is."

He's holding back a smile that is begging to come out. His dimple gives him away. "Myles," I groan.

"Hershey," he says, giving me a stoic facade. He leans forward a little more. "I want to take you out, but I can't do that if you're going out with another"—he hesitates—"*guy*." He growls out the last word.

My eyes dart back and forth between his blue ones while I debate what to say. He's still wearing that old hat, backward of course, causing a thick piece of hair to tumble across his forehead in a way that makes me want to reach across this table and wisp it to the side. Sliding my eyes downward, I feel an ache between my thighs as they settle on how good Myles' broad shoulders look in that white button-up shirt. The sleeves are rolled past his forearms where his tattoos are exposed.

Taking a big breath, I meet his eyes again. "I like to horseback ride and play beach volleyball in my spare time." *Yes, I chicken out and go for the easier question. Shoot me.*

He smirks. "Interesting." Putting one finger on his chin, he says, "I go to JT's to ride." Leaning back in the booth, his broad chest pulls at his shirt threads.

I move the straw in my cup in circles, and the ice clinks as it follows. "I miss it. I haven't found a place to ride since moving here. I have a horse back home, but I had to leave her at the family farm when I moved here." I blurt. *Why is he easy to open up to?*

He messes with his rolled sleeve. "You can come to JT's and ride with me. He has a few extra horses." I swear hope blooms in his eyes.

"Oh, no." I wave him off. "I couldn't do that." I turn my head and look at the other customers eating around us. I didn't mean for him to invite me over to JT's house. That would be awkward. Kind of like the elephant in the room right now.

"JT wouldn't mind. He'd love to have you over. His horses need to be ridden," he says.

"Maybe." I look at my hands fidgeting in my lap before peering up at him through my lashes.

His cheeks raise as the corners of his mouth follow. "I'll take it."

I reach for a broken chip, but his hand grabs hold of mine before I can. I can feel calluses from obvious hard work. His thumb lazily strokes across my knuckles. We both look down at our hands. My small hand looks dainty in his. Jerking my hand away, I tuck a few stray hairs behind my ear.

Leaning forward on the table, he says, huskily, "I gotta know."

My body is on pins and needles, wondering what he's going to say. Clenching my thighs together, I take a breath and look at him.

"Are you with James?"

Gone is the playful smirk he had just moments ago. All I see is the seriousness in his face. His jaw is tight, and his gaze is firm. Like this information is what his life depends on. Like he's holding back until he figures out this little snippet. That thought alone sends excitement through my body.

"No."

15

MYLES

MY EYES ARE GLUED to her curvy ass as she jumps into her Bronco and backs out of the parking space. Standing here like a love-struck teenager, I can't help feeling lighter than I did this morning. Everything about Hunter draws me in. Her laughter when she talks about her nights with Jess, filled with a lot of chocolate. Her lips as they tug upward and her eyes cast down when I say something a little forward. Her determination to succeed because failing has never crossed her mind. Then there is her perfect body that could bring any grown man to his knees, but she doesn't even realize the power she wields.

I jump into my truck when she turns onto the main road. I crank my truck on the first try. "Atta girl, Gertrude." I really have to get the engine looked at. It's like a catch twenty-two if she will crank. I can't count how many times I've called JT to come pick me up because she wouldn't turn over. But that's the cost of owning a vintage truck.

Leaning on one hip, I get my phone out of my pocket and call JT. I back out and turn in the direction of my house and wait for him to answer.

"Hey, man. How did lunch go?" JT asks casually. "Does she

still hate your guts? Oh, please tell me she threw your drink in your face." His booming laughter rattles my ear.

"Shut up." I laugh, turning onto another street.

He chuckles.

"Do you have Hunter's number?" Part of me hopes he does and the other part hopes he doesn't because why would JT have her number unless he's trying to flirt with her?

"Nope."

I let out a slow exhale of relief. "Well, what about Jess?"

"Uh. Why?"

I don't miss the way his voice drops all hints of playfulness at the mention of Jess' name. Interesting.

"I want to ask her out." I pause and when he stays silent, I smirk. "Bro, seriously, what do you think I want her number for? I need to get Hunter's."

His laugh rings through my ears. "She didn't give it to you?"

"Well, it kinda slipped my mind until she drove away." I thrum my fingers on the steering wheel.

"Alright. I'll see what I can do. Don't be disappointed if she'd rather get my number. I'm prettier."

I lift my eyes as if looking to the heavens will help me figure out why I'm getting punished. It's probably something I did in a past life. "Why am I friends with you?" I tease.

"Ah, you love me."

I shake my head. "Will you just get me her number?"

"Anything for you my brother. I just can't promise I won't use it first."

"Text me when you have it."

"Righty-o."

I laugh as I end the call. He can be so weird. I pull into my driveway. It's a small house, but there's not much I need besides a place to sleep, eat, and watch TV. It's perfect for me. And my favorite thing—it's on a lake. So between JT and me, we have everything we need. He has horses with some wooded trails leading to a creek, and I have a lake with a boat. We spend most of our days off on the lake in the summer. I need to schedule another boat day. I always thought the bachelor life was for me until Hunter. Now I can imagine her on the boat, adding so much life to our group. I walk into my house and jump in the shower.

Water runs down my face while I stand under the stream and images of Hunter flood my head. The girl with large green eyes and curly brown hair that almost reaches her butt. I want to reach around and grab the back of her neck and rake my fingers into her hair, giving it a little tug, I'd bring that face up to expose that gorgeous neck. I'd wrap my other arm around her body, pressing her firmly against me. I can almost feel her against me as the water rushes down my body. My cock throbs, and I know picturing her like this is too much to handle. *Fuck.* My hand wraps around my length, and I stroke to the fantasy of her. I think about burying my face in her neck while I kiss my way to her sassy mouth. I slap my palm against the tile in the shower to brace myself. Images of her looking up at me through her thick lashes as she slowly kneels down in front of me, flicker through my mind. I throw my head back and groan. Her tongue drags across her lips before licking the bead of pre-cum off the tip. All I can think about is grabbing a fistful of her long hair as she brings my shaft deep inside her mouth. I find my release in no time, thinking of hitting the back of her throat and hearing her gag. My heart slams against my ribcage, as I take a minute to catch my breath. Fuck, if just imagining her gets me this worked up, the real thing might actually kill me.

After the shower, my shoulders are less tense. Today's sale may be my favorite, but it's always the longest. So I never leave without a little soreness. I wrap a towel around my waist and stretch my neck back and forth to alleviate any leftover knots. Leaving the bathroom, I head to the kitchen to heat some leftover Chinese food. The microwave dings at the same time a text chimes through my phone. I grab my food and lift a large forkful into my mouth. It's hot, forcing me to blow out a burst of air as I toss it around inside my mouth until it cools. After swallowing, I pick up my phone. It's JT.

JT:

Am I good or am I good?

"Shared Hunter Smith's contact"

MYLES:

It's why I keep you around.

Going into the living room, I put my food on the coffee table and sit on the couch across from the TV. I save her number in my phone and open a new thread to text her. My thumbs hover over the screen as I think of what to say. I've never felt the pull toward a woman like I do with her, and now that I've surrendered to it, I feel desperate. Everyone says you'll know when you find someone you want to be with. I've always loved my job, and the thrill of the auction is addicting. But doing it with her makes it that much better.

She looked beautiful today, pushing against a stubborn cow's side, trying to get it to move. And her wild hair, it makes me want to run my fingers through it, grabbing a handful while I kiss those perfect, full lips. I couldn't take my eyes off her the whole time we were at the restaurant.

MYLES:

Hey. It's Myles. I may have gotten JT to get your number for me.

I click send and wait. I tap my phone against my palm. I don't know if she will respond right away, but my heart rate picks up at the possibility. I put down my phone and finish eating. As I reach for the remote, my phone vibrates, and I toss the remote to grab my phone.

HUNTER:

Wow. Stalker much?

I chuckle.

MYLES:

Borderline. At least I don't know where you live yet. But I'm sure JT can find out that little tidbit too.

HUNTER:

Should I be afraid he has that much power?

I smile as I lean back on the cushions.

MYLES:

I definitely think someone should at least break his nose just to make the playing field more even. No one should be that good-looking. He can ask someone for the most personal information, and all he has to do is smile for them to fork it over.

I smirk at the thought. I remember a time growing up when he asked a teacher about a book we were supposed to read. He hadn't read it, but he smiled and the teacher just thought he was interested in the book to provide feedback and wanted to discuss it. I sat with my head buried in my textbook, laughing my ass off while he got the answers he needed.

HUNTER:

I don't know what to say to that.

MYLES:

You should see what his smile does to my mama. She's obsessed with him.

HUNTER:

Jess says you two must have been popular in school.

I chuckle at how wrong she is and rub my fingers through my damp hair. I wasn't hated in school, but I definitely wasn't popular. JT was the only person I hung out with.

I press on her contact information and click on her number. Bringing the phone to my ear, I hear it ringing and then her voice comes through the earpiece.

"Hello?"

"I was not popular."

"I find that very hard to believe. You may keep to yourself, but everyone at work speaks highly of you."

I shake my head in disbelief. "I find that hard to believe."

"Oh, I did, too. Don't worry."

Her laughter echoing through my ear brings a smile to my face. It has to be one of the most beautiful sounds. "What about you? Were you popular?"

"Ahh," she moans. "I guess I was, but I didn't think so."

"Okay." I chuckle. "What are we talking? Prom queen or head cheerleader?"

"I don't really want to answer that."

"You were both. Holy shit." I lean forward, pressing the phone harder to my ear. I can't believe I hit the nail on the head. "Damn, so all the guys wanted you and probably some girls too."

She snorts. "Oh my god. You're unbelievable."

"I know. It's hard to be so unbelievably handsome." I lean back into my couch, putting my arm behind my head to lie against. "I mean, you are gorgeous, so I think you can relate," I say. "But what the hell was that sound you just made? I bet no one knew you made those sounds when they voted for you. Prom queens don't snort." I can't slap the smile off my face listening to her consistent laughter coming through the phone.

"I just can't with you right now." She sighs. "So you weren't Mr. Footballer?"

"Oh, no!" I laugh. "I worked all through high school. So I didn't have time for extracurricular activities."

"Why did you work so much, and where did you work?"

I can hear the excitement in her voice from that little tidbit. She wants to know more about me. It's sweet, but I have a hard time talking about that period of my life. It wasn't an easy time.

"My mom raised me by herself, and we needed any extra money I could bring in. I worked at a restaurant called Ramshackles as a busboy, and I also worked at the local skating rink."

"Oh, I'm sorry you had to do that. What is Ramshackles?"

The fact that she doesn't pry further makes my heartbeat slow to a normal rhythm. I don't want to talk about my childhood, or worse, my deadbeat father. But I'm in no rush to stop talking to her. It's a feeling I'm not used to. I usually only talk to my mom on the phone, and that's a completely different type of conversation.

"I'll have to take you some time. They have some of the best chicken wings." *Man, now I'm craving some.* "It's a pretty chill place, and they have their menus printed on newspaper. It's a whole thing."

"Are they still open?"

"Oh, yeah. It will be a sad day if that place ever closes. It was the place to go when I was in school. On senior skip day, we all had lunch there. I worked that day to pick up extra hours since it was a day off for us, but my boss let me eat with my class when they showed up." There is something about Hunter that makes her easy to talk to. She already knows way more about me than most people I come in contact with.

"That was nice of him. What's your mom like?"

I shake my head. *How do you describe that woman?*

"She is the loudest, most intrusive person you will ever meet.

If she wants something, there is no holding her back. If she sniffs out something she doesn't know, she won't let you rest until all your secrets are for her to keep, and I mean *ALL*." I laugh again. "She is also the kindest woman with the best hugs. She would love you."

"She sounds like a wonderful lady. I'd love to meet her sometime."

Hunter wanting to meet my mom warms my chest.

"So how was your day?" I always thought these types of questions were cheesy, but I guess I hadn't met a person that I was interested enough in to want to know their answer.

"It was great." I hear her happy sigh come through the phone. "I love cattle auctions. It reminds me of home."

This piques my interest. Most women hate dealing with cows or getting dirty with all the cow poop around. At least, the women that I've been around.

"Because of your dad?" I ask, looking up at the living room ceiling and watching the fan spin in circles.

"Kind of. They are also where I got started." She gives a small laugh.

Stretching my legs out, I go to put them on the coffee table, but I'm still only wearing a fucking towel. I walk to my room and get joggers, boxers, and a T-shirt.

"My dad used to take me to work with him when I was little," she explains. "I would sit and listen to him. A lot of the buyers would let me bid on the cows for them. It was kind of like a second home for me. It's also where I became an auctioneer."

I put her on speaker while pulling on my clothes. "Sounds like fun and some special times with your dad. Are you two close?" I ask.

"Yes, we are, but..." she pauses. "What are you doing? You sound far away."

"Oh, sorry." I finish pulling the shirt over my head. "I'm

getting dressed. I just took a shower and wanted to get into comfortable clothes."

"Oh."

Her voice is quiet, as if admitting my nakedness made her timid, a part of her I haven't witnessed before. I like knowing she has a softer, possibly shy side. I wouldn't mind getting to know that piece of her a bit more.

"So what's your favorite day of the week?" Her answering laugh makes me grin, as I head into the kitchen to grab a soda from the fridge.

There's my girl.

"Well, yesterday I would have said Tuesdays, but in a month, I'll probably say Mondays."

"Why Tuesdays?"

"Because Manheim Orlando is the auction I can sell cars the fastest, and because"—she hesitates—"never mind. What's yours?"

"Oh, no." I walk back to the living room and fall back onto my couch. "Let's hear it."

"It's nothing." Her voice is getting quiet again.

"Tell me, Hershey." I'm loving this comfortable feeling I get talking to her, but it's going to bite me in the ass if I scare her off. I swing my legs off the couch, leaning over, burying my face in my hand. I hold my breath, waiting to see if she'll answer me or bite my head off.

"It's because I get to work with you, okay? Even though you've been an asshole, you've also been fun to work with. Sometimes you're even nice. But I get to see you, and I like it. Is that what you wanted to hear?" she quips at me.

Her unexpected answer pulls a surprised chuckle out of me. It's cute when she gets so riled up. But she really just said that. She likes working with me.

"Oh. Ha. Ha. What's so funny?"

"You're cute when you're embarrassed."

"You seem to see all the bids, and it makes the day flow more smoothly. Don't read too much into it."

"Well, seeing you is the best part of my day, too. And I think you should read into it," I admit. She doesn't say anything, and it makes me think I might have taken it too far. My mind races, trying to think of something lighter to talk about. "So what's your favorite sport, or do you not like sports?"

"Wow! Already assuming I don't like sports?"

"I'm not assuming. I'm asking. Are you the type to watch a sports game, or am I in for many nights of Hallmark movies?" A smile creeps across my face. I already know I would rather watch a Hallmark movie with her than watch a game by myself.

"Well, I actually do like sports."

"I remember you like playing beach volleyball. Is that all you enjoy watching, or are there other sports that get you screaming at the TV?"

"I love the thrill of live games. It doesn't matter which sport. I like to cheer obnoxiously, so you may be embarrassed to watch any game with me. Except golf, that's not for me. But I do love Hallmark movies. So choosing would be hard. I guess it would depend on which teams are playing, to determine whether it overrides one of my favorite movies or not."

We continue talking until the sun peeking through my curtains slowly goes away. I can't remember the last time I talked to a woman on the phone this long. She doesn't hang up until we need to go to sleep. We both have an early morning. The best way to fall asleep is dreaming of Hunter. The even better part? Seeing her shortly after I wake. The more I learn about her, the more I want to be around her. I'm not wasting another second not being with her. Unless she tells me to fuck off, I'm all in.

16

HUNTER

JESS BURSTS into my room just as I violently press the snooze on my alarm.

"Good morning!" Jess sings.

Scooting up onto my elbows, I level her with a hard look. "What?"

"Oh, I'm only wondering how last night went." She plops down onto my bed, bouncing a few times. A smile spreads across my face, and she screeches. "I knew it. Ah"—she places the back of her hand over her forehead, acting as if she'll faint. "Young love."

I laugh as I nudge her with my feet. "Knock it off. Come on." Pulling my sheets off, I let my feet hit the floor.

"Wait." Putting her hand out to stop me, she looks frantically at me then at my phone. "That was only your first alarm." Reaching up, she puts her wrist against my forehead. "Are you feeling okay? Hold on." She grabs my chin, turning my face side to side. "You look like you got laid!" she says bluntly, making us both laugh.

A huge smile spreads across my face as I think about my talk with Myles. I've never talked so long on the phone before. I didn't even think continuing a conversation for that long, without an awkward pause, was even possible. But the whole phone call felt easy. We shared things about ourselves, and I learned a lot about Myles' life. The love he has for his mom is obvious. It's the sweetest thing listening to him talk about her. It was adorable, and I couldn't get enough. He made me feel like he wanted to know everything about me too.

"Whatever." I bat her hand away. "I slept great on my new bed. That's it."

"Uh-huh. I'm not buying it." She was obnoxious the whole time we talked. Peeking into my room, she'd check to see if I was still talking to him, do a little silent dance, and walk away with hearts in her eyes.

"Go. We need to get ready for work."

Jumping up, she skips out of my room and hums a Taylor Swift song.

I fell asleep thinking about all the stories he told me. I don't think I've ever slept so well. I've never had a man open up so much about himself before. All Steve wanted to do was talk about himself, but he never said anything real. Myles laid everything out for me. It should have scared me, but I only wanted more. As I got more comfortable, I asked as many questions as he did. By the end of our call, I wanted to melt into a puddle on my new bed.

Since I'd gotten some cash tips from the dealers, I went shopping and found a beautiful oak bed and nearly replaced my whole wardrobe with more Florida-appropriate outfits. Jess made me show off all my new outfits in a mock fashion show in the living room.

Toeing on my slippers, I walk into the kitchen where Jess stands in front of the stove, scrambling eggs for her breakfast.

"Are you driving today?"

She spins around to face me. "Yup."

I walk around her, opening the pantry to grab a protein bar.

My phone pings with a text message, and I dig it out of my pocket. I hold it up, seeing it's from Myles, and I can't stop the smile beaming across my face. I go to open it when Jess lunges for me, grabbing the phone right out of my hand. "Hey!"

"Who could this be?" She lets out a gasp, holding a hand to her chest. "Why, it's Myles Johnson!" Jess drawls in the most horrible Southern Belle accent.

"Give me my phone!" I reach to snatch it away from her, but she spins around to avoid me. Unfortunately, she knows the passcode on my phone and opens it.

"Jess, I swear to god. I'm going to kick your ass."

"Aww! He's sweet," she says after reading it. She finally stops moving around and hands me my phone. Grabbing it, I look at what he said.

MYLES:

Last night was the most fun I've had in a while.
Looking forward to seeing you today.

Smiling, my eyes return to my roommate, who is giving me a knowing look. My smile falls into a smirk. I take a big bite of my bar and bounce back to my room to get ready. Jess' laughter follows me down the hall. Nickelback trails closely behind me and jumps up on my bed to take a nap. I ruffle his head and start getting ready for work.

I spray leave-in conditioner in my hair and put on some black jeans and a fitted green cotton shirt. Even though it's hot as hell most days, I have a hard time not wearing pants to an auction. I let my hair do its normal crazy thing and do my minimal makeup. Looking into the mirror, I quickly grab my eyeshadow palette to add more and another coat of mascara. I finish the look with little brown booties and my brown leather purse. The weather is supposed to get into the record highs for the area, so I bring a ponytail to easily throw up my hair.

Jess and I ride together on Tuesdays because we work at the

same auctions. We squeeze into her little Volkswagen red bug since it's her day to drive. The sixty minute drive usually goes by quicker with the two of us chatting away, but today it feels longer than normal. I rest my elbow on the window and lazily watch the trees go by on the long country highway.

"Oh, for the love of god. Will you stop bouncing your knee?"

I startle at her loud voice and look at her, then down at my knee, which is still bouncing like the energizer bunny. "Oh." I push my feet firmly into the floorboard, and nervously bite my thumb nail. "Sorry." I look back out the window.

Jess sighs. "You have such good nail beds, and now you are going to ruin them." She reaches over and grabs my hand to get it away from my mouth. "Talk to me. What's going on in your head?"

A little smile plays across my lips. I'd be lost without Jess in my life. "I guess I'm just nervous that yesterday was a fluke, and he's going to turn back into the jackass he was before."

She nods and squeezes my hand. The auction sign peeks into view as she whips into the huge parking lot. Putting the car in park, she turns to look at me, grabbing both of my hands with hers now.

"I get where those feelings are coming from." Tilting her head to the side, she presses her lips into a small smile. "But I have a hard time believing he would put that much time and effort in, just to ignore you today." Releasing my hands, she reaches up to twirl a piece of my hair as if she's thinking of more to add. "Well, it's not unheard of because guys are stupid, but I don't see it happening." Patting my knee she says, "Now, are you ready?" I laugh and shove her before crawling out of her tiny car.

We walk past the guard, flashing our badges. My head goes all different directions, but I have to force myself to keep my steps as big as Jess' so I'm not speed walking to get inside. Excitement takes over the closer we get to the front doors that are beyond the gated property.

Yesterday morning, I had thought Myles was a moody jerk.

By the afternoon, he was wearing on me. A lot.

Last night, I went to bed seeing Myles in a whole new light. When I think of him, I now see him as the guy that the girls were describing. I can't help the way I'm feeling. I may be naive, but I have to find out if this is real.

The chaotic hustle and bustle sets in as dealers scramble to get their bidder numbers and a run list for whatever lane they want to buy on. Office workers are all behind their desks and counters ready to help as many people as possible. It's always pure chaos before and after the sales.

Jess and I go in different directions once inside, her to an employee break room to clock in and me to my meeting. Walking through the large office, I spot Myles standing outside the doors to our meeting, holding something. My heart races. Biting my lower lip between my teeth, I walk toward him. He's looking at his phone and doesn't see me coming. His outfit is different today. He may have on the same hat and worn jeans as always, but his black polo shirt leaves more of his tattoos on display than ever before. It's sexy, especially with his hat on backward. There has to be a story behind it and why he's never replaced it. I make a mental note to ask him.

The closer I get, the more my anxiety spikes. He's leaning against the wall, and I'm not sure what to do. Do I walk over to him and stand in front of him? Try to hug him? I'm going to make this more awkward than it should be. I take a deep breath and lean against the wall next to him, painting on a face of confidence.

"Morning."

His head jerks toward me, and a smile slowly grows across his face. "You never texted back. I was worried you were blowing me off."

My shoulders fall. "Crap. Well, I knew I was going to see you, and I had a lot on my mind." I suck at texting or talking on the phone, but now I regret it. I missed out on an entire morning of talking to him. *Okay, don't be dramatic. I missed out on a few hours of texting him.*

He grabs my chin and tilts it up, giving me no choice but to meet his gaze. "Hey, I'm messing with you. But it sucked not getting a morning text from the most beautiful girl. I'll settle for a kiss instead," he says, taking a step closer to me.

My eyes bug out of my head, and my jaw drops.

"Hey, I was only kidding." He laughs awkwardly, raising his hands up, still holding a little brown bag and a drink. "I wouldn't do that to you."

How embarrassing. I tuck my hair behind my ear and look down. I should have known. He caught me by surprise. I would be lying if my heart didn't skip a beat, thinking about pressing my lips against his.

He leans over, bringing us a mere foot apart. "The meeting will start soon. I got you something. I took a guess at what your favorite food would be."

He gives me a mocha frappuccino and a bag with a donut inside covered with chocolate frosting. I stare into the bag, unable to form words to thank him for such a sweet gesture.

"I would have given you a chocolate bar"—he gestures to the bag—"but I figured this would be better for breakfast."

Is that an embarrassed smile? How did he know? I *LOVE* chocolate.

"How did you"—I stop and look down at the food. He leans over, ghosting his fingers over the side of my face and tucking a stray hair behind my ear. It makes my heart race again. My eyes meet his, and it feels like his body is folding over mine, creating our own little bubble. He's so close, but also not close enough.

"You are always eating or drinking some kind of chocolate whenever I see you. So I took a guess." An award-winning smile stretches across his face. "Was I right?"

I give him a nod and whisper, "Yes." I never get embarrassed, but he has a way of bringing new feelings out of me. I'm confused, but I like him. Well, I like *this* side of him he's been showing me, which is polar opposite from the guy he was at first. I feel like I can open up to him without judgment. That thought alone scares me, but Myles has a way of getting past all my defenses. "Thank you."

"No problem. You ready to go in?"

I nod and walk around him through the doors and find an open spot in the meeting next to JT. He looks at me with a knowing smile, and I force my gaze to the front of the room.

My senses heighten as energy flows through me, and I know Myles is standing right next to me without even looking. The entire left side of my body is on alert, eagerly awaiting his touch. A magnetic energy pulsing through me, begging me to step closer. I take a deep breath to focus, but instead, his woodsy scent invades my senses. I jump when Griffin's booming voice echoes through the room, grabbing my attention.

Everything Griffin says is repetitive from week to week, so it's not enough for me to ignore Myles when he shifts closer to me. I feel his arm graze against mine. I shift back and forth on my feet when his breath caresses my ear, placing his hand on my lower back, causing that area to be the focal point of ignited fire. It reminds me of a hot tub. It's hot, but you can relax into it, enjoying every bit of the tingling.

"You look beautiful today," he whispers.

My eyes flicker over to look at him. I open my mouth to respond, but nothing comes out. I'm left standing there speechless. I clutch my hands in front of me so I have something else to focus on. *What is up with me? I've never gotten butterflies from a guy before.*

JT leans over into our space. "Thanks, darlin'," he whispers in Myles' direction. "I just got my hair done."

I clamp a hand over my mouth to stop the laughter from bursting out of me. I look over at Myles, and he's just shaking his head while standing back to his full height. But I can see the small smile at the corner of his mouth.

"Alright," Griffin says, snapping me back to reality. "Let's have a good sale."

AS SOON AS the lane is over, Jess looks at me with the biggest smile. "Okay, you two could not keep your eyes off each other. What is going on? I think James picked up on it. I mean, he would be blind not to," she says, only making my heart sink.

We sold a bunch of cars. Nothing was different, except Myles would turn and make eye contact with me every chance he got. I swear, he looked at me more than the dealers. But he didn't miss a bid. We always work together flawlessly. But I don't want this to cause any problems with dealers, and I don't want James to have any negative feelings because we didn't work out. I would like to remain cordial, so I don't want to rub whatever this is with Myles in his face.

"James and I haven't talked since our date. After the movie, we both knew there wouldn't be another date. He didn't want to admit it, but it wasn't working. I don't think he will have an opinion on Myles, especially since we're only *talking*." At least, I'm hoping he won't care. I know he had stronger feelings than I did, but that date was a disaster. I'm sure he changed his mind, especially since I haven't received a text from him in days. He also didn't talk to me this morning, only giving me a friendly wave.

"Girl, talking isn't the only thing you are doing," she says, wiggling her eyebrows.

I purse my lips and give her my sassiest look. "Yes, Jess. That's it." I pause and my face turns into a small smile. "At least for now." She grabs my arms and squeals, making me laugh while walking off the auction block. I notice Myles going over to give Aaron a break on JT's lane. I love watching him up there. He is so smooth. Out of the corner of my eye, I see James walking over to me.

"Hey, Hunter."

"Hey, James. You got a lot of good cars today," I say, readjusting my purse on my shoulder.

"Yeah, I did. I wanted to say that I'm sorry about what I said about cattle auctions. I was wrong. I'm happy you're finding your place here."

James is a nice guy. I know it won't be long until he sweeps a girl off her feet. It just won't be me.

"Thank you. That means a lot. I'd like to remain friends if that's alright with you?"

His shoulders relax, and he exhales. "Yes. I'd like that."

"Great. I'll see you later, then?"

He nods, and I lightly touch his forearm and walk around him to where Jess stepped away to give us some privacy. Before walking by, I wave to JT, and he gives me a nod with his usual easygoing smile. I look up at Myles, but his back is to me, facing the dealer by the open garage door.

Jess and I walk inside the office, and I wave to a few dealers as we go. She cuts through a side door to clock out so we can go to the next auction, and I find my way to the front door to wait for her like I usually do. My phone pings with a text message. Fishing it out of my purse, I see Myles' name light up on the screen, and I swear my heart does a flip.

MYLES:

Hey, don't leave yet. I want to ask you something.

HUNTER:

Okay. I'm by the front door.

I look up and see Jess walking over, saying bye to a few office workers on her way. She is wearing a brightly colored floral skirt and a purple shirt. There is no missing her. The girl was born to stand out.

"Ready?" she asks.

"Myles asked me to wait for him. He said he needed to ask me something. Can I meet you at your car in a minute?"

Her face lights up. "Of course! Can't wait to see what he says." She winks and walks out the door, talking to the security officer who's standing there.

I roll my eyes and pull out my phone to text my dad while I wait.

HUNTER:

Hey, Dad. Yesterday, I had my first day at a cattle auction. It was great. It made me miss you. Love you.

My phone pings almost immediately. He's always quick to respond.

DAD:

That's my girl! Good job, sweetie. I'm proud of you. Love you too. Your mom wants to know when you can come home for a visit.

It's amazing how my dad and I have a good relationship. But then my mom uses him to talk to me because our relationship is nonexistent. It's sad, but it's all I've ever known. I wish she could be proud of me. I just don't want her approval enough to do what she wants. I'm not willing to marry someone or be someone who goes to the country club all the time. I know she loves her lifestyle, but it's not one I've ever wanted. I tuck my phone back inside my pocket. I'm not ready to give him an answer right now.

"Hey."

I look up excitedly at the sound of his familiar voice. Myles walks a few more steps before he is standing in front of me. He has a twinkle in his eye, making it hard to look away.

"Can I walk you out?" Myles gestures toward the door.

I cock my head at him. "That's what you wanted to ask me?"

"No." He smiles and opens the front door, his other hand gently splaying across my back, sending goosebumps across my body. He doesn't remove his hand while we walk outside.

"I wanted to ask if you would go to lunch with me before the next sale?" He looks down at me and his blue eyes meet mine.

"Oh. Well, I rode with Jess."

"So ride with me," he says quickly. Gently cradling my elbow he stops walking, bringing us to a stop so he can look at me while talking. "Please?"

His eyes are begging me to say yes.

"Okay. But Jess will probably go all crazy roommate on your ass when I tell her." I laugh, but I'm not kidding either. He chuckles, and I can't help looking at him. His smile is vibrant.

He squeezes my elbow. "I'm not worried."

He steps a little closer and tilts my chin up to look at his face. The way he's looking at me, makes me feel it deep down in my toes. It makes me want to melt into him. Would he think it's weird or too soon if I take another step forward and wrap my arms around his waist? Sometimes you yearn for a hug. I've only ever wanted hugs from my dad. But I'd love to be wrapped up in Myles' arms.

I clear my throat. "Um. Okay." I look around before meeting his gaze again. "I'll text her to let her know." Getting my phone out, I send her a quick text. I'm about to put it away when it starts ringing. Seeing Jess' name on the screen only makes me chuckle. Of course, she's calling me. "Hey, Jess."

"OH, MY GOD! You're going with him?" She screeches, making me cringe and pull the phone a little further from my ear. My eyes trail up to meet his again, only to find him smirking. I know he heard her. It would surprise me if people within a mile radius didn't.

"Yes. I'll see you at the next sale, okay?"

"You have to tell me every—" Myles wraps his fingers over mine and brings the phone to his ear.

"Hey, Jess," he drawls.

I hear some squeaking coming from the phone at his ear.

"Okay, no alcohol before 5 p.m." He nods. "Yes, I'll have her in Orlando for the next auction." He winks at me. "Got it."

The squeaking continues, and I can't help but bite my lower lip. I liked how he wasn't afraid to get the third degree from my best friend. Myles immediately zeros in on my mouth, and his eyes look like they are a shade darker than usual.

"Bye, Jess."

He ends the call without taking his eyes off my mouth and slowly brings his fingers up. I have to keep myself from making a sound when he touches my lip and pulls it free from my teeth.

"How about we go get some Italian?" His voice is gravelly.

"Okay." My voice cracks when I answer. His eyes are still completely focused on mine, and I can't seem to stop myself from slowly leaning closer to him.

"See you two at the next sale," Aaron calls out, making us take a step back and look at him.

"Yeah. See ya." Myles slides his hands into his pockets.

I let out a breath and blink a few times. We got so close to kissing. Where is my head? I never had the urge to kiss James. Even with Steve, it took a while, but he finally went for it without asking. Honestly, it was like kissing a fish. It felt like I was drowning, and I didn't want to do it again.

"Come on, I'm parked this way." He rubs the back of his neck, taking a few steps backward. He slows his pace to match mine. His arm makes slight contact with mine, and the goosebumps appear.

He opens my door for me and reaches his hand out because his lifted truck makes it difficult to hop in.

"You ready?" he asks.

"Yes, why wouldn't I be?"

"Because this is where everything changes for us." He leans in, putting one hand on the roof and the other on the door. His body towers over the space, pressing against me in the seat. I look at him, not shying away from the close proximity.

I cross my arms over my chest. "You seem sure of yourself."

"Oh, I am." He pauses and tucks some of my hair behind my ear, making my eyes flutter. "Plus, I've been waiting all morning to get you alone."

He slowly leans over and kisses my cheek with his soft lips, and my face grows hot.

"Let's go, Hershey," he whispers, stepping away to shut my door.

I release a long exhale. I've never liked pet names, but I like that he gave me one. Something has awakened inside me, and I'm not sure what to do with this new feeling.

I watch him as he struts around the front of the truck and gets in. Starting the truck, he takes a peek at me and smirks.

"What?"

"Oh, I'm wondering how long it's going to take you to realize you like me. Because Hershey"—he leans across the seat, his breath tickling me when he says,—"It's written all over your face."

My jaw hits the floorboard. I'm shocked at how forward he is. He's not holding back. I straighten myself in the seat and look out the windshield.

"Is not," I murmur.

"Okay." He doesn't move. He's still leaning over in my space. "Whatever helps you sleep at night, but I want to point one thing out."

I wait for him to continue, but he doesn't. I look over at him and raise my eyebrows, making him chuckle.

"You could have gone with Jess, but you agreed to come with me. There's no need for you to put up your barriers now." He sits up and faces forward, putting the truck in reverse to back out of the parking space. "So should we get some food before it's too late?"

"Waiting on you," I tease.

He chuckles and shakes his head. "I didn't quite realize the mouth you have on you." He arches a brow and laughs when he sees me drilling glare holes right into his head.

"Oh. You knew. Don't even try to act like you didn't. Now I'm hungry. Can we go already?" I motion toward the road to get him to drive.

"Yes, ma'am."

17

———

MYLES

"So tell me about your dad." I take a bite of my stuffed shells covered in melted mozzarella cheese and marinara sauce.

Her face relaxes as I watch her think of her dad. "He's the best. Of course, there was a lot of pressure living in his shadow, but he's always encouraging me. I remember a time where he handed me the microphone and said, "Take it home." Then he walked off. Everyone stood there gaping. He never handed over his microphone to anyone to finish the sale. There were fifty head of cattle left. Everyone knew me, but had never heard me sell anything. He didn't even give me a warning."

I gape at her. "Woah. What did you do?"

A smile plays at the corner of her lips. "I took a long deep breath, squared my shoulders, and brought the microphone to my mouth. I kept my eyes scanning the men, only looking for their bids. I knew if I looked at their faces and saw the look of shock or frustration, I would fuck up. So I didn't focus on anyone and just sold the cows." She shakes her head and chuckles softly. "It was exhilarating."

"That's awesome your dad had that much faith in you." I take a sip of my sweet tea.

Conrad Smith had been working his way up since he was eighteen years old, starting as a ringman. Over the years, he worked hard and became the best cattle auctioneer. He'll make special appearances for TV auctions, but I heard he's hard to convince even with all the money they throw at him.

"He's always helped me pursue my dreams, despite it causing fights with my mom."

My eyebrows furrow. "She doesn't want you to?"

Her lips flatten into a straight line and there is a hard look in her eyes. "She wants me to live her dreams. Wants me to marry well and pop out kids. Even though I don't think having kids was really part of *her* dream."

I can't help but be confused. I'm close to my mom, so it's hard for me to imagine a woman choosing not to support her daughter. But I'm in a similar situation with my dad, so I feel for her. My hands roll into fists under the table. "I'm sorry." I'm not sure what else to say.

She waves me off. "That's enough about her."

"Okay. Then tell me, is it true your dad nailed some guys for selling sick cows?" I lean my elbows onto the table.

Laughter erupts out of her. "Yes! Oh my god. That was the best. I was there."

"What?"

"Those guys were sleazy. My dad had suspected something for a while. He finally got the auction to do a few tests. They would do anything for him, but they were worried about pissing people off. They finally realized that pissing him off was worse. I watched as he walked out with the cops who arrested them. Apparently there was a lot more shit going on than just selling sick cows."

I shake my head with disbelief. It's hard to find an honest man in this industry. It's typically not as bad as selling sick cows, but more often than not you can throw a rock and hit a seller who will lie about the mileage of the car or if it's been damaged.

I CAN'T SEEM to keep my eyes off this girl. Her hair blows around with each breeze that comes through the window. It's hard to keep my eyes off her today. Her hips perfectly sway as she walks, torturing me with each step. I can still feel how soft her lips felt beneath my finger. Just thinking about it makes my cock twitch. Her mouth is begging to be on mine. I want nothing more than to wrap my arms around her and press her firmly against my body, so I can feel every inch of her against me. Every time I learn something new about her, it makes me want more. Lunch with her went without a hiccup. The only thing I regret is not reaching across the table to hold her hand. I want to take it slow, no matter how much it's driving me mad.

I watch her from across the lanes. Hunter flows from one increment to the next, never fumbling over her words. She points from bidder to bidder, with JT sending out the cars and motioning to the dealers that they were out bid and needed to raise their money. I can't tear my eyes away, wanting to soak up every detail of her in her element. Aaron mumbles something each time my eyes are on the other lane. I've sent more than one car out before I was supposed to. My mind runs through different scenarios, figuring out how to spend more time with her. I could call her, but being with her is a million times better. I'd like to take her to JT's. It's peaceful to go to the creek after a long day. I look over toward her again as her last car rolls in. I pull out my phone to send her a text.

MYLES:

You're so beautiful. Don't leave. I want to talk to you again.

Tucking my phone away, I take a few more bids with Aaron.

Glancing at Hunter, I see she has her phone in her hand and a smile on her face, as she turns to look right at me. She didn't have to search. It was as if she knew exactly where I was without having to think about it. I give her a wink and watch as a sly look creeps across her face. She glances down, tucking some hair behind her ear. *I don't think this girl realizes how much I like her.*

LEANING against the cement wall of the building outside, my eyes jump to the door, waiting to catch a glimpse of Hunter. Feeling nervous around someone feels foreign. The front door opens and her hair whips around in the wind. *There's my girl.* Her eyes search around before she turns and lights up when she sees me.

"I figured you would be waiting for me out here." She casually walks toward me.

"Where else would I be?" I wink. Her cheeks turn a little pink, and she looks down at her feet. I love seeing this new side of her. She is a feisty, sharp tongued little thing, but if you say something sweet, she turns to jello.

"Okay, Mr. Smooth. What did you want to talk to me about?"

Her cheeks are still a little pink, but she squares her shoulders, trying to regain her composure. It only makes my smile grow.

"Come riding with me." Reaching out, I pinch the bottom of her shirt. I run my thumb back and forth over the soft material and grin down at her. The urge to hold her is strong. I'm losing my control the more I'm around her. Hunter's eyes grow wide.

"Really?" she lets out softly.

"Yes, really. How's…" I get cut off when the door opens and JT bursts out.

"Hello, beautiful people!" JT says. His face morphs into the face of a kid who found a full cookie jar. "Well, what do we have here?"

I sigh. He's not going to leave us alone. Once he found me behind the bleachers with a girl in high school. He knew we went to make out because what else do you do behind the bleachers? But did he leave? No. He's always been the worst wingman. The girl eventually left when he sat on the ground and picked up a stick to whittle which he was known to do it for hours. Of course, JT laughed his ass off the entire way home, and that was my first and last football game.

Crossing my arms across my chest, I say, "I was inviting Hunter to your house, actually."

"For real?" JT focuses on Hunter, as if waiting for her to stay otherwise. I knew he would be happy to have her over.

"Yeah. Just waiting for her to say yes."

Her eyes jump back and forth between us, her lips slightly apart. "Uh," Hunter says. Her eyes zero in on someone behind us. She skirts around, careful not to bump into us in her haste. I turn just as she grabs Jess' arm with a death grip. "Only if I can bring Jess."

Jess turns to Hunter. I notice Hunter squeeze her arm harder, making Jess wince. Hunter stands tall, still observing us to see what our answer is. I'd love to have them both, but it is JT's place, so I turn the question over to him. He looks right at Jess and clears his throat before turning to me.

"Oh, now you're asking if you can have friends over to *my* house and ride *my* horses?" He studies me, and his eyebrow twitches.

"You're right," I say, facing Hunter and Jess again. "We're free Friday afternoon. Does that work?"

JT chuckles. I knew he was just giving me a hard time.

"That sounds like a lot of fun. Right, Jess?" Hunter squeezes Jess' arm again.

"Okay." Jess locks her eyes on Hunter. "You've got to stop with the whole squeezing thing. I'm going to lose feeling in my arm. I'll go, okay?" She turns to scrutinize us, pointing her finger at our faces. "But if either of you tries *anything*, I'll spray you with my bear spray. I watch a lot of True Crime. I may enjoy working with you, but I don't trust you as far as I can throw you. Got it?" Glaring at us, she squeezes Hunter's arm to silence her, waiting for our reply.

"Yes, ma'am," JT and I say in unison.

"Good!" Jess' face lightens and smiles. "I can't wait."

Hunter shakes her head, but I can see a little smile peek through the corner of her mouth. They've grown close since Hunter moved here. I'm glad she has a friend to look out for her.

SITTING on my couch in sweatpants, I flip through the channels on the TV. I choose an episode of *Game of Thrones*, only to flip it to a movie. But I turn it off after five minutes. Picking up my phone, I press the contact for Hunter. My thumb hovers over her number. I turn it off and toss it to the other end of the couch. I get a glass of water in the kitchen, drain the whole cup, and walk back to the couch. Looking down at my phone, I feel like it's taunting me. I could call her right now, but would she want me to? Grabbing my phone again, I tap her contact.

"Ugh." I'm about to toss the phone for a second time when it starts ringing. It slips from my fingers, but my hands save it from crashing to the floor. Hunter's name dances across the screen. I don't even let a ring go by before I click the accept button.

"Hello?" My voice cracks, sounding like a teenage boy going through puberty. Clearing my throat, I say, "Hunter?"

"Hey, Myles."

"Hey, I was just thinking about you." The tension in my shoulders melts away as I plop down on the couch and lay on my back with my arm tucked behind my head.

"You were? Well, I have a question for you."

I love that she decided to call me. It makes it that much sweeter knowing she felt comfortable enough to initiate contact first. "What's your question?"

"Did you name your truck?"

I laugh. That was the most random thing she could ask me, and I love it. Crossing my feet at the ankles, I answer her. "Yes. Her name is Gertrude, and she is the best. She gets a little temperamental, but if I give her enough love, she'll take me anywhere I want to go. She's a lot like me."

Hunter's alluring laugh sounds in my ear. There's no place I'd rather be than talking with her.

"ALRIGHT, it's my turn to ask a question first," I say to Hunter. We talked for three hours last night. I had the best night of sleep after hanging up with her. Today, we didn't get to talk much after the sales. We rushed to our second Wednesday auction because our morning sale lasted longer than the Daytona 500. We had no time to get anything but fast food. Hunter waved and told me she'd see me at the second sale, while she and Jess jumped into her Bronco and pulled away. Sadly, the second auction wasn't any better, and we were on different lanes. Her lane wrapped up an hour before mine did. I texted to let her know I would call her tonight.

"Okay. Hit me," Hunter says.

"Hugh Jackman, Matthew McConaughey, or Ryan Gosling. Kiss, marry, or kill. Go."

"What? That's impossible." Her voice sounds like she's physically in pain. "I can't. Next."

"Nope," I say, popping the 'p'. "Answer."

"Ugh. I can't believe you're making me do this."

I chuckle, waiting for her.

"Fine. Kiss—Ryan Gosling. Marry—Hugh Jackman." She pauses. Whispering, she says, "Kill—Matthew McConaughey."

A laugh bursts from my mouth. "I can't believe you'd do that." I feign my shock.

"You're an evil man, Myles Johnson."

THERE'S nothing better than falling asleep with your phone against your ear, listening to an angelic voice. Neither of us wanted to hang up, so we both fell asleep while on the phone. I kept hearing Jess come into Hunter's room and grumble something about trying to sleep. Waking up this morning wasn't easy after staying up so late. Plus on Thursdays, I have to get up early enough to make the almost two-hour drive to Tampa. After two large cups of black coffee, I made it to work and through the sale. I practically ran into the office to look at the run list, hoping we didn't have a shit ton of cars. Hunter and I made plans to go to lunch between sales if we had time.

I check the time on my phone as soon as she sells the last car. My lane ended about five minutes ago, so I've been waiting around until she finishes. We only have about an hour and a half to get to the next sale. So it's not a lot of time.

Hunter and I walk through the blazing heat to my truck. When I open the passenger door, Hunter stops right in front of me, peeking up at me through her eyelashes.

"Thank you."

The words almost bring me to my knees. I'm wrapped around her finger, and she has no clue. I lean my face in toward hers after she gets settled into her seat.

"Anything for you."

Hunter's eyes lower and focus on my lips. She leans in ever so slowly. I hold my breath and don't move a single muscle. It feels like someone couldn't move as slowly as she is, but I remain still, wanting her to choose this for herself.

A horn blares, causing her to jump back and clear her throat. I peek over my shoulder, finding JT driving by, waving his hand with mock enthusiasm. I flip him the bird over my shoulder before closing Hunter's door.

I sigh and walk around the truck to my door. Gertrude roars to life once I turn the key. "How does Chipotle sound?"

"God, you never have to ask. Chipotle always sounds good."

I nod and without thinking twice, I reach over and hold Hunter's hand while pulling out of the parking lot, half expecting her to pull her hand away, and half hoping she'd never let go. My stomach flips when she doesn't let go and only gives me a light squeeze. I want to pump my arm in the air, but I just sit and enjoy the feel of her hand in mine. I casually trace little circles on the inside of her wrist with my thumb, feeling like I'm flying high.

FRIDAY MORNING, I wake to my phone pinging. Rubbing the sleep from my eye, I blink to help focus my vision.

HUNTER:

Good morning. I wanted to let you know that Jess and I are sick. We went to urgent care and tested positive for strep.

My heart sinks. I was hoping to take her horseback riding. Strep is one of the worst sicknesses for an auctioneer. I prop myself up in bed with my pillow and text her back.

MYLES:

Fuck. That sucks. Do you need anything?

HUNTER:

No, we got the medications we need from the doctor, and we had food delivered to the house. Thank you. It's been hurting so much to talk. The doctor said I need to limit talking for a few days if I want to heal faster. I hope to be back to work by Wednesday.

I rub my face with my hands and groan. This is going to suck.

MYLES:

I won't lie. I hate this, but I want you to get better.

HUNTER:

Believe me, I hate it too. You need to keep your distance. I don't want you getting it too. I'm going to take a nap. I'll text you later.

MYLES:

Okay. Sleep well.

WEDNESDAY FINALLY ROLLS AROUND. I swear, the past five days have been the longest of my life. Since Hunter had been so sick, her doctor was nervous about her going back to work. He had her go in this morning for a last check, to make sure her throat was okay. Her throat had closed so much that she had to get steroids, and even then, the raspiness remained. The doctor was afraid she would relapse and get a worse case of it. My days were filled with waiting for her next text and going to JT's farm. Thankfully, she texted me saying she got the all-clear from the doctor and would see me at the second sale in Orlando.

I walk in with her favorite coffee in hand and some Reese's peanut butter cups. I know she's standing on the lanes, waiting for the meeting to start. I tune out the side conversations around me as I pass through the office. My eyes only see the doors that lead to the lanes.

Swinging the door open, I see my girl. She's standing with her back to me, her weight on one foot, making that hip amplified in her dark denim blue jeans and black polo shirt. Jess is standing in front of her. I want nothing more than to wrap my arms around her and never let go, but I'm not sure that's appropriate while we're at work. How I'm going to make it through a whole day without enveloping her in a hug, I'm not sure. I pick up my pace until I'm standing behind her. There's only an inch or two of space between us.

Leaning toward her ear, I whisper, "Hey, Hershey."

Hunter spins around, and her eyes light up. She reaches to hug me but pauses to look around. My heart races as hope flares in my body, thinking I won't have to wait all day to get my first hug from her. Disappointment flashes across her face as she looks over my shoulder. I turn and see the GM walking forward to start our meeting. I have to physically hold up my shoulders at the sight.

I turn back and hand over her goodies. Her eyes meet mine as she mouths, "Thank you."

I give her a small nod and bring my attention back to Marcella, the GM.

The sale is uneventful, and I can't take my eyes off Hunter. JT snickers every time he catches me looking over at her. He enjoys working with her too. She's flawless at her job. There's no way to deny that she's an astonishing auctioneer.

Afterwards, I stand outside the auction, like I did last week, waiting for her to come out. So much has happened between us this past week. I am more smitten than ever, and she seems to like me back.

Hunter strolls outside. She spins around, finding me in the same spot, and her face lights up. Pushing myself off the wall, I walk toward her.

"Okay, before you say anything"—I put my finger up. She closes her mouth and folds her hands in front of her. "How's"—I trail off when her phone goes off, making the most annoying sound known to man. She reaches into her back pocket to pull it out and sighs before silencing it.

Her eyes focus back on me. "How's—?" Before I can answer, her phone blares again. She huffs, and her face morphs into agitation. "Hold on a second."

The cheery tone in her voice is gone. *Who is causing this much grief?* She walks away, and I can't quite hear her, but I can see that her body is as tight as a bowstring.

"Hey." Jess walks out of the office, toward me. "What's going on with Hunter? She looks tense."

"I don't know." My eyes don't leave Hunter. Rubbing the scruff on my chin, I say, "Someone called her, and she seemed like she didn't want to answer it."

Hunter's voice carries across the parking lot as she yells. "What are you talking about? How bad is it?—Okay. I said, okay!—Yes. I'll let you know when I can get a flight." She stops talking, but her pacing has increased. "Would you stop! I said, I'm coming.—Okay.—Yeah. See you soon." Hunter turns around.

Gone is the face that was filled with so much happiness and excitement.

Gone is the sparkle in her eye.

Gone is the determination that shows through her body language every day.

She looks like someone ran over her dog. As she makes her way back to us, I have the strongest desire to pull her into a hug, but Jess beats me to it.

"Hey, what happened?" Jess asks.

Hunter, still enveloped in her hug, reaches her hand out, grabbing mine as her eyes peer at me over Jess' shoulder. I methodically draw little circles on her wrist. Tears pool in her beautiful green eyes, and I see nothing but desperation on her face.

"What's wrong?" I ask softly.

She sniffles. "My mom told me my dad—." She wipes a few tears away and sniffs again.

It's killing me to see her like this. I want to hold her and take away all the hurt in her eyes right now. I have never wanted to physically take pain away from someone so much in my life. My chest physically aches looking into her eyes.

"He, um, he had a heart attack." A sob breaks free from her lips, tucking her face into Jess' neck.

"Oh, Hunter! I'm so sorry!" Jess squeezes her a little tighter.

Inhaling deep breaths to calm herself down, she looks at Jess. "Can you take me home? I have to pack."

Did she just say pack? Shit. Of course, she's going to go be with her dad, but shit.

"Pack?" I confirm.

"Yeah." Hunter tucks some hair behind her ear and peers up at me. "I need to get on the next flight back to OKC. I have to be there for him." The tears stream down her face.

Of course, she has to go, but how long will she be gone? When will I see her again? Will she be okay with her mom? Questions race through my mind as Jess nods.

"Yeah. Let's go." Jess pulls Hunter toward the car but pauses and lets her go. "I'll wait for you in the car. Okay?" She squeezes Hunter's hand and looks at me.

I like Jess even more than before, which was already a good bit. It's like she knows exactly what her friend needs. Without either of us saying a word, she knows Hunter wants a moment with me.

"Hey," I whisper. Putting my hand against her cheek. She looks up at me and jumps into my arms. I release a long breath, loving the feeling of her against me. Without hesitation, she curls herself into my body. It's the most amazing feeling in the world. She's so tiny, but she molds into me perfectly. I don't ever want to let her go.

"I'm so sorry." She cries softly against my chest, wetting my shirt with her tears. We stay like this for several more minutes before I place a few small kisses on top of her head, the sweetness of her lavender and vanilla contradicting the sadness of the moment.

I want to breathe her in all night.

I want to stay wrapped up in her arms.

I want to protect her from hurt. But I can't, and I feel her slightly pull away.

"I have to go," she whispers.

I know she does. She needs to be with her dad. They are close, but I know she's going to be with her mom too. After hearing how they talked on the phone, there's never been a stronger urge to protect her.

"Yeah. Will you tell me if there is anything I can do?" I press my lips into her hair, basking in the feel of my lips on her.

"You're doing it," she whispers again.

I squeeze her a little tighter before she lets go. She looks up at me with her arms still wrapped tightly around my waist. A tear slides down her cheek. I catch it and wipe it away with the pad of my thumb. Leaning down, I place a soft kiss on her forehead. She leans into me, making my heart soar.

"Call me. Okay?" I'm falling hard for this girl, and I'm not ashamed to admit it. I can see what an amazing woman she is.

She's hard-working, caring, loving, and thoughtful. Anyone would be lucky to have her in their life. I'm lucky she's giving me a chance after how much of a jerk I was to her.

She nods, pulls out of my arms, and reluctantly trudges to Jess' car. Part of me screams to chase after her, demand to join her on that plane, and protect her from whatever unknown awaits. Instead, I wave one last time before they disappear down the road.

18

HUNTER

THE CLOCK on the dashboard slowly ticks by. Our hour-long drive is silent. Jess keeps reaching over to squeeze my hand. I know she's here for me if I want to talk, but I have so many things bouncing around in my head. I'm afraid if I open up about one thing, they will all come flooding out. My dad is the only thing on my mind. My mom isn't nurturing. He's going to need someone to be there for him. Pulling out my phone, I book the first flight available to OKC. I don't know how long he will be in the hospital, but I want to get there before he's released. My flight leaves Orlando at five a.m. Pinching the bridge of my nose, I take a deep breath to calm myself. I know it's not a great flight, but it will get me there first thing in the morning. Now that I have my flight booked, I text each of my bosses, letting them know I need the time off. They all reply, telling me to take as much time as I need. The advantage of having Conrad Smith as your dad is that all your auction bosses know him.

It sucks having to take so much time off back-to-back, but my dad comes first. I need to be there for him during his recovery.

Looking out the window, I focus on all the familiar mailboxes flying by. I can't seem to get my knees to stop bouncing, and they only move faster the closer we get to home. I can't stop thinking about everything I need to do. As soon as we pull into the driveway, I burst through the front door and whip out my luggage from my closet. I throw the first few outfits I see into my suitcase. It's challenging not knowing how long I will be there for. I only bought a one-way flight. By the time I'm done packing for an infinite amount of time, my luggage is bursting at the seams, so I sit on it, struggling to get the zipper closed.

Collapsing onto my bed, I'm mentally exhausted. My brain calculates when I need to leave for the airport. Nickelback jumps up and lays next to me, putting his head on my chest. It warms my heart that he knows exactly what I need. He'd been sitting at my door waiting for me to stop moving around so he could lie with me. I wish he could take me to the airport.

I should ask Jess to drive because I don't want to leave my Bronco in the parking garage. But I have to be out the door by two-thirty tomorrow morning in order to get there to check in and get through security in time for my flight. I hate to ask that of her. I know she has to work two auctions tomorrow.

My mind immediately goes to Myles. Butterflies fill my stomach, thinking about the possibility of him taking me and getting another hug. I felt like I was spiraling with all the thoughts running through my head after the call from my mom. Then he held me close, and it was like he was grounding me. The world quieted, and my mind cleared. I felt safe. His strong arms enveloping me made me feel like everything would be okay as long as I had him. I've never had that type of hug before. A hug has never affected me in the way that one hug from Myles did. I felt strength seep into my body as he tightened an arm around my waist and cupped the back of my head with the other. When he buried his face against the side of my head and whispered everything would be okay, comfort cloaked me like a warm bath, and I felt the stress melt away and my airways open. And with the deep breath I inhaled, I knew my feelings for Myles had grown exponentially.

I'm scared for my dad. He's always been there for me, and I'm not ready for that to change. The "what-if" questions are terrifying.

I hear my phone ding with a text message. Giving my fluffy companion one last head scratch and belly rub, I grab my phone off the nightstand. Myles' name flashes on the screen. As soon as I touch the green button, a rush of calm surges through my body. How can one man bring me so much peace? Every time we talk, he's been an open book even though I can see it isn't the easiest thing for him. He's was so guarded around me at first. It's nice to see a side to him that few others see. There are a lot of people who know they can depend on him if they need help, but they don't know his true personality or what he's like outside of work.

MYLES:

Hey. I'm here for you if you need me.

The first smile since being home stretches across my face. I don't know what we are right now, but I want more. I love this version of Myles. But now I need time to sort out my feelings. I quickly type out a text before I can second-guess myself.

HUNTER:

Will you take me to the airport in the morning?

MYLES:

What time is your flight?

HUNTER:

5 a.m.

Bringing my thumbnail to my mouth, I chew the tip. It's inconsiderate to ask this of him. Pushing myself from the bed, I pace the room and hold my breath, waiting for him to tell me he can't, or worse, say yes out of pity.

MYLES:

I'll pick you up at 2:30.

My breath whooshes out of me as my shoulders relax. I'm torn between guilt and relief. Guilt wins in the end.

HUNTER:

I know you have to work tomorrow, so please don't feel obligated. It's okay if you can't or would rather not. I don't want to pressure you.

Resuming to pace around the room, I tap my phone against my open palm, waiting for him to reply. The alert for an incoming text sounds immediately.

MYLES:

Hunter, I'll be there. I would have told you if I didn't want to or couldn't.

I sigh with relief. My anxiety about the morning is already beginning to quiet down, knowing he'll be there with me.

HUNTER:

Thank you!

I quickly send him my address so he knows exactly where to get me, and I won't have to tell him in the morning. I can't help but smile, knowing I have one good thing to look forward to before this trip. I need to keep my mind busy to avoid picturing my dad lying in a small hospital bed, while my mom is likely snapping at the poor nurses close by. Is it too much to hope that she will be on her best behavior? Heaven forbid this causes her to miss one of her many frilly social events. I can't remember her putting anything ahead of herself.

Jess knocks on my doorframe, a small smile on her face. I do my best to push all the unwanted memories that flood my brain out and focus on her.

"Hey. Would you want to lounge on the couch, watch a Hall-mark movie, and eat a lot of ice cream?" When I don't jump at her invitation, she says, "I have chocolate." Holding up a pint of chocolate ice cream, she presents two spoons from behind her back.

Jess knows me so well.

"I would love that. Thanks, Jess." A small smile stretches across my face, and I get off my bed and head into the living room. We've had many a movie night, snuggling on the comfy sectional with our blankets and snacks, letting the stresses of the day fade away. Nickelback jumps up onto the couch with me with the sweetest puppy dog eyes, laying his chin on my stomach and gazing up at me. I pet him and let out a slow breath. Something about him always brings me comfort, especially right now.

My phone dings and seeing Myles' name flash across the screen brings a smile to my face before I even know what the message says.

MYLES:

What's your favorite color?

"Is that Myles again?" Jess looks over at me, arching her brow as a smirk perks the corners of her lips.

"Yes." Unable to contain my smile, I look down at my phone as my cheeks warm.

"He seems to have done a complete one-eighty on you. First, he didn't like you, and now, he can't seem to get enough. Are you feeling better about him flipping the switch on you?" She knows how to lay it all out there.

"Honestly, yes. But we have talked a lot, so I get why he wasn't nice in the beginning. He shared with me his reasoning, and he has a lot going on that none of us realize. Like, he's trying to provide for his mom. He was mad at the situation, and he took it out on me. I'm not trying to excuse his behavior. I just—I understand it better. He's trying to make it up to me. He doesn't have to, but I've enjoyed getting to know him better this past week and so far I like what I see." I can't help but spill my guts to Jess. She's heard me rant many times about Myles. It only seems natural I tell her where my head is at right now.

"I want you to be careful, but I will say I like him a lot more than James." She snickers, and I roll my eyes. "You glow when Myles is around or even when he's just the topic of conversation."

"I don't know what it is about him." I tuck a stray hair behind my ear. "I want to be in his arms, Jess. Like earlier, I could have stood there with him hugging me for hours. I've never wanted anyone to hug me like that, but I felt safe. It felt right. But what does that mean? And now I'm going back home. I don't know how long I'll be there." My eyes fall. Having to leave tears my heart into pieces. I'm scared he's going to lose interest if I'm gone too long. My dad would tell me I don't want the type of guy who lets a little distance change the way he feels. Even so, it's a hard situation. It's new and something I want to pursue. Having to leave makes the future a little more uncertain.

Jess smiles. "This is what I was talking about. *This* spark is what was missing with James! I have no doubt you're going to figure this out."

"He's picking me up to take me to the airport in the morning," I tell her and start smiling again.

"Yessss! That makes me so happy. I'm glad he'll be able to give you a hug and a little extra comfort before you go." Jess saying that only makes me love her more. "Now, let's watch this movie." She takes one of the bowls of ice cream off the coffee table. Before grabbing mine, I text Myles back.

HUNTER:

Green. Yours?

MYLES:

Last week, I would have said black. But now it's green.

HUNTER:

Why the change?

MYLES:

Because it makes me think of you. Your eyes are the most beautiful shade of green I've ever seen.

Talk about swoon.

"Hey. What's going on over there?" Jess asks. "I can see by the smile on your face he texted something sweet," she sings out.

"He asked me my favorite color. Then he told me his is green because it reminds him of my eyes. Where did he come from?" I laugh.

"Aww. He's so sweet. You're lucky you get to know the guy behind the quiet exterior." We laugh together and finish our ice cream as the characters in the movie start to fall in love.

MY ALARM GOES off at 2 a.m., but I struggle to muster the energy to get out of bed. My thoughts go to Myles. He'll be here soon to pick me up, and I want to look somewhat presentable. He hasn't earned the privilege of seeing the disaster I am in the mornings, yet. I get out of bed and throw my hair up into a large, messy bun on top of my head, which my mom is going to love when I get there. I'm sure it will be the first thing she comments on when she sees me. I'm there for one reason, and it's being by my dad's side as he recovers. Plus, my flight is in the middle of the night. I'm not trying to impress anyone, except Myles, of course. And I have a feeling he might appreciate the *fresh face* look.

There's a soft knock at the door, just as I'm finished getting ready. I have on jean shorts, a comfy baggy gray shirt that drapes off my shoulder, and white tennis shoes. My bags are already at the front door, so I'm ready to hit the road. I open the door to a smiling Myles holding a plant and a green sweatshirt in his hands. He's wearing shorts and a black T-shirt with his hat on backward. This has quickly become my favorite look on him. He looks relaxed and comfortable.

"Hi." I crinkle my nose at the plant and chuckle.

"Well, you said your favorite color was green. I was going to get you flowers, but they didn't have green. So I got you a plant instead. I also brought one of my old college sweatshirts from USF. I know it'll be big on you, but I wanted you to have some part of me with you for comfort." The thought he put into these gifts melts me. I tuck my bottom lip beneath my teeth in an attempt to stop the grin spreading across my face. Nobody has ever put forth so much effort to try to make me feel better.

"This has to be one of the sweetest things anyone has ever done for me. Thank you!" I grab the plant and put it on the kitchen counter. I scribble a note to Jess threatening her life if she lets it die while I'm gone. He walks up behind me and wraps his arms around me. My heart works in overdrive as I attempt to control my breathing. This gesture is sweet and one I really need. His cheek rests on top of my head as my hands hold his arms wrapped around my middle.

"How are you holding up?" he asks, softly.

I squeeze his arms and turn to face him, lacing my arms around his neck. "Feeling like I'm living in fight or flight mode." My eyes sting with the growing tears in them.

"I know." He hugs me closer.

I close my eyes as I rest against his chest. It's crazy how fast this is moving. I never expected this, and now I can't imagine not having his arms for comfort. I'm already dreading being away from him and having my new found safe place miles away.

"These yours?" Myles points to the bags crowding the side of the doorway. "I'll go put them in my truck."

"Yes, thank you!" I finish my note and grab the rest of my things.

Once outside, Myles already has my bags in the back of the truck and is waiting for me by the open passenger door. He helps me into the cab, then leans in and gives my cheek a quick kiss. Grabbing the seatbelt, he leans across me to lock it in. My heart is pounding out of my chest as I'm surrounded by his woodsy scent.

Myles leans back, his eyes dropping to meet mine, a wicked grin curling his lips as he dips his head closer and whispers, "I love your hair down, but seeing it up"—he loops a finger around a loose tendril and gives it a tug—"makes me want to kiss a path all the way up your neck until I get to your lips. It's a bit distracting."

The feel of his lips grazing my ear sends goosebumps rolling down my body, lighting every nerve on their way down. I have to bite my lip to keep the moan threatening to burst through from escaping.

Myles' gaze drops to the lip pinned between my teeth, before slowly bringing it back up to my eyes. "Something to look forward to when you get home." The playfulness of his deep voice reverberates to my core. Before I can respond, he winks and shuts my door.

On the drive to the airport, the conversations flows easily. He casually reaches over to hold my hand, and it's the first time I am relieved to have the contact. Myles rubs a soothing circle across the back of my hand, relaxing every jittery nerve spasming through my body. He asks about my family and loves hearing more about my dad and his love for auctioneering, but also his love of riding and roping cattle. I tell him about the farm and the horse I miss. He tells me about his mom and stories about him and JT growing up together. I can't believe how much trouble they got into. His poor mom. I can only imagine what they put her through.

As the airport gets closer, I dread leaving. I'm torn between not wanting to go, and wanting to be there for my dad. I haven't talked to him. I know he's still in the hospital, and my plan is to go straight there. My mom and I don't communicate well, so it would be better to get the information myself from the doctors. Knowing her, she might downplay it.

"Hey, you got a little quiet. You okay?" Myles says, squeezing my hand as we pull into the parking garage.

I look over at him and give him a small smile. "Yes, just thinking about what I'm headed into. Thank you for driving me. You've made this so much easier." I squeeze his hand. He pulls into a parking space and turns toward me.

"No place I'd rather be." His eyes sparkle.

His actions have shown how much he means those words.

"Come on, let's get you inside and check your bags."

I can't believe he's not just dropping me off at departures. *Where did this man come from?*

We get all my bags out, and he grabs my hand before walking me inside. There's not many people here so it doesn't take long to check my bags. He ventures off to buy me a mocha frappuccino. A few minutes later, as we stand off to the side near security, he looks at me.

"Come here." He wraps me up completely in his arms. I immediately relax into his warm, large body.

"Thank you for being here," I mumble into his chest. Breathing in his smell, reminds me of being in the woods. I close my eyes, doing my best to commit it to memory as he kisses the top of my head.

"Always." Pulling away, Myles hooks his finger beneath my chin, tipping my head up. "I'll be right here when you get back, Hershey. Go, take care of your dad, then come back to me."

He slowly leans down and his soft lips press against mine. It's the sweetest kiss I've ever gotten. Quick yet tender. He pulls back to look into my eyes and gives me a smirk, but I'm not ready for this moment to end. I press up on my toes and put my hands around his neck, bringing him down to me. His eyes show a glimmer of shock and then they darken. It's like he didn't expect me to want more. Our lips meet again, but it's not gentle this time. One of his hands holds the back of my neck as the other snakes around my body to pull me closer. His tongue slides against my lips, and I open, allowing him to deepen the kiss. It's everything I could have ever imagined. I completely forget where we are or that there are people around. All I can think about is Myles' lips and hands. I weave my hand up, pushing his hat a little to the side to tug the hair on the back of his head. He groans into my mouth, squeezing me harder. My legs are weak. I would drop into a puddle on the floor if it weren't for Myles holding me against him. I feel his desire pressing into my stomach. He slows our kiss, and I whimper, not wanting it to end.

"We can do this as much as you want when you get back. You can't miss your flight." His eyes search my face before landing on my lips. "If you don't go now, you'll miss it." Cupping my face, he kisses me.

I've never wanted a man as much as I want Myles. "Maybe that's what I want right now." I kiss him again, and he moans, kissing me back harder before breaking for air.

"You're killing me, Hershey," he complains, pressing his forehead to mine. "Please, I'm trying to be good here. It's not something that comes easy for me." I smile up at him. Missing my flight doesn't sound so bad, but I know I'll regret not being there for my dad, and I don't want to rush into anything with Myles. I nod and run my hand down the rest of his chest.

"I'm not sure when I'll be back," I whisper, looking down. Having to leave without a definite return date sucks. I look back into his eyes. "I bought a one-way flight." My heart sinks a little at my honesty. He nods and lightly kisses me on the forehead. Then he wraps his arms around me for another hug.

"He needs you right now, and I'll be here, waiting." He leans back and lifts my chin so he can look right into my eyes. "When you get back, I'm taking you on a ride, and I want this"—he points to me and then to himself. —"to be more. Okay?"

"It already feels like it is," I admit. This all feels like it is so much more.

"It is, but I want you to take your time, to be sure. I don't want you to have any regrets," he explains while his eyes never leave mine. He cradles the side of my face with his hand and gently rubs his thumb against my cheek. "I want you to be as sure as I am." He kisses me softly, but it's over before I can make it more. "Now, get out of here before I change my mind." He winks.

"Okay," I whisper and grab my purse and carry-on bag. I walk away but pause before joining the line to look at him once more. He smiles at me, and I return it. Then I turn back around and walk through security. That felt a lot like a last goodbye. I don't want it to be, but I've also never actually said goodbye to someone at an airport. I guess we gave the few people around us a good show, but I have no regrets. I know I want more with him. I guess I'll have to show him I don't need time.

19

MYLES

THE TOP of her hair vanishes as she disappears through security. That had to be the best first kiss of my life, and I didn't want to stop. It was hard letting her go. The way she grabbed my hair had me going crazy. I've never reacted to someone like this before. The hard-on I have right now is making things very uncomfortable. It doesn't help that I'm in an airport with people all around. I adjust myself in the least obvious way to get a little relief before turning around to leave.

It has never been this easy with a girl. There weren't any awkward moments on our drive. Everything just flowed. I want to know everything about her, what makes her happy, sad, or angry. She's such a hard worker. I never knew how hard it is for females in the auction world. I mean, I knew a little bit, but now I know that it really sucks for them. She never gave up and that shows the kind of person she is. She's amazing, and I am blown away that she's even giving me the time of day.

After I get back to my truck, I glance at my phone to see I still have about four hours until the auction sale starts. I'm right around the corner from it, so I drive to the parking lot and decide to sleep while I still have a little time left, but I shoot Hunter a text before closing my eyes.

MYLES:

Hey, Hershey. Let me know when you land safely. Enjoy some time with your dad.

HUNTER:

Thank you! I will be back before you know it.

I hope she will be. I put my phone down and lean my seat back. Putting my hat over my eyes, I drift off thinking about a little brunette green-eyed beauty the whole time.

I startle awake to a knock on my window. I rub the sleep from my eyes because I was dreaming a little too well. After getting excited at the airport, then dreaming of her, I'm a little uncomfortable right now especially having someone at my window. It has been a long time since I've even been with a woman, so my current predicament isn't all that shocking. I turn to see JT smiling at me, arching an eyebrow. I roll down my window.

"What?" I bite out.

"What are you doing?"

"What does it look like, asshole? Sleeping." I grab my bag of clothes on the passenger seat and then open the door..

"I see that, but why are you sleeping here? Don't you usually sleep... I dunno, in your bed?"

It's too early for his sarcasm. "Fuck off." I roll up my window and shut the door. "I dropped Hunter off at the airport before the ass crack of dawn, so I was getting some sleep," I say as thoughts of Hunter invade my mind again. I check my phone, but there's nothing.

"I assume it's going well with you two? I mean, she had you drive her to the airport." He looks at me a little cautiously.

He knows I never wake up well, and he's used to me biting his head off when he has the nerve to wake me.

"Yeah. Things are good." Not too happy she's gone for a while, but there isn't much I can do. I give him a knowing look with a wink.

"Ahh. You bastard!" He guffaws and shoves me, and I laugh with him.

Thinking about kissing her makes me feel ten times better. After being miserable for so long, I like being this happy. I can't remember the last time I was.

We walk into the auction, and Marcella says I'm going to run Hunter's lane while she's away. It's bittersweet because I wish Hunter were here, but this is an opportunity to run my very own lane. I'm not just giving auctioneers breaks, it's my lane. It feels surreal. But I have to admit, I'd still rather be a ringman if it meant Hunter were here.

"Hey. Congrats. You're finally getting what you've always wanted," JT says while we walk to our lane.

Since JT was scheduled to be her ringman, now he's mine. At least I know the day will go by quickly with him by my side.

"Yeah. It's great." I know I sound a little less than pleased.

"Okay. You don't sound like all your dreams are coming true." He smacks me on the shoulder. "Yeah, it's not a permanent thing, but at least you get to run the show for a little while. Right?"

He knows better than anyone how much I've wanted this. He's watched how hard growing up was for me because I always felt like I needed to help my mom. It made me grow up faster than the rest of our class in high school. I wasn't worried about the petty drama. I was making sure my mom didn't have to work harder than she already was. No one in our class ever understood why I was always busy. They didn't know how much I worked outside of school. They thought I had a part-time job like the rest of them, but little did they know I was picking up every side hustle to help my mom. I don't think *she* even knows how much I worked back then.

"Yeah. You're right. I just"— I trail off and shake my head.

"Eh, nevermind. Let's do this." I put my fist out, and he bumps it. He's right. She will be back. I need to enjoy this time. Although I wish she were here to see it and for us both to have our own lanes at the same time. That would make this moment even sweeter, but I'm going to show these guys what I've got since I finally have my chance.

THE SALE IS RUNNING SMOOTHLY, and we're selling a shit ton of cars but a nagging distraction gnaws at my chest. Hunter's flight should have landed by now, but I've heard nothing from her. It's making me lose my focus, and JT keeps his eyes on me to make sure I stay on track. I need to do well, so I need to push all the outside thoughts out of my head. I pocket my phone and get back to business. The rest of the sale blows by, and many of the selling dealers give me tips and praise for my performance which did my ego some good.

"Hey. You did good, man." JT slaps me on the back.

He's always the first one to cheer me on. No matter what it is, I can always count on JT to have my back, but he's also the first one to give me a hard time when I fuck something up too.

"Yeah. It felt good."

"You got a little *distracted* for a bit, but you came back," he says, laughing.

"Yeah, yeah. Alright, let's go get some food before the next sale." I slap him on the back in return. Looking at my phone and still not seeing anything from Hunter, I tell myself that she probably just forgot. I know she has a lot on her plate with her dad. My gut nags at me, wanting to make sure she's safe.

The day flew by on the lane, but it has slowed to a snail's pace as I wait to hear from Hunter. The bright side was the Lakeland sale also let me take Hunter's place on her lane. It seems like they don't want to permanently fill her spot, just a temporary fill in. I'm not complaining. Both sales went great, and the GMs let me know they were happy with how I did. I'm hoping they will keep me in the back of their minds if another position opens. There's no telling what they'll do though.

I'm exhausted after being up a good chunk of the night, so I head home instead of out with the guys to shoot some pool. Once I'm home, I put on joggers and a sweatshirt and throw a frozen pizza in the oven. I'm too exhausted to make a full dinner. I check my phone again, but there's still nothing from Hunter. I'm just going to text her. It's been a long day, probably for both of us.

MYLES:

I'm thinking about you. Hope everything's okay.

I get my pizza out and continue watching the first season of *Game of Thrones*.

I must have fallen asleep because I wake up to my phone's ringtone blasting. Rubbing my eyes, I look at the screen to find Hunter's name.

"Hello?" My voice is laced with sleep.

"Myles? Were you sleeping? I'm sorry! I didn't mean to wake you. I didn't text you back because my mom took my purse and bags to the house without me realizing. Then, when I finally got home, I texted you. When I didn't hear back, I thought I'd call before I went to bed. I'm sorry. Please go back to sleep," she blurts out.

I have a hard time following along, still a bit groggy. "Hershey, slow down. It's fine. I fell asleep on the couch. But I'm up now, so talk to me," I urge her. I don't want her to go now that I'm finally hearing from her.

"Okay. How was work?"

"Work was fine, but I want to hear about you. Are you okay? What's going on with your dad?" I don't want to talk about me. I need to hear all about what is causing her to ramble a hundred words a minute.

"Oh, um. He's okay, I guess. They said it was a minor heart attack, but he's still in the hospital. It was hard to see him like that. It made me realize how much I've missed him. He was in and out of sleep, and I couldn't bring myself to leave until visiting hours were over."

She sounds exhausted. I want to be with her so she can curl up in my arms, and I can comfort her.

"How's it going with your mom?" I know they don't get along. I have to know if she's okay.

She lets out a breath. "Normal," she grumbles.

"I'm here, Hunter. I'll listen if you want to talk. I was worried about you today, so it's good to hear your voice."

"It's good to hear your voice, too. It was a tough day. My mom isn't the easiest to be around, and my dad's too weak to be the usual buffer between us. But the doctors seem to think he could go home in about 48 hours. I'm hoping for that."

I can't help but smile. I love listening to her and hearing about her life and family. I can tell how much she cares for her dad. Stretching back out on the couch, I get comfortable.

"Tell me something real." I change the subject to distract her from her current situation. "Something few people know about you." She laughs, and it's music to my ears.

"Hm. That's a hard one for sure because I'm an open book." She pauses.

I'm excited to hear whatever it is she's about to tell me, but I'm stalling because I don't want to get off the phone with her.

"Okay, when I was little, my parents would have me pull weeds outside. I always hated it, but I had to fill a grocery bag."

"How is that something not many people know? Don't all kids do that when they're younger, either as a punishment or chores around the house?" I was always doing yard work around the house to help my mom, which meant I was always dirty. I used to get made fun of when I was little for wearing shirts with stains to school because my mom was too busy working. She didn't have much time to make sure the clothes I wore were clean.

"Well, the thing is, I would always take a lot longer to do it because I had a crazy imagination. So I would pretend the weeds were people and instead of dolls talking to each other, I had the weeds talk to each other, like little weed people." She laughs while explaining her story.

"Wow. . . so you were kind of a weirdo?" I laugh through my question.

"Ha. Ha. Yes, I was. I'm not ashamed of it. I loved creating my own little world. It made a very annoying chore more fun. But it made it take way longer than it should have," she pauses and a few beats pass before she says, "Well?"

"Well, what?"

"Your turn. I told you something real. You had to know it was coming back to you. You have to tell me something now."

I rub my hand over my face. I didn't think this through. I wasn't expecting her to ask me the same thing.

"Okay. Well, something real would be," I pause, because I don't want to scare her, but this is the most genuine I can be. "I really like a wild-haired brunette that I can't stop thinking about."

She's so quiet that I can't hear a peep from her end.

I tap my fist against my forehead and squeeze my eyes shut. "Hunter?"

"Really?"

"Yeah, really."

"*This* scares me." Her voice is quiet. "The whole thing, I want to believe it's all real. I'm just scared," she admits. "I don't want to get hurt."

"I know you are. I am too. Let's be scared together," I say. "I wish I could hold you in my arms." As long as she doesn't shut me out, we can make this work.

"Me too, Myles."

"Why don't you get some sleep, and I'll talk to you tomorrow. Alright?" I don't want to get off the phone, but I know we both are sleep-deprived. Hunter has the added emotional exhaustion that comes with travel, an entire day at the hospital, and strained conversation with her mom.

"Okay. I'll call you when I can tomorrow. Goodnight, Myles."

"Goodnight, Hershey."

She ends the call. Man, I have never felt like this before, but I wasn't completely honest with her. This doesn't scare me. If anything, it makes me crave her more.

20

HUNTER

THE UNIVERSE DECIDED I didn't need a calmer day. I'm staring at my dad while sitting on a brown scratchy fabric couch. The doctors give him the rundown of how he needs to take better care of himself, starting with his diet. He isn't too happy about all the foods they tell him to cut out, but it's a necessity for his health. My mom half listens while her eyes flicker from my frizzy hair down to my worn-down shoes. Her glare saying, "How dare you wear those clothes out of the house."

She, on the other hand, is dressed to perfection. Her hair is pulled into a low-style bun, not a single hair out of place. Her blue dress is completely free of lint, hair, and wrinkles, and nude heels with no scuff marks. She always wears some type of jewelry. Today, she has on pearl stud earrings and a gold necklace with a single pearl at the bottom. *Always classy.* I thought I could enjoy alone time with dad, but I guess not. There's always my mom, doctors, or nurses coming and going, no actual moment of peace. So as I sit here trying to stay out of everyone's way, I allow my mind to wander to the phone call with Myles last night.

I can't believe how blunt he is sometimes. I'm thankful I know what he is feeling, but I am scared he may be lying. Or that he will grow bored after a while, and I don't want to get hurt. Even though I ended things with Steve, it wasn't an easy breakup. He knows my parents, and his parents are in the same club as mine. He convinced his parents to talk my mom, so she pressures me to be with him. Believe me, they didn't need to pressure her. She was already doing it herself.

"Honey, are you even listening to me?" I look up, startled, as my mom snaps her fingers near my face to get my attention. Her stare is just short of a glare, her lips pursed.

"Um. No, sorry. What were you saying?"

"Ugh. I swear. Your head is always in the clouds. I don't understand why"—

My dad clears his throat. "Why don't you repeat what you said, Beth? She was thinking of other things, and honestly, I'm not sure what you were talking about either," he says.

I wish he wasn't hooked to so many tubes and wires so I could lean over and give him a big hug. He always tries to take the smoke out of the fire she spits out. It never works, though.

"Fine," she bites out.

Mom also hates when he does that. She's always thought of it as him and me versus her. In reality, he's always trying to get us all on the same team.

"I was saying there is a gala next Friday. I want Hunter to go with us."

I blink. I must be in another reality. How is my mother expecting dad to attend a gala, which means wearing a tux, in his current state? Also, he doesn't like to show it, but the heart attack took a lot out of him. He's sleeping more and doesn't have the energy to walk around much. Sometimes I wonder how on earth I'm related to this woman. I focus my attention on Dad, and he takes a deep breath.

"Mom, you can't be serious right now."

She only gives me a confused look.

"Dad's not even out of the hospital, and you expect him to go to a gala with you? How's that realistic in any way, shape, or form?" I fold my arms across my chest and give her a disgusted look.

"What do you mean?" She looks at him with a look of fake shock. "He's getting out in about 36 hours now. The gala is more than a week away. Why wouldn't your father go? We have had this on the schedule for months. We have our tickets. The only thing we need to figure out is how to get you one. But since I'm on the board of the foundation hosting the gala, it shouldn't be a problem."

I stare at her with my mouth open.

"Honestly, Hunter, close your mouth. It's not ladylike to gape at someone in such a way." She looks down and plucks an imaginary hair off of her skirt.

I snap my mouth closed and blink a few times. She's actually serious. I look over at my dad, but he isn't saying a word. He's looking down, trying the best he can to stay out of it. He doesn't want to rile her up before he needs to. Of course, he's used to her being like this. I'm sure it didn't shock him in the slightest.

"Well, if Dad is well enough to attend a gala, I'll go home. I'm only here to make sure he gets better and has the care he deserves." It felt good to stand up for myself. Referencing Florida as my home slipped out, but it gave me peace. I'm happy to call it home. OKC has never felt much like where I belong. I miss the home I've made for myself. I want to get back to it, but I'm not pushing Dad, unlike my mother.

"Honestly, you can stay another week. There's no reason to leave so soon. Everyone will love to see you again. Especially a certain person who you left so high and dry."

She continues spitting out evil. I don't even want to listen to her anymore. She always makes me feel awful about myself. Of course, I did something wrong to one of her friends, and she's holding it against me. New day, same manipulation.

"What are you talking about, Mother?" I sigh.

"Steven. The poor boy has been heartbroken since you left him. He doesn't understand what he could have done to make you leave him the way you did. It wasn't right. He misses you," she says.

I have to hold myself back from gagging. He didn't miss me when he was jumping into bed with someone else right after the breakup. He must have conveniently left that part out.

"Mother, we have been over this. He wasn't with me for the right reasons, and he started getting abusive. I will not be with someone like that," I state, looking her directly. She can see how serious I am, but I don't think she cares.

"Oh, please. Girls these days are so dramatic." She waves her hand to dismiss what I've said. "He loves you, so you should see him. In the meantime, I will get you a ticket, and I want you to find a dress. It should be exquisite. I expect nothing less."

She continues acting like my opinions don't matter. I can't stand being around her when she's like this. Aren't mothers supposed to be nurturing and loving toward their kids? Mine must have missed that memo.

"Okay, we can talk about all this later. I want a nap," my dad cuts in.

I let out a sigh of relief. Maybe she will finally leave me alone for a little bit too if she has to be quiet.

"Fine. I have to get going anyway, darling. Have a good nap," she says and kisses my dad on the forehead. Her eyes flick back to me. "I can make you a hair appointment before the gala, honey." Turning, she leaves the room.

I look over at my dad. I'm having a hard time not blowing up.

"I know." He puts his hand up and nods. "You don't need to say anything. I know. Now get some lunch, so I can sleep." He reclines his bed to get more comfortable.

"Fine. But call if you need me." I stand and walk toward him to kiss his cheek.

I leave with my purse, but I can't seem to focus enough to find somewhere to go. I'm nothing like her. I used to think I was born with my unruly hair only to piss her off. Growing up, she was always trying to tame it, but once I was old enough to do it myself, she started her passive-aggressive remarks to shame me. Despite her comments, I never stopped wearing my hair as natural as possible. It was one way I could control how I looked.

After aimlessly wandering down different halls, I finally find the cafeteria. My stomach lets out a monstrous growl. It's after 1 p.m. People in blue scrubs buzz around on lunch break. Exhausted, somber families gather around small portions of food. Most are not alone, and it makes me wish I had someone here with me. I bet Myles is done with his lane by now. I miss him. Yes, he puts on this rough exterior, but I've come to know the man beneath that. That man is kind, caring, considerate, thoughtful, giving, and I don't want to even think about his body. My hormones might get carried away.

HUNTER:

Hey there. I'm thinking about you.

MYLES:

All naughty things, I hope.

I laugh. Of course that's his response.

HUNTER:

Can't wait to come home.

MYLES:

Me too. I have a saddle with your name on it.

THE DAYS GO by in a blur, and we are able to get Dad home and comfortable. Mom insists on hiring a nurse to help twenty-four-seven because she doesn't want to do anything herself, but she's covering her true intentions by saying it's because she wants him to get the best care he needs. He's allowed to do short walks each day. So I take that on as my duty. We start on small walks around the house, then we venture down to the mailbox. Now he's able to go around the farm, which has made him the most excited. He misses his animals and wants to be around them as much as possible.

Before I know it, a week has passed. Dad is doing so much better. He's able to go on a decent walk now and doesn't take as many naps throughout the day. I know he wants to get back to work, but the doctor said he needs to take off at least a month. He isn't happy about it, but it's important for him to get stronger before returning to work.

Each day, I make it a point to call or text Myles. We haven't talked as much as I was hoping, but when we do talk, it's the highlight of my day. I cannot wait to get back to see him. He promised to pick me up at the airport. I'm thankful to have him in my corner right now. I've also talked with Jess each day, but those talks are filled with giving her all the details about me and Myles. She's obsessed. She wants to know everything, and I love having someone to talk to about him. I haven't been able to tell my parents about him, because I know my mom would only give me a harder time. My dad would be happy that I've found someone, but my mother isn't over my breakup with Steve. I'm going to miss my dad when I leave, and I wish I could talk to him about Myles in person. I know he would love him. They could probably talk for hours about the auction world.

"You're doing great, Dad." I look over at him as we take our daily lap around the farm. His complexion is less pale, and the dark circles under his eyes are gone. He even has a little pep to his step. I know he wants to check the training progress on a few of his horses.

"I know. You can stop hovering now. I love having you here, but sweetie, I'm okay." He looks at me with sincerity.

I know he's physically okay, but it's been a tough week. It was extremely scary seeing him vulnerable in the hospital bed, connected to so many wires. I will never forget seeing him look helpless in the hospital bed, and I never want to see it again. He looked so fragile that I was afraid to touch him. He needs to get as healthy as possible before I leave.

"I know you're okay, Dad." I take a breath. "It was hard seeing you like that, but I'm glad you're doing better. I want you to keep doing the things you need to get strong. No stress for you." I level him with a stare. He laughs, but he knows I'm serious.

"Okay, but I need one favor, sweetie." He looks down with a little uncertainty in his eyes.

It piques my curiosity because he rarely asks me for anything.

"Of course. Anything for you." We stop walking to face each other.

"Go with your mother to the gala tomorrow."

I shake my head, ready to tell him absolutely not, but he holds his hand up stopping me.

"Just hear me out. This is selfish of me, but I don't think I'm ready to be around the club members right now. I want to relax a little longer before diving back into her world."

I cannot believe this is even a topic of conversation. There's no bone in my body that wants to go anywhere close to that gala. I also can't believe that he feels pressure to go. He's doing better, and I will do anything to make sure he doesn't risk his progress.

"You definitely shouldn't go. There is no question about that at all, Dad. You need your rest. Mom will have to go by herself. She'll be fine." He's crazy if he thinks I'm going to a gala with her. We'd be at each other's throats.

"I know it will be hard for you, especially considering how

difficult your relationship is, but she hates going alone. Let me break it down for you like this." He hesitates and gives a strained face. It's like he's physically pained by the words that are about to come out of his mouth. "If you don't go for me, then I will have to go."

My blood boils. I don't like when people force me into situations. Mom always tried to back me into a corner in some way or another to go to these functions. It was one of the main sources of contention between us. Now I feel like my dad is, and it doesn't sit right with me.

I finally look him in the eye after giving myself a few moments to calm down. "Fine. I'll see you at the house," I say, turning and walking away. He knows what he's asking of me is wrong. He knows he gives her anything she wants, and now it feels like he's stabbed me in the back.

"Okay, sweetie," he says softly after I'm already far away from him.

Now I have to get a fucking dress to wear to a stupid event I will hate. I want to go home and cuddle up on our comfy couch with Jess and watch a Hallmark movie. I also wouldn't mind if Myles came over and brought me some Reese's. Now that Dad's better, it's time for me to start planning my trip home.

21

MYLES

"DUDE, come on. You look like someone ran over your fucking cat," JT says while we're walking into our Wednesday morning sale in Orlando.

I haven't been very good company recently. Hunter's only been gone for six days, and I've turned into a miserable sap. Although, I wasn't much company before that either. I *at least* went out with the guys and hung out at JT's. This week, I've jetted home after work to make sure I was available for Hunter's calls. The guys would have my balls if they knew. I'm guessing they're getting close to putting the pieces together. I want to make sure I'm there for Hunter. She's going through a hard time, and not only that, but I can tell it's taking a toll on her. She hasn't shared much about how her mom's treating her while she's there, but I know it's not good. Every time I ask, she brushes it off and makes it sound like she doesn't see much of her. I know she's there for her dad, but her mom is in the same house. She has to see her often enough to make an impact.

"I know, man. I'm tired," I lie, not wanting to tell him the real reason.

"Ha. Yeah. You can say that all you want, but I know you. I

know what you look like tired, angry, hungry, and this is none of those things. Is someone missing a certain lady I like to call Fun-Size?" He gives me a knowing look.

Sometimes I hate how well he knows me.

"Yeah, yeah. Whatever." I roll my eyes. "Let's get to work, asshole." I walk faster into the office to get away from him, but his laughter invades my ears, making me clench my teeth. All the young women in the office turn their heads to look at him. We usually get a lot of looks when we show up to work. Most of the dealers are men. The same is true for ringmen and auctioneers, but most of the office workers and block clerks are women. It's not unheard of for relationships to form here, because we all see each other often. I have no desire to be with anyone else, but that doesn't stop JT from flirting his ass off. Jess sits behind the counter, and I wave at her before going to our meeting even though I'm early. Knowing JT, he'll hang back and talk to any girl that piques his interest.

I grab some breakfast and coffee in the cafeteria before the meeting. I've been wanting my own lane for longer than I can remember, but it doesn't change the sinking feeling I have now that Hunter isn't here. I check my phone and go back and forth, deciding if I should call her or not. I know she's used to waking up early, but she doesn't seem like a morning person. Since she's been gone, she usually talks to me later in the day or night. Not that I mind, but I wonder if she's awake right now. After going back and forth, I finally say to hell with it and call her.

"Hello?" Hunter answers, her voice groggy with sleep.

"Hey, Hershey. I'm sorry. I should have texted to see if you were awake." Now I feel like shit for waking her up. I'm selfish for wanting to hear her voice to start my day.

"No. It's fine, Myles. Is everything okay?"

Sheets rustle on her end, and it only makes me wish we were cuddled up in bed together. I can only imagine how gorgeous she looks with her hair a mess and a baggy T-shirt on.

"Yeah…" I pause. We've had tons of great conversations, but I don't want to scare her away by coming on too strong.

"Yeah? What is it?" I hear the concern in her voice.

"I wanted to hear your voice before my day got started," I finally admit.

She lets out a sigh. "I'm glad you called." My shoulders relax, and I smile.

"Yeah? Even though I woke you up? I've noticed you don't seem like much of a morning person." I laugh.

"No." She laughs with me. "I'm definitely not, but…" She pauses then, and it makes me stiffen.

"What is it?"

"I'm ready to come home." She sighs.

My shoulders relax. "Did anything happen? Is your dad doing better?" She's always sounded a little off while she's been away, but she's never sounded this down before.

"Well, kinda. My mom is pushing my dad to go to this function. He can't go, but since he doesn't want to disappoint her, he asked me to fill in. I hate these things, and my ex is going to be there. My mom won't stop trying to push us back together. Then, to top it all off, my dad has always had my back with this stuff, and now it feels like he doesn't," she blurts out fast.

I'm sitting straight and stiff now. I don't like to hear her like this. I want to hold her and protect her. But what makes my blood boil is the mention of her ex and her mom pushing them together. What is that about?

"Hey. Calm down and take some deep breaths." Once I hear her exhale a few times, I go on. "Just don't go. Your dad definitely shouldn't go, but that doesn't mean you have to take his place if he doesn't. But if you need backup, I'll be on the next flight there to go with you." Where the fuck did that come from? But I would if she wanted me there.

"You're the sweetest, Myles. But, no. It's okay. He just isn't a good guy, and I'd like to avoid him as much as possible. My mom doesn't understand or want to believe that he's the main reason I moved."

Taking my hat off, I rake my fingers through my hair. "What do you need? I want to make sure you're safe."

"I think I just needed to rant. You've been the bright part of my days while I've been here. Thank you for calling."

Her voice sounds lighter, like she needed to talk to me just as much as I needed to talk to her.

"I feel the same." I look up and see JT signaling the meeting is about to start. "Hey, I'm sorry. I gotta go. I'll talk to you later?"

"Yeah. Have fun on *my* lane." She laughs.

I can't help but smile. "It's not the same without you here. I'll talk to you later."

"Bye."

Her voice sounds so small. It's not the headstrong and sassy girl I know. She's been sounding less and less like herself, and it makes me worry about her. But now, I'm worried she's going to be around this ex of hers whom her mom loves. I can't get that out of my head. I should have asked more questions, like what kind of function is this? Will there be a lot of people so she can completely avoid him? Do I need to come and punch him or talk some sense into her mother? At the airport, I told her to go and make sure this is what she wants, that I am what she wants. But everyday we talk, I feel it. We are more, and I have to protect her.

My body hums as I storm over to JT with all these thoughts swirling around in my head. My blood pressure rises as my ears start to burn. I swear steam might come out of them. I thought calling to hear her beautiful voice would make my day better, but now all I picture is her being around that piece of shit. Even though Hunter says he's a bad guy, she must be really downplaying it. He did something bad enough to make her move, not just hours away, but states away from him.

"You okay?" JT whispers to me once I reach him.

"Yup." I pop the p.

He smirks. "Yeah. You look it." I glare at him, and he covers his mouth to hold back his laughter. It only makes me scowl more. I catch sight of Jess walking by, and I immediately get an idea. Our meeting ended quickly since there wasn't anything different for today. I jog over to my lane, and Jess is setting up the computer. I see her grunt with a frustrated look on her face. When I'm right behind her, she bends over to reach for something on the ground, still sitting in her chair.

"Hey, Jess!" I say, a little louder than I intended to.

She gasps and startles, making the chair fly out from under her. She falls right to the ground. My shoulders meet my ears as I cringe.

"Ouch!" Jess rubs her hip and looks over at me. "What the hell, Myles! That fucking hurt."

"Sorry. I didn't mean to make you fall. I just wanted to talk to you." I take my hat off and rank my fingers through my hair, then reposition my hat.

"You couldn't have gotten my attention at a normal volume?" She glares while getting up.

I rush over and pick up her chair. "Sorry. I'm a little off today." That's an understatement, but I'm not going to admit that to her.

She looks at me and squints, which makes me square my shoulders more under her assessment. Her shoulders slump. "You heard."

My eyebrows shoot up.

"Yeah. I know. She told me she's going to be around her ex. Your face is easy to read. Your friend is like Fort Knox." I see her eyes flash to JT, who is walking across the lanes before sighing. "I'm worried about her, too."

I decide to let that last little tidbit go about JT. "Can't say that I like it."

She laughs and shakes her head. "No. She won't get back together with him, but that doesn't mean her mom won't try hard to make it happen." She fidgets with her shirt. "I know she's ready to come home, but she promised her dad she would go with her mom to the gala tomorrow."

My eyebrows draw in. *It's a gala?*

"She's going shopping today for dresses. I'm excited though. I'm making her send me the pictures so I can help her pick one out." She smiles and goes back to the computer to get it ready for the lane to start.

She's about to buy a fancy dress and go to an event that her ex is also attending. Her mom's going to push them together, and there's nothing I can do to stop it. I want to go to Oklahoma, bring her home, and keep her away from that guy. I'm ready for her to be back. *Fuck.*

I'M STARING BLANKLY at the TV screen, trying to watch the last episode of the first season of *Game of Thrones*. My phone rings, and I smile when I see Hunter is calling. I've had a rough day ever since I heard the news that she'll see her ex again tomorrow. I couldn't focus, and I've been racking my brain all day, trying to figure out what to do to help her.

"Hey! How was your day today?" I say when I answer the phone.

"It was good. Dad's making a lot of progress walking around the farm. Pretty sure he doesn't need my help anymore. He barely needs the help of the nurses that come, either."

I sit up straight. "So you're coming home soon?" I try not to sound too hopeful, but I don't think there's a way for me to hide that.

"Yes, and I'm bringing you a new hat."

"Yeah, I'm not changing my hat." It would be hard for me to switch hats even if she was the one to get me a new one.

"What's the story with it, anyway?" It's been fun that every day we've been able to uncover more about each other.

"Well, when I was younger, I didn't have a dad to show me how to fix things or anything, really. My mom was always at work, so I was at home a lot by myself. I had a neighbor, Mr. Arnold, who didn't have any family close by. He was a handyman, and he hated that his grandkids weren't around so he could teach them different odds-and-ends jobs. He noticed I was by myself a lot and didn't like that I didn't have a male figure in my life. So he took it upon himself to teach me. I basically went to his house every day after school."

"Wow. That was nice of him. I'm glad he could teach you. Were you like an adopted grandson to him?" she asks.

I smile. "Yeah. He always called me that. He said he adopted me, and I didn't have any say in the matter. I was stuck with him. I think he only said that to make me feel better about going over there. He knew I wanted to, but I didn't want to upset my mom and make her feel like she wasn't doing enough. So he would tell her he *needed* my help for things." I miss the old man. He was grumpy, but he meant the world to me.

"How long did you know him for?"

"I started when I was about nine years old, and he passed when I was fifteen. I would have had to stop going over there, anyway. That was when I started working to help my mama." I sigh and scratch the back of my neck. "He left me something in his will, and his family knew about it. They weren't upset, but they weren't exactly happy about it either. I didn't even go to the lawyers to see what he left me. I told his kids that he gave me enough, but I only wanted his old hat. They, of course, had no problem giving it to me. So I've been wearing it ever since."

"Wow. You must have meant a lot to him. He sounds like an amazing man."

The entire day, I have thought about Hunter, and her going to this fancy event. Jess hinted at Hunter needing to stay away from her ex. I have to know why. I have a sinking feeling that something bad happened, and I'm too far away to make sure it doesn't happen again. I rake my fingers through my hair.

"Hunter, tell me about your ex."

She sighs. "That's a long story, and a complicated one. I met him at work. He buys cattle for a big company, so he would kiss my dad's ass trying to get a better deal. My dad treated everyone the same, never showing favorites, but that didn't stop Steve from trying to get on his good side. One day, Steve started paying me more attention, and I thought it was harmless. We ended up dating, but slowly, I stopped recognizing myself. He made me feel as if I wasn't important and only his wants and needs were. Eventually, I believed I was there to please him, but no matter what I did, he was never fully happy with me. One night, we went out on a date, and he drank too much. I didn't order what he wanted me to order for myself, and he backhanded me as soon as we were alone in the parking lot. I stood there, shocked, as he drove off. He had been a little too handsy or tightened his grip on me a little too hard in the past, always apologizing later, but this was the first time he physically hit me, drawing blood. I called my dad, barely able to talk through my tears. I've never seen him so angry as when his eyes landed on my bloody lip."

"Hunter." My voice barely comes out above a whisper, while my body aches to hold her.

"My dad wanted to press charges, but I knew I wanted to leave, had to leave. My dad respected my wishes and helped me find a job far away. I know it killed him to have me go, but he has always supported me above all else."

"I'm so sorry. You should have never had to go through that." I sit on the edge of the couch. "Hunter, I don't want you around him. I'm not saying that to tell you what to do, but I'm worried about you. Your dad won't be at the function to help you, and it doesn't sound like your mom will be much protection."

"It's okay. It's a large event. I'll make sure to never be alone with him. He wouldn't do anything in front of people."

I can hear her yawning. "You should get some sleep."

"No, we just started talking." She whines a little, making me chuckle.

"Yeah, but I woke you up early this morning. You missed out on some shut-eye, but I'm here for you. I would never lay a hand on you. I just want you to know that."

"I know you wouldn't, Myles."

We continued to talk for a while until we both physically couldn't stay awake any longer.

"I'll talk to you tomorrow. Get some sleep," I say through a yawn.

"Okay. Good night."

"Night." I hang up the phone, turn off my TV, and get ready for bed. I don't know how she does it. Even though we had some intense topics of conversation, we were able to end the phone call on a good note. I can feel that she will be coming home soon, and I can't wait.

22

HUNTER

"WOW! THAT ONE LOOKS AMAZING." The sales associate cups her cheeks as she looks at me.

I'm pretty sure she's only trying to make a sale and get me out of here. Believe me, I want to be gone. But I refuse to show up in a dress that isn't something I'm confident about. I've tried on a simple purple strapless that Jess said made me look like a crayon, an orange knee-high dress with some tulle around the skirt, which she said looked like a loofah. Then a red one that hugged all my curves. All she sent back was a picture of Myles. His eyes looked like they were bulging out of his head. I didn't realize she'd been sharing the photos with him. The red one I sent to tease Jess. I didn't want to buy it. It was too tight, and it had a deep plunging neckline. Of course, teasing her would bite me on the butt because she had shown Myles.

The dress I have on though, I actually like. It's a floor-length, dark olive green strapless dress with a high slit. My favorite part is the little peekaboo cutouts along the bodice. I love the way I look in it. Now that I know Jess is showing Myles, I adjust the dress to show my best angles. I want him to like the one I pick. I send her the picture and go to my clothes back on. I don't want to try on any more, so I hope Jess sends a thumbs-up. My phone rings.

"Well? Do you like it? I'm over trying these things on, Jess. Please don't make me try on any more." I let out a frustrated breath.

"Yessss! That's the one, Hunter." She pauses. "Myles absolutely loves it too, but he has a green monster on his back called Mr. Jealousy." She sings out, and I hear Myles in the background groaning at her and telling her to knock it off.

He's jealous? But why?

"Jess, what are you talking about? You're being ridiculous." She isn't even listening to me. She's too busy teasing Myles. I'm glad they're friends and hearing them bickering over the phone makes me smile. They've both told me that they've worked together more over this past week. Jess even said that JT has been talking with her a little more often. "Whatever. I'm going to check out. Have a good sale." I hang up the phone before she can say anything else. I want to get the day over with.

Pulling my black camisole over my head, I shimmy into my jean shorts. I grab Myles' green sweatshirt and bring it to my nose. I smell his woodsy scent, and it makes me miss him so much more. I pull it over my head, I have to push it up my arms for my hands to be free. It's almost down to my knees, but the comfort I feel wearing it and having his smell around me is unmatched.

Myles ends up texting me, saying I look beautiful in the dress, and a huge smile stretches across my face. I want to go home and jump into his arms, which only makes me think about his body and tattoos. He told me a little about them and showed me some over Facetime. He has large trees with mountains on one arm. On the other arm, he has a creek with trees and a few animals. I didn't ask, but I'm almost positive his inspiration was JT's place, based on what he has told me about it.

I really want to go riding with him when I get back. I told my dad I would leave to go home this weekend. He didn't say much. We actually haven't talked too much since he pressured me into going to the gala. I think he figured I wouldn't mind it as much as I used to. Well, he was wrong. There is not a single part of me that wants to go, and I definitely have no desire to see Steve again. I already know both of our mothers are on his side, so it's going to be hard to avoid him. Just thinking about being stuck at a table with him, my mom, and his parents makes my skin crawl.

I shake the thoughts away. I just have to get through the event, then I'll head home. I can do this. Suck it up for two more days, and I'll be home free. I'll miss my dad, but he's doing so well. He's walking more and more every day to get back into better health. I know he still has about two more weeks till he can work again, but he promised not to go back until he's healthy enough. He should retire, but I think he would have another heart attack if I suggested that.

I WALK to the front door Friday night, greeted by my parents. "Wow! Sweetie, you look great." My dad kisses my cheek.

"Thanks, Dad." My hair is styled in a loose updo with small pieces framing my face, but there are at least a thousand bobby pins woven into the curls. I went to the hair appointment my mom made, but I told the stylist she had to do what I wanted. The stylist was nervous, not wanting to upset my mom since she's such a loyal customer. In the end, she said she wanted to touch my wild hair and have fun with it. I was thankful for that.

The makeup artist was not as easy to convince. I had to keep a close eye on her and request a mirror to watch as she applied everything. She almost painted on bright red lips, but I quickly took a different color she had on her tray and applied it myself.

She glared at me for that, but I wanted nude lips that match my heels and clutch. I rarely wear jewelry, so I threw on simple hoop earrings. My mom's eyes zero in on my ears, like she wants to rip them out. Everything's as close to my style as I could get, but still fancy enough for the gala.

"I see Michelle and Abigail didn't give you what I asked for. What are those large silver things in your ears?" she asks.

I have a sinking feeling she's going to fire Michelle and Abigail, but I'm pretty sure they will eventually be grateful to me for that.

"You ready to get this over with, Mother?" I ask, ignoring her dig about my earrings. I turn when I hear a knock at the door, and my mother's face tips up into a smile. Not a warm smile, but one that makes you want to run and hide because it means she's up to no good.

"Hello, Elizabeth! It's so good to see you! Conrad, you look great," Steve says, stepping inside, kissing my mom on the cheek and shaking my dad's hand.

I watch as Steve plays the part in front of my family. My heart races and a ringing rumbles in my ears. I have to clasp my hands together, so I don't bolt from the room. I knew I would see him, but I didn't think he would show up at the house. Of course, my mom would pull a stunt like this. She looks at him with her shoulders back and a smile forming on the corners of her mouth. My dad levels a hard look at Steve and crosses his arms. I swear I hear a growl rumble from his throat.

"Hunny!" Steve says, his nickname for me, making my skin crawl. He tries to wrap me in a hug.

I finally snap out of my shock in time to back away from his grasp. I quickly walk around him, putting my dad's body between us. I turn and glare at my mother, who still hasn't lost her prideful look, then turn toward Steve. The look he gives me for denying him almost makes my knees buckle. But I take a deep breath and stare right into his hateful eyes.

"It's Hunter." I correct, and he feigns indifference. "Mother, what the hell?" I bite out. She looks at me with wide eyes. But her expression turns hard as her eyebrows pull together, and she glares at me.

"Watch yourself. This is my event, and I will invite anyone I please." She gives me a pointed look.

I want to scream. How the fuck did I get myself roped into this?

"Steve was sweet enough to accompany us to the gala. He came here to be your date."

I glare at her. *Like hell, he's my date.* I turn when there's another knock at the door.

"Let me guess, another ex-boyfriend?" I snap at her sarcastically, but her eyebrows raise as she looks to the door. She opens the door, and the breath gets knocked out of my chest. Myles stands in the doorway looking devastating in a tuxedo. His hat is nowhere to be found. I feel the irresistible urge to run my fingers through his perfectly tousled hair. He looks around, but when his eyes land on me, his body relaxes. His face breaks into the most handsome smile I have ever seen. Before anyone can say anything, I rush toward him and launch myself into his arms. He drops the bag I didn't even see he was carrying and holds me tight, nuzzling his face into my neck.

"Um. Excuse me? Who are you?"

I barely hear my mom trying to get our attention. I don't care. I want him to whisk me away. I can't believe he's here! He loosens his hold on me, which only makes me tighten my grip on him. His rumbling laughter vibrates through my body, igniting something deep inside me. I have never wanted someone as much as I want him right now.

"I'm not going anywhere, Hershey. You can let go," he whispers. I reluctantly unwind my clenched arms from around his neck, but tuck myself into his side as I face my mother.

"Mom and Dad, this is Myles Johnson. Myles, these are my

parents, Beth and Conrad." I point to each of them, smiling at my dad. Myles moves forward to shake their hands. Without hesitation, my dad shakes it, but my mom only stares at it as if she's repulsed by him, then sets her glare back on his face.

"Why are you here?" Her eyes look him over for a flaw that she won't find. "Hunter, did you invite this man to a closed event? I'm sorry you came all this way, but the event is full."

My heart sinks because I was so happy to have him here, and now she's not going to let him come. I look up at Myles, who doesn't look worried at all. He glances down at me and gives me a wink. I can't help but look at him in confusion.

"Well, you see, darling." My dad's voice makes us all look at him. "I called Mr. Johnson and told him our little girl would like him here as backup since I couldn't go. Seeing as how I can't use my ticket, I gave him mine." My dad gives me a wink. I drop my hands from Myles and give my dad a big hug.

"Thank you, Dad," I whisper and squeeze tight. I can't believe my dad did this for me. I was so upset with him, and this feels like his way of apologizing for not having my back. I have so many questions about how he even knows about Myles, but that isn't important right now.

"Anytime, baby girl," he whispers back.

"Well, that's a great idea and all, but Hunter is using your ticket." My mom purses her lips.

She doesn't want him to go, but if she won't let him go, then I won't go either.

"You and I both know you bought her a ticket as soon as she arrived. Now I'm tired, and this young man came all the way here. You guys are going to be late. So quit arguing and go have fun at your event." With his arm still around me, Dad levels her with a look, warning her he isn't backing down.

I let go after another squeeze and tuck back into Myles' side. My mom keeps opening and closing her mouth like a fish. My dad rarely puts his foot down with her, so she's not sure how to handle this.

"Um." Steve clears his throat. "Hunny, your mom was planning for you to ride with me in the limo. I'm sorry, your friend won't be able to join."

I forgot Steve was still here. My mom's face brightens by this turn of events. She's still hoping she can turn this around in her favor by forcing me to spend time with Steve.

"It's Hunter, Steven," my dad bites out, which only makes me want to hug him again. "Here, Myles." He pulls out a set of keys from his pocket and tosses them to Myles. "Drive my Mustang. It's in the garage. Hunter will show you." He gives me a smile. "Go have fun tonight. I would like to get to know this fella in the morning." He turns toward Myles.

"Thank you, sir," Myles says, keys in hand. "You ready?" Myles looks at me with those big blue eyes. I thread my hand in his and give him a big smile.

"Now that you're here, I'm definitely ready." Turning, I say over my shoulder, "See you there, Mom."

My fingers intertwined with his ground me as I lead us out the door to the garage. I'm completely shocked to see Myles. When he said he would come, I thought it was a crazy idea. But now that he's here, I realize I was hoping he would show up the whole time. Before I open the garage, Myles tugs me back and pulls me into his arms. Now that we aren't in front of my parents, his hand goes to the back of my neck and his other on my lower back pressing me into him. I couldn't be happier than I am in his arms. My whole body feels extra sensitive, finally having his hands on me again. He gently pulls away to look into my eyes.

"Is it okay I came? Your dad called, and I jumped at the chance to see you."

He looks a little nervous as he messes with the sleeves on his wrists before putting his hands in his pockets, and it makes me smile. I put my hands around his neck and pull him down to kiss him. He hesitates for a second, but gives in. His lips press into mine softly, but I wasn't searching for a small peck. I haven't been able to stop thinking about our kiss at the airport. My tongue slips against his lips, and he opens his mouth, his tongue playing with mine. I moan into his mouth, and his grip tightens. I don't ever want this to end. The way he's holding me, with his thumb tracing along the curves of my jaw, makes me feel like I'm all he wants in this world. I snake a hand into his hair, which elicits a moan in return. His erection against me only makes the heat between my legs grow. Reluctantly, we slow it down, as he sweetly brushes his lips across mine. Wanting to get just a few more kisses, Myles presses his lips to my forehead, each cheek, and my chin before placing one more lingering one on my mouth and stepping away. He couldn't be more perfect.

"I guess you don't mind that I came." He smiles, rubbing his nose against mine.

"I love that you're here," I admit. "Now, I would love to stand here and keep kissing you. But I haven't ridden in my dad's mustang in so long. Let's go!" I bat my eyelashes at him.

"Let's get out of here." He lets go for only a moment before pulling me back into his chest. He lowers his face down and brushes his lips against my ear, causing goosebumps to rise and making me shudder. "I haven't gotten the chance to say this yet, but you are the most beautiful thing I've ever seen." He delicately presses his lips right below my ear, making my heart flutter. He lets go of me, so I can open the garage on the keypad, keeping his hand on my lower back. My fingers hover over the keys, my brain fuzzy trying to remember the code as I focus on every place Myles touches me. The numbers come to me by some miracle, and I punch them in.

We drive to the gala, and I smile more during the thirty minute drive than the entire week I've been here. I still can't believe he's here! I glance at my phone, realizing Jess was in on the surprise, as she asks for pictures of us. I can see how happy Myles is, too. We pull up to the valet, and I swear Myles must have been to one of these events before. He's so at ease and casual while he walks around to escort me inside. I don't know how he got a tux at the last minute, especially since this one looks tailored to his body. He doesn't seem to be bothered by the tie either. I know even my dad, who goes to these events a lot, complains about the ties. Myles doesn't fidget with anything, and it puts me more at ease. I didn't want to come to this event, but having him by my side is the absolute best thing that could have happened. We walk toward the gala, only to be bombarded by photographers trying to take our photo. We pose for a few, but Myles's eyes never waiver from me, even when each photographer tries to get his attention.

I'm not sure what kind of charity or organization this gala is for, but they didn't spare any expense. The entire clubhouse is decorated to perfection with silk white streamers, swooping across the ceiling and down the walls. The focal point is the massive crystal chandelier in the middle. The main event is in the ballroom. Exquisitely decorated dinner tables fill the room, adorned with silk white tablecloths, crystal glasses, and fine china. Each table dons a massive bouquet of white roses and greenery. An open bar is off to the side, while servers walk around with trays of food and drinks. A large dance floor is in front of a stage where the band plays.

These events have always made me anxious. But being next to Myles with his hand on my lower back, I feel like I might actually enjoy myself. He leans toward me, and my whole body ignites in anticipation. His lips tenderly press below my ear. It's now my favorite spot for him to kiss. I melt into him, forgetting we are in a room with over a hundred people.

"Incoming," he whispers. My eyes flash open and look around.

I find my mother walking toward me with a scowl on her face, and Steve and his parents close behind. *Oh, for the love of god.*

"Darling, I hardly think you are being appropriate at a charity gala."

Steve sneers at Myles, which makes me grip Myles' arm as if I dare not let go. He laces his fingers with mine and squeezes, and I slightly relax.

"Hunter, your seat is over at table four, but Mitch, *you* are at table twelve."

She looks at us, convinced her little scheme will keep us apart. I can't believe she is still bent on separating us. I know she's going to push to get what she wants. I am her daughter, after all, and I guess that's where I get my stubborn trait from.

"Come, Hunny, I'll walk you to our table," Steve pipes in, thinking I won't dare question my mother again.

He's always tried to control and ridicule me when I wanted to do something he didn't. He made me feel less than. All the horrible memories of losing myself slowly when I was with him come flashing back to the forefront of my mind. I look up at Myles, and he gives me the slightest nod, letting me know he will support me no matter what I decide to do.

"Oh. Well, if there's no room at our table, I guess I'll sit in *Myles'* lap." I glare at my mother for choosing to say the wrong name. I look up at the handsome man holding my hand, and he kisses my cheek. I hate that this is how he's meeting my mother, and I'm ashamed that she's treating him this way.

"Sounds good to me. I have no plans to let you out of my sight," Myles says, loud enough for everyone to hear as he gazes sweetly down at me.

"Hunter!" Steve's mother calls over to me. "This is hardly the place to pitch a fit. Now you had your little break in Florida. Stevie has been miserable without you. It's sad you've been breaking his heart this way." She rubs her son's back like he's a toddler that needs consoling.

I roll my eyes.

"Oh, please. Steve, how long did it take for you to jump into bed with Brenda?" I question him. "Less than twelve hours? Do your parents know I ended things with you for getting too drunk and putting your hands on me? Now, if you'll all excuse us." I turn toward Myles, dismissing everyone else. "Would you like to dance with me?"

Myles' smile lights up his face. "After you." He motions toward the dance floor but turns to the others. "If you will excuse me, my girlfriend and I have a slow dance calling our name."

He gives them all a big smile, and now I feel like I've stopped breathing altogether. *Did he say girlfriend?* Myles presses his palm against my lower back, and escorts me to the dance floor. He surprises me by grabbing my hand to twirl me out and back to him, making me laugh. I softly land back into his arms, and he tucks me into his chest. He slides his hand down my lower back, skimming my ass as he rests it where I can feel his long fingers grip my hip. Some may think it inappropriate for an event as fancy as this, but I have no complaints. I lay my head on his firm chest, letting a sigh escape when he rests his cheek on top of it. Myles holds me close and the room, along with everyone in it, melts away. Nothing else matters right now. It's just him and me swaying to "Just the Way You Are" by Bruno Mars and for the first time in a long time, I feel completely safe.

We're so lost in each other that we only realize three songs have gone by when the announcement for dinner is made and we have to take our seats. I reluctantly pull myself out of his arms. But Myles tenderly grabs my chin, tipping it up so he can press the softest, most perfect kiss against my lips. He leans back, grins and gives me another quick peck. Leading me off the dance floor, he keeps his hand on the small of my back. The added strength is appreciated when I see my mother storming toward us.

"Okay. I was able to seat him at our table. Now would you come sit down before you make a scene and embarrass me further?" She hisses, but plasters on a fake smile for anyone watching to save face. My cheeks heat in embarrassment. I don't want Myles to see this side of her, but unfortunately, she doesn't have many other sides. When he begins rubbing slow circles on my back, the tension in my shoulders lessens, helping me take a deep breath and follow her.

Dinner goes by as smoothly as it can. My mother attempts to seat me by Steve. But Myles is two steps ahead, pulling his seat out for me and placing himself in the chair between Steve and me. He spends the entire dinner with one hand on my thigh, his fingers dragging lightly across my leg where it's exposed by the slit in my dress. At first, he rubs little circles, but then his hand slowly roams higher and higher. With every inch, my body tingles. Steadying my breath, I try to focus on the conversation at our table and not the rough, muscular hand inching its way up my leg. His fingers leave a path of fire behind them as they stroke and tease their way closer to the warmth gathering between my thighs. The ache he's creating has my hips begging to buck forward to help him reach the target. Glancing over at Myles I expect to see him giving me a mischievous grin, but the man is talking stocks with the couple across the table. Or is it horses? Fuck, I can't think straight. When his pinky grazes over my lace thong an unexpected squeak falls from my mouth. The table goes quiet as everyone looks my way. I cover my mouth and try replicating the squeak, before forcing a smile and saying, "Hiccups."

My mother arches her brow before turning back to the lady next to her. I relax and Myles takes advantage of my lapse of awareness, pressing his pinky against my center.

"Oh god!" I squeal, leaping from my chair.

"Hunter, what is wrong with you?" my mother demands.

"Sorry. I suddenly have to use the little girl's room."

My mother rolls her eyes. "Thank you for announcing it to the entire room." The bite in her voice tells me I'm going to hear about this later.

I ignore her and grab the jacket collar of Myles' tux while I lean over to whisper into his ear. "Meet me in the hall in two minutes." He smirks, and I rush away from the table. The hall is almost empty. Since I spent so much time at the club when I was younger, I know exactly where I want to go. I wait for Myles and as soon as he comes through the door looking for me. I grab his hand and almost start running to a side door.

"In a hurry?" he asks with a laugh.

Once he's through it, I spin around and jump into his arms. He catches me and looks around.

"Are we having a rematch?" He laughs, his eyes landing on the pool table.

"Shut up, and lock the door, Myles," I say, my voice coming out breathy.

His eyes darken like he'd never imagined this would happen, but he has never been more ready.

Something stirred in me after he called me his girlfriend. A pleasant little fire ignited between my thighs, his tight embrace fueling the heat as we danced. But when Myles' fingers climbed their way up my leg and sensually touched me beneath a table full of snooty, aristocratic elites, it felt as if he was dousing the flame he'd already stoked with gasoline, and I'm ready to combust. I want him *now*. He seems more than happy to oblige.

23

MYLES

THIS WOMAN never ceases to amaze me as she leads us into a small billiard room with bookshelves all over the walls. There are no windows in here and only one door. She's stunning, and it's been hard to keep myself off of her. When she jumped up from the table, my heart sank, thinking she wasn't happy with how forward I was. I thought she was about to rip my head off, but when she leaped into my arms and told me to lock the door, I realized I was mistaken. Hunter's eyes blaze, burning every doubt I have and make me damn near come in my pants.

I slowly put her down, and she steps away from me. I quickly lock the door and work on taking off my bowtie. I hate suits, and tuxedos are far worse. Thankfully, I had one from a black tie event last year. I would wear anything for this woman, even something that feels like it's trying to slowly choke me. I stalk toward her, backing her up against the pool table. I'm right in front of her, with nowhere for her to go. This green dress has driven me mad all night. I've tried to hide the bulge in my pants, but it's nearly impossible around this gorgeous woman.

Reaching around, I bend and grab her thighs, lifting her until she's sitting on the edge of the pool table, then I step between her legs, pressing myself against her center. She moans and winds her legs tightly around my waist. Rubbing my fingers over her lace thong was torture enough. I could feel her getting wet, and it caused my brain to short circuit. I have no idea what the fuck anyone at the table was talking about. My eyes were on the people in front of me, but my focus was only on her. I loved the way her breath caught when I first touched her. My heart was pounding so hard in my chest I felt the pressure in my ears. I run my hands up the sides of her legs and she jumps, her eyes wide as they bounce between mine.

"Talk to me. We don't have to do anything you don't want to do." My thumb caresses her cheek. If she says stop, I won't think twice. I'd help her off of this table, straighten her dress and walk her back out with a smile on my face. Not that I haven't dreamed of worshiping her body all night, but I want it to be right. I want her to be ready.

"I just..." she stops, capturing her lip between her teeth and gazes around the room as if she's scared to look at me.

I lightly place my hand on the side of her neck, my thumb brushing against her jaw. Then tilting her head, I smile. "Talk to me," I say, then place a soft kiss on the tip of her nose, hoping to ease her anxiety so she knows it's safe to express how she feels.

"Well, I've never actually enjoyed"—she licks her lips—"you know," she finishes sheepishly.

"Um." I scratch the back of my neck. My mind reels trying to understand what she means by that. "You've never liked what? You didn't like it when I pressed my fingers against your clit under the table?" Hunter's eyes go wide. Her neck flushes, the color traveling up her cheeks as she tries to look away. But I hold her chin in place as I continue to stroke her jaw with my thumb. I haven't moved the hand resting on her thigh because her leg is still wrapped around my waist. I know she can feel how hard I am. I'm trying not to move. The slightest friction makes my dick twitch, and it's pressed so close to her center, I can feel the heat radiating from her. I know she wants me, but something's holding her back.

God, feeling her heated core under the table had my head spinning. Hunter is the most stunning woman I have ever been with. Her body makes me want to go to my knees before her. She doesn't even realize the hold she has on me. I wasn't sure if I was being brave or just flat out stupid earlier, but my hand had a mind of its own. I never want to stop touching her, but I would if she told me to.

"No, I liked that." Her cheeks turn brighter, and I have to hold back a smile. "What I'm trying to say is that I've never cared for sex. It was always something I had to do. I didn't like it." Her fingers play with the buttons on my shirt. "I actually have never liked being touched or kissed at all until I met you. Everyone I know enjoys sex, they crave it." A sad smile plays at the corner of her lips. "I've always thought that maybe something inside me was broken." Hunter takes a deep breath. "I just—I wanted you to know in case I can't...because I've never—"

"Are you trying to tell me you've never had an orgasm? Ever?" I ask, reigning in my shock as I try to wrap my mind around it. How is this possible? Even if she always had a selfish partner, there are things that she could do on her own. But damn me, if my mind doesn't immediately want to use one of those *toys* on her myself.

She chews on her bottom lip, glancing down at her hands now in her lap. "No, I don't even know if I can"—the deep breath she takes causes her cleavage to swell over the top of her dress making my mouth water—"I've never come close."

"Well, then I must be one lucky son of a bitch." Her beautiful green eyes jump, meeting mine as her mouth parts. "I can't wait to show you exactly what you've been missing." Tucking a curl behind her ear, my lips brush against hers. Winding an arm around her body, I pull her tight against me and kiss her harder. She melts into me, opening her mouth, and allowing her tongue to stroke against my lips and that's all I need. I deepen our kiss, losing myself when her fingers find their way into my hair. I don't care how far we go while we're here. But one thing is for damn sure, she's going to feel amazing by the time I'm done with her. I'm not leaving this room until she has her first orgasm. My heart picks up speed at the thought. Letting my hands fall down, I grip her ass as I pull her against my erection. Her breath catches as a soft moan tumbles from her swollen lips. Fuck her sounds are going to be the end for me.

I grip her ass as I teasingly rock into her. The whimper she makes kicks my libido into high gear, and I grip her chin firmly before crashing my lips into hers. I move my hand, grabbing the back of her neck, while my other grips under her bare thigh. I want her. I think all the time we were separated has made me want her even more, and I have to fight the urge to strip her bare and fuck her till she's screaming my name.

Hunter's fingers fumble with the button on my shirt like she can't wait another minute to have my clothes on the floor. All I can think about is her lying down for me naked on this table. But I'll give her anything she wants. She fumbles with the first buttons, so I help her with the rest. Once my shirt is off, I watch as she scans me, her nails gently scraping over my bare chest and down the center of my stomach, setting the path they make on fire. When she changes direction, bringing them up to circle my pecs, and lightly caressing my nipple, I feel an intense wave shoot to my groin.

"Mmm," I growl as I reach around and unzip her gown. Hunter lifts her hips as I push the silky material over her curves and down her legs, then toss it over my shoulder. *Fucking hell.* She's not wearing a bra, and my whole body freezes as I take her in. I didn't expect that. I bite my lip to keep the moan building inside my throat from escaping. Her hourglass curves are perfect. I try not to rush the experience of seeing her body for the first time, because it's a work of art. My gaze glides over her smooth sloping hips, down to her lace thong that enhances her entire body, making it hard to concentrate. My eyes make the journey up her body, admiring her perky round breasts and the way they dip into the valley of her flat stomach. I nip at her neck and at the delicate spot below her ear, then slide my tongue down the length of her throat before gently scraping my teeth across her collarbone. As her moans deepen, my erection stiffens knowing how affected she is by my touch.

Reaching for her perfect breasts, I palm them between my hands before covering one with my mouth and sucking. I tease the nipple of the other between my fingers, rolling and pinching until her head falls back and she tumbles backward onto the table. She leans back on her forearms as another moan spills from her lips and her hips grind against mine.

Seeing the way she reacts to nipple stimulation fuels the fire already racing through my veins. I want to hear her scream my name. Dipping my head back to hard nipple, I lay my tongue flat against it and slowly drag up over the pebbled point before capturing it between my teeth and gently tugging. Hunter jerks forward, and I quickly slide my hand between us, splaying it against her stomach and holding her there.

Another whimper rumbles in the back of her throat as she winds her legs tighter around me and grinds against me trying to find her release. I pinch her nipple and scrape the other a little harder between my teeth as I thrust against her center wanting her to feel how hard she makes me.

"Oh, Myles," she wimpers. "Fuck."

Her encouragement and breathy voice makes my cock throb harder. I continue rotating which nipple gets attention and then lick and kiss my way between them, down her stomach. Peeking up at her face, her hooded eyes are fixed on me, pleading. I make it to her hips and give little nips, and she jolts again making me press her down once more. She lies completely flat, her chest rising and falling as she tries to watch me. I kiss right at the edge of her black lace thong and keep moving down. I inhale, sticking my nose right between her soft legs, and she moans loudly. She makes the most perfect sounds; I could come listening to her alone. I look up at her and place my fingers on the thin lace strip on her hips, silently asking if I can take it off. She gives a few small nods like she's begging me to.

Unable to hide my smile, I slowly slide her thong down her legs, and she unwraps herself from around me, just long enough for me to get it off. I grab her ankles before she can wrap them around me again, placing her feet on the edge of the pool table. Keeping my eyes pinned on hers, I lower myself to my knees, and I swear her eyes turn to flames. Blowing a little air onto her, I watch as she throws her head back, sucking in a breath. I lean closer and take a long and slow lick up her center, giving a little pressure at the top. She grabs my hair, tugging as her breathing grows heavier. She tastes like heaven, and I'd do this all night if she let me. Seeing her unravel for me, it's the sexiest thing to watch.

"You like that?"

"Yes." She gasps. "More." Her voice comes out a mere whisper.

I laugh. My greedy little thing. I spear my tongue right into her, and she almost rolls away from me. I play with one of her nipples and keep licking her, sucking on the part where her nerves peek. She's moving against my mouth, and I suck harder, making her gasp. Easing a finger into her, I pump into her slick core. She gasps louder, as she arches her back like a bow. Her body is taut with anticipation. I continue sucking, and add a second finger. Her center is slick with her arousal. Her body is practically begging for more as her breathing goes erratic. She whispers a few more curses in between soft moans. I feel her walls start tightening around my fingers. Body freezing, she holds her breath. Fuck, I'm so turned on right now. She gasps as her body spasms, and she rides out her orgasm. Once she is completely limp, I give one last long lick up her center. I look at her right in the eyes as I slowly pull my fingers out of her. Bringing them to my mouth, she watches as I suck them clean. She lets out a small gasp. Her green eyes bore into me, and I can't pull my focus away from the rising and falling of her full breasts. It's the most beautiful thing to watch.

"That was the sexiest thing I have ever experienced, Hershey." Her soft smile eases any worry I had while she sits up and wraps her arms around my neck. Her nails lightly scratch parts of my back, making my whole body ignite in goosebumps. Pressing my lips against hers, I kiss her hard. I'm falling for this girl. She takes my breath away.

Pulling back, she bites her lip and asks, "Can we do that again?"

I love that she knows what she likes and isn't afraid to ask for it. "We can do that anytime you want." Grabbing her ass, I nip at her bottom lip. She pulls back letting her hands graze over my chest to my stomach. She traces my abs with her fingers. Her eyes peruse my bare chest, taking in every inch.

I wait for her to make the next move, intrigued by the curiosity she's showing. It blows my mind that Hunter has never experienced this kind of pleasure. How could any man be so selfish?

She looks up at me as she takes my belt and unbuttons my pants. They hit the floor, and I kick them aside along with my shoes. Her eyes widen, now that I'm just in my briefs. Another moment goes by without her making any moves, so I help her out. "Would you like me to take these off now?" I motion toward my underwear, and she bites her lower lip and nods. Smirking, I lean toward her and kiss her neck as I pull them off.

Without hesitating, Hunter reaches for me and her soft touch makes my eyes roll back in my head. She drags her hand up and down my shaft, and I have to stop myself from exploding right here and now. I lean my forehead against hers and feel like the world around us is spinning. Her thumb gives a little pressure underneath as she trails it right over the tip where I already have precum. I have no restraint because this woman could make me cum with a few pumps of her hand. A deep moan drags out of me, as I try to stay in control the best I can.

Gripping her face with my hands, my mouth meets hers, and I almost lose myself again. I snake my fingers into her hair, making a few pins come loose.

"Condom"—she breathes out. "Please tell me you have a condom." Her wide eyes search mine.

I look at her and kiss her again before heading for my jacket and getting one out of my wallet. She plucks it from my hands and rips it open with her teeth. She gently rolls it onto me and my eyes lift to the ceiling, and I bite my lip. She grabs onto my shoulders and pulls me closer, digging her nails into my back. I swear she's marking me, and I don't give one fuck. I look into her eyes and she's practically begging me for more. I reach between us to line my cock up at her entrance. I kiss her again and slowly push into her. She's still soaking wet and so tight. I moan with the feeling of pure ecstasy. Nothing has ever felt more right in my life.

She grabs onto my neck to bring us closer and wraps her legs tighter around me. It gives me the best angle to go in deeper. I bottom out inside of her, seeing stars at the edge of my vision. She lets out a loud moan right as I get as deep as I can, pausing as she adjusts to me. I start to move, and she pants right in my ear. Wanting her to come again, I reach down and rub her clit. She loses herself, biting her fist to keep quiet. I don't know how long I can last for her, but I'm going to try to hold on for as long as possible. I keep pumping into her, and she releases her grip to put her hands on the table behind her, giving me the perfect opportunity to start kissing and sucking her nipples. It only makes her moan more. I'm not sure if my thumb on her clit or my tongue on her nipples finally pushes her over the edge. She tightens around me and lets out one final moan, and I can't help but follow her over the edge with my own release. As soon as I finish, I have to prevent my legs from giving out. I lay her down on the table, while I lay on top of her. I'm careful to keep my weight on my forearms so I don't crush her.

We're both breathing hard. I swear that was the best sex of my life. Even after hearing her talk about how much she had never liked sex before, I didn't question that she'd love it as much as I would. What the hell were men in the past doing that they couldn't make it happen?

"You okay, Hershey?" When she doesn't say anything and continues breathing hard, I look at her. Her spasms have finally subsided along with mine. She looks perfect, lying there with her eyes closed. Eventually, she opens her beautiful eyes to look at me. Her lips form the most perfect small smile while her cheeks turn a little red.

"Yeah. I'm perfect," she whispers.

My shoulders sag with relief, and a smile takes over my face. She smiles, but it turns into a frown, making my heart nearly stop.

"We should probably get back out there or even head out."

I nod my head realizing where her mind is going. We've already been gone a while, and it won't be long before someone comes looking for us.

"Yeah. I guess we can't stay locked away in here all night, can we?" I laugh which makes her smile again. I lift myself off of her and walk over to the trash to throw away the condom. I turn around and she is still sitting there naked as can be, staring at me. I walk toward her and lean in. "Like what you see?" I place a kiss just below her ear, and she smiles, biting her lower lip, and nods. I look at her perfect body sitting there on full display just for me. I lift her off the table, and she glides gloriously down my body, and damn, if my dick doesn't start to get hard again. She smiles like she knows what just happened.

We both get dressed, and I help her with her zipper, then she helps me with my bowtie. I don't want to leave this room. I know her mother's most likely searching everywhere for her. I hope we can get out of here without being seen. I doubt it, though. Her mother seems to have the worst *perfect* timing. We both give each other a once-over to make sure nothing is out of place, and we head out the door together, holding hands.

24

HUNTER

"HUNTER! There you are! Honestly, where have you been? People have been asking to see you. I didn't think you would embarrass me this much," my mother spits out.

I was hoping we could run to the car and get away. But of course, my mother was right there waiting, like she knew we were in that room.

"Oh, Myles, you won't know these people. Why don't you go get yourself a drink so you aren't bored," she says, dismissing him.

Of course, she's still trying to separate us. He opens his mouth to say something, but I cut him off.

"I actually think I'll go with Myles to get a drink. Please tell whoever it is, hello, for me." I turn my back on her, and Myles looks at me with those amazing blue eyes, trying to hide a smile. He tucks me against his side and kisses me on the cheek. We walk away before my mother can say anything else.

"Any drink in particular?" he asks.

"Rum and coke, please." I look up at him, so grateful he is here.

"Got it. Need to rehydrate you after all that *exercise*," he whispers the last part so only I can hear, and my body ignites in flames.

I have never felt anything like what we did together in that room, and on a pool table, no less. I still can't believe it! I've always felt like I was broken. Steve made me feel like I was too much work because I took too long. It made me feel like I wasn't worth it. He didn't care if I enjoyed it. He only wanted his release. Then I stopped even trying to get my own afterward because I felt frustrated and not cared for. Myles made me feel everything. Never would I have expected to have one orgasm, and he gave me two mind-blowing ones! I look over at him, leaning across the bar, grabbing our drinks. I have never felt more happy than I do when I'm with him.

"Come dance with me," I hear a voice say, shattering my happiness.

"Steve, go away." I groan. I don't want him to talk to me, let alone touch me. He grabs me around my elbow and starts pulling me toward the dance floor.

"Don't be like that. We had something good once. I don't know what you're doing slumming it with this new guy, but you at least owe me a dance for walking out on me."

He is such an entitled prick. I stop and look at him, refusing to move any further. I won't do something I don't want to do, and I do not want his hands on me.

"I said no. Now leave me alone."

"Why are you such a spoiled brat? We were perfect, and our parents want us together. Why can't you be quiet and give everyone what they want?" he's almost shouting, causing several heads to whip our way.

My mother is one of them, and she has a weird look on her face. I wish she would come and stand up for me, but she has never believed me when I told her what he's really like. I look around at all the people whispering to each other. I look toward Myles, but he's too busy ordering drinks to notice. I don't want to make a scene, so I take a breath.

"I don't want to be with you, and just because you want it doesn't mean it has to happen. Now you're making a scene, and you know how our parents feel about making scenes at events." He shoots back the drink he has in his hand which has to be his usual double shot of Scotch. He wobbles a little and sets his glare on me.

He looks me up and down then toward Myles, his eyes blaze. "Fucking slut!" he shouts, attracting even more attention.

I flinch. It's never a good thing when he shouts. The last time he did—I shake my head at the thought. I left the state for a reason, *him*. I refuse to let him hit me again. I try to back up, but I fall into warm, comforting hands. I breathe in, able to recognize that smell anywhere.

"Steve, I think you should take a walk," Myles' deep voice says from behind me. His hands remain on my waist, giving me a little squeeze.

"Yeah. Yeah, I don't know why Conrad brought you here. He clearly has something wrong with him to make him think it was a good idea to send for you," Steve spits out to Myles.

I grab hold of Myles' hands to keep them in place. I don't want him to leave or go toward Steve when he's like this. Myles only squeezes me like he's saying he's not moving anywhere. My eyes land on my mom, who excuses herself from the women she was with to storm over here. It's a combination of shame and relief that courses through me at the sight of her.

"That. Is. Enough. Steven," my mother says firmly. "I am ashamed of you. Robert and Cheryl, take your son home. He's not welcome back here." She motions toward his parents watching from a nearby table, apparently dismissing the whole exchange.

I can't help but look at her in shock. She's always loved Steve.

I hope she finally sees the man he actually is, even though this was tame for him. He wasn't even that drunk yet. Steve's parents pull him out of the room. He continues shouting obscenities at me and Myles. A tear escapes down my cheek, and I wipe it away, not realizing I'd started crying. I never wanted to embarrass my mom or make a scene at her charity gala. I hate that this happened because of me. Small warm hands touch my shoulders as Myles slowly steps back but holds my hand instead, and I look up to find my mom is standing right in front of me. Her hands squeeze, and she gives me a small nod. She's never shown affection toward me or any type of concern. I had figured she would walk away and try to salvage the night, but here she is right in front of me. Myles squeezes my hand as if to tell me this is real.

"Alright, now I have an event to get back on track. You two enjoy your evening, but I don't blame you if you want to go home. It's completely your choice," she says.

She never gave me a choice growing up. I always had to stay till the very end. I know this is her way of saying she supports me, and relief floods through me, making my shoulders relax. I watch as she walks toward the stage. Myles brings his arm around me, pressing me into him. His free hand holds the side of my face as he looks deeply into my eyes with concern.

"Are you okay?"

I nod, closing my eyes and taking a deep breath. It feels like the first freeing breath that I've had in a long time.

"It's okay if you aren't, you know?" His thumb traces my jawline.

Any pressure I was feeling in my chest vanishes, and I smile at him. "Yeah. I am."

"Okay. Well, what would you like to do?" He takes hold of my hand and twirls me.

I smile, loving that I have a choice. "Let's go home and spend a little bit of time with my dad before we leave tomorrow." He arches a brow, and I add, "I'd already planned to go home tomorrow. Are you wanting to stay?" I laugh.

"Uh no." Myles kisses me. "Let's get out of here."

MY EYES FLUTTER OPEN, and I stretch my stiff muscles. Large tattooed arms surround me, making it difficult to move. Myles' deep, steady breath caress my cheek, and all I want to do is snuggle in deeper. His chest is on full display, and I can't help but try to memorize every detail. My eyes trail down his body, from the small scar on his shoulder all the way to the hair below his belly button leading to what I already know is an impressive dick.

After the gala, we came back to be with my dad. Myles and my dad hit it off, as I already knew they would. They talked for hours about work, cars, and animals. It's been amazing to see them become close in such a short amount of time.

At first, my dad was not happy with my mom and how she had Steve come to the house and what she tried to pull at the gala. He was relieved to hear how she had Steve leave. There's still so much hurt from growing up with her, but I think we're on the path to creating a better relationship.

I'm still in shock my dad got Myles to come. Apparently, my sneaky roommate had a lot to do with it. My dad called to have Jess come here to go to the event with me, but she explained that she had a better idea. He wasn't surprised to hear I had someone like Myles in my life and was eager to meet him. I texted Jess a lot about everything that went on at the gala and sent her multiple candid pictures.

Myles and I stayed up so late with my dad that we immediately fell asleep once we got into bed. He snuggled me close to him. In his arms, I feel like everything is right in the world.

Unfortunately, we need to get up because we do have a flight to catch. My dad was able to get Myles and me on the same flight. He dismissed Myles' offer to pay for his return flight. He said it was the least he could do. I lean over to look at the time on my phone, and it's nine in the morning. Our flight is at one. I know we have time, but I'd like my mom and Myles to at least have a few moments to talk and get to know each other a little more before we hop on a plane. I also need to make sure Dad is ready to be here without me.

Myles groans as I scoot away from him. Blindly reaching out, he drags me back against him and nestles in again. I giggle as his stubble tickles my neck. He trimmed it for the event, but I'm glad he didn't remove it completely. I love how good he looks with some scruff on his face.

"Hey. We need to get up." I try to break away again, but his grasp only tightens. He moans again.

"No. I want to stay like this all day." His voice is laced with sleep. Myles hooks his arm around my waist, dragging me across the bed until my back meets his chest. I can feel the warmth of his skin against mine where my tank top rides up behind me, sending a wave of desire through me. I push my butt against him, wiggling my hips to get his attention. I feel him harden against my ass, and he groans deeply into my ear.

"Myles," I say a little more breathy than I mean to. "We should get up." He wiggles a little closer and kisses my neck. It feels so good, my eyes flutter shut. He nips along my shoulder, and now it's really starting to get hot in here. "Um," I gasp. "I don't..." My mind goes blank as he continues to nibble and lick until a moan pours from my mouth. Rolling me onto my back, Myles straddles me and stares down at me with his sparkling blue eyes and gorgeous smile. His thick thighs are covered with low-riding sweats, but his chest is bare, and I can't help but stare.

"You were saying?" he asks with a little smirk.

Instead of answering him, I reach and grip his waist, pulling him down until our lips crash together. Bearing his weight on his forearms, Myles trails his fingers down my body. I'm wearing a thin tank top and loose shorts, so he has easy access to reach under and cup my ass. He groans. My left hand scratches up and down his back, and the other tangles in his soft hair. My legs wrap around his hips and I move against his length. I feel an ache growing in my core, and I need him inside me. I tug on his sweatpants with my feet, and he stops kissing me to laugh.

"What are you doing?"

"I want these off," I state firmly, and his eyes darken.

"Yes, ma'am," he whispers against my lips.

Shifting off the bed, he pulls his sweats and boxers off in one swoop. I gasp as I look right at his cock. It's even bigger than I remember, and man, he's so ready. I trail my eyes up his body to meet his face.

"Please, fuck me," I beg him. He lowers himself over top of me again and brushes a few loose hairs out of my face. Softly, he kisses my lips, and I can honestly say I've never felt more treasured than when I'm with him.

"You don't even have to ask, Hershey. I'll do whatever you want," he says, softly.

His words make me melt as he scoots down and pulls my tank top above my breasts. His eyes meet mine, and I see that devilish look there. He lightly nips my nipple, eliciting a gasp. He looks up, and I see he wants this just as much as I do. Bringing his hand up, he rubs his finger over my lips, gently asking them to part. As I open my mouth, he puts his finger into my mouth and sucks on my nipple. I suck on his finger at the same time and release it with a pop when he pulls it out of my mouth. I watch as he rubs his finger around my other nipple to get it wet and starts twisting and pulling it. Who knew someone playing with my nipples could make my whole body feel like it's on fire? I rub against him, needing relief. He crawls back up to kiss me again, this time angling my head so he can kiss me deeply. I can't help but get lost in him. He kisses me so passionately that I start to feel dizzy. He breaks the kiss to sit up on his knees. His fingers trail up my sides as they bring my tank top all the way off, and when they skim back down my body, leaving a trail of goose bumps in their wake.

Once he reaches my sleep shorts, he hooks his fingers under them and my lace underwear. I lift my body so he can take them off. He doesn't seem to be in a rush as he slides them down my legs. Gripping one of my ankles, he kisses up my leg. He only stops and puts it down once he gets to my knee. I practically whine. He rakes his eyes over me and lets out a long exhale, and I track his ab muscles contracting.

"You're perfect," he whispers, and my eyes fly to his.

I squirm under his stare and direct words. I've never laid naked under a man while he looks at my whole body. The honesty in his words are almost too much for me to handle. He grips my body and lowers down again, crashing his lips into mine. I feel him bare right at my entrance. I want more. I want him inside me now. I start to move and can feel him right at the peak where all my nerves are the strongest. He growls into my mouth.

"I'll come right now unless you stop."

I pause but look him right in the eyes.

"Then get a condom, and fuck me, Myles."

He smiles and kisses me again. I put my hand around his throat and lightly squeeze, letting him know how serious I am. He takes the hint and his laugh rumbles through my body. Leaning over the bed, he grabs a condom from the side zipper of his overnight bag. I take it from him and rip open the foil with my mouth. He stares at me as I roll it down his long length, and he lifts his head and sucks in a breath. I give him a little push to the side, and he takes my cue to move over. I guide him to sit with his back against the headboard. He places his hands on my waist to have me straddle him. I lower myself as slowly as I can, inch by glorious inch. His body tightens, and he lets out a groan along with me. *Fuck! How did I not like this before?* He lets me take control of our rhythm. I move slowly at first going as deep as I can, to barely just the tip inside me. His eyes roll back with the feeling.

"You're a fucking temptress," he says through another moan.

He keeps his hands firmly on my waist and squeezes. It wouldn't surprise me if it left a mark. It all feels so good. As I pick up the pace, I look him right in the eye. I want him to watch me come while he's inside me. I place my hand on his shoulder to help me balance and then reach down with my other hand to massage my clit. With how little I've enjoyed sex, I've never even considered playing with myself, but something compels me to try. His eyes go wild watching me.

"Fuck. You are the sexiest thing I've ever seen."

I rock my hips faster, and I feel myself getting closer. It feels too good, the sensation is almost too much to handle, like I'm flirting right with the edge. He puts one hand on my ass and squeezes, bringing us a little closer together. It pushes me right over into my release. I throw my head back, and I let out a final moan as my body spasms. He continues moving us through the aftershocks, and he lets his release come right after mine. I collapse into his chest, and we lay still for a few moments.

"God, where have you been hiding all my life?" he asks into my hair. It feels like we're truly made for each other. He kisses my temple. "Didn't you say we have to get ready to go?" He laughs. I look up at him giving him a glare.

"Oh, now you heard me?"

"Always the smart mouth with you." He grabs my chin and lays a gentle kiss right on my lips. He pulls away but looks right at my lips. "I love it." Then kisses me again.

"Okay. Now we really have to get going. I'm sure my parents are wondering why we slept in so long."

His body turns to stone and his eyes go wide. "Fuck, Hunter. I forgot they were here. You don't think they heard us do you?" He looks like his face is turning white. I laugh. It's too late to worry about that now.

"No idea. But if they did, we'll find out soon." I crawl off his lap and turn to find my clothes. He leans over right as I get up and spanks me hard. I gasp as I turn around with my mouth agape, but now I'm getting turned on again. *Two can play this game.* I lean over and get right in his face. "Hey," I whisper, making him look at me quizzically. "Save that for later." I wink at him and bite my lower lip. I stand up so he can see my naked body on full display. He growls and lunges at me. I try to run away, but he already has his arms wrapped around me as we fall back into the bed. He's lying on top of me, not holding any of his weight. He kisses me hard, and our tongues tangle in the best possible way. I bite his lower lip. I can feel his primal energy, and I can't help but want him deep inside me again. He breaks our kiss, and I whimper.

"Okay. Let's get going, or I'll never let you leave this bed again." He kisses me one last time before jumping off the bed.

I roll onto my stomach and watch as he disposes of the condom. Leaning down, he grabs his clothes off the floor. My eyes trail over his strong body from his broad shoulders down to his tight ass. He catches me looking at him, and he walks towards me with a smirk on his face. Gripping my chin, he presses his lips to mine before walking into the connected bathroom. Rolling onto my back, I pull a pillow into my chest and sigh as I lie here for a moment. How did this become my life?

Thankfully, my parents don't imply anything about hearing what was happening in our room. Dad's nurse comes by, so I can make sure he's all set before I leave. But I give the nurse my number in case she needs anything. She shook her head and assured me that he is doing great. During breakfast, I feel like my mom actually attempted to get to know Myles a little. Also, she gave him a real smile, not a clubhouse smile, but a genuine one. I wasn't sure she remembered how to smile like that. I'm relieved that she is showing signs of wanting a better relationship with me, but I know it's going to take a lot of time to heal a lifetime of wounds. We had a perfect morning with them, but I'm excited to finally get home. Myles said he has a surprise for me for tomorrow. He made sure I didn't have any plans, so we could be together all day, and I've never been so anxious.

25

MYLES

Glancing to my side, I watch Hunter sleeping soundly against my shoulder, her arms intertwined with mine. Our plane took off about an hour ago, and her eyes fluttered closed soon after. Pulling out a book from my bag, I scan the cover. Her dad gave me a few books to read about auctioneering. He was supportive of trying to help me get the promotion, and I'm grateful for his help.

Every so often, I steal glances at Hunter, and I can't get over the fact that she's mine. I soak up all the uninterrupted time to take her in. She's wearing jean shorts. I love seeing her in what she wears to work, but these tiny shorts aren't leaving much to the imagination, making my thoughts run wild. They show off her sexy legs, and it's hard for me to keep my hands to myself. Her baggy T-shirt hangs off her shoulder. Because of our morning fun, we didn't have time to shower. She threw her hair into a large messy bun on top of her head. She didn't have time to put on makeup either, and I love it. She looks beautiful with the few freckles peppering her skin. I could look at her all day and learn new things about her body, which I plan to get to know more as soon as possible. The thought causes my dick to jump in my joggers which is the last thing you want to wear while having a boner. I adjust myself casually and go back to reading to keep myself distracted.

About an hour later, we walk through the Orlando airport. People run in all different directions with their suitcases dragging behind them. There are many families wearing their Disney souvenirs, and kids holding their favorite movie stuffed animals. The airport has never been one of my favorite places, but I couldn't be more happy to be home, especially while holding Hunter's hand. Looking over my shoulder at her, I watch her beautiful face light up, a smile growing across her face. The moment is broken when someone shouts Hunter's name. A giddy Jess runs as fast as she can toward us. Hunter's laughter echoes around the airport as she drops her stuff before launching into a run. They wrap each other into a hug and laugh again uncontrollably. Behind their giggling forms, I notice a familiar face walking closer. It seems like Jess left JT in the dust to get to Hunter faster. Picking up all our luggage, I walk to my friend and clap him on the shoulder.

"What are you doing here?" I ask.

JT motions to Jess. "She told me that she wanted to be here when you arrived, so I offered to drive her." He shrugs.

I watch as JT looks at Jess. He doesn't just offer to bring a girl to the airport for no reason, but I'm not going to push him on it. "But neither of you had to come. I left my truck here," I tell him while watching the girls squeal and talk over each other. I have no clue what either one is saying though.

"Yeah, I know. I tried to tell her." He motions toward Jess. "But she wouldn't hear it. Said she had to be here because she needed more *details*. Any clue what she's referring to?" He turns to face me, lifting an eyebrow.

"Nope," I say, popping the p. "Alright. Let's grab the girls and get out of here. There's no telling how long they will squeak." We walk toward the loud women, hoping to be able to herd them toward the parking garage.

JT grabs one of the bags off my shoulder. "It doesn't seem like either one has taken a breath since they started"— He pauses assessing them —"talking? Is that what they are doing?" He finally looks at me with his brows furrowed.

I shrug. "Your guess is as good as mine. We better get used to it though."

"Yeah? Why's that?" he asks, then whips his head back to me.

I ignore him and look at the girls. "Come on, you two. We gotta get outta here." They both sigh seemingly forgetting that they live together. They lock arms as they waltz to the parking garage, while JT and I follow close behind. I watch as Hunter whispers something into Jess' ear, and Jess gasps, bumping her hip into Hunter. Of course, that makes them break out into a fresh fit of giggles.

As we walk up to our vehicles, Jess says, "JT and I will meet you two at the house. I made dinner and there's fudge brownies with vanilla ice cream for dessert." She winks at Hunter.

Hunter squeals, hugging Jess for the hundredth time since we landed. This girl can be one of the most professional auctioneers one minute, and such a giggling schoolgirl the next. JT slings his arm around Jess' shoulder, breaking the girls apart. Hunter and I look at each other with surprise and watch as they walk away.

"What is going on there?" I ask and look at Hunter, who's already whipping out her phone.

"I don't know, but I'm going to find out."

She immediately starts texting Jess. My eyes go to Jess and watch her pull her phone out of her back pocket, peaking over her shoulder to look at Hunter. Jess turns toward us, walking backward, and JT looks at her like she lost her mind. He drops his arm and she raises her hands and shrugs her shoulders as if to say, she has no clue. Grabbing our luggage, I throw it into the back seat and open the door for Hunter to climb in. She's standing there, texting Jess, her fingers flying over the screen.

"Hey, Hershey," I say, but she doesn't acknowledge me. "Uh, you ready?" I laugh. She whips her head toward me, a smile stretching across her face. God, she's beautiful.

"Coming!" Pocketing her phone, Hunter launches herself right into my arms, barely giving me any warning to catch her.

I grunt.

"Oh, am I too heavy for you? I guess you did miss a gym day while we were gone. Already out of shape, old man?" she teases, patting my stomach.

"Ha. Ha." I lean over, pressing my lips against hers. As I place her back on her feet, she spins around and lifts a leg to climb in the truck and those damn shorts tease me again. Without hesitating, I let my hand fly as it smacks her curvy, tight ass. She squeals, whipping around to face me. There's fire in her eyes, and the corner of her lips lift. I see the challenge in her face as if to say she will get me back, but it only makes me more excited. I peck her on the lips and close the door.

My hand lays on her thigh the whole drive, drawing little circles with the pad of my thumb. She keeps her hands on my forearm, either scratching or tracing my tattoos the whole drive back to her house, asking rapid fire of questions when she finds a tattoo she hasn't asked about yet. My hand periodically gives hers a light squeeze, and I can't help but think how I could get used to this life. She rattles on about how Jess evaded her questions about JT, which makes my eyebrows furrow. Knowing JT, that's not like him. He usually tells me about a girl he's sleeping with. The only time he has ever been quiet about a girl is when he actually likes them which has only happened once since I've known him.

"It would be amazing if they got together," Hunter says, her fingers squeezing my arm.

I continue to rub my fingers up and down and around her thigh. It's relaxing. "Yeah? How so?"

"Well, we could double date. Oh, there will probably be days where we are all sleeping at the same house. We could also all go riding together. You said you have a boat. Oh, it would be so much fun to go boating together. Could we do that soon?" She looks over at me with a hopeful look in her eye.

I chuckle and shake my head. She definitely has the lungs of an auctioneer, being able to talk fast without taking a breath. "Yeah. So you think we're always going to be sleeping together?" I ask, having a hard time keeping a straight face.

"What?" She whips her head to face me.

"I mean, you're assuming an awful lot about me if you think I sleep with anyone in my bed." My cheeks ache from holding back the smile. Glancing her way, her face is scrunched, lips pressing into a thin line. I burst out laughing, unable to hold it in anymore.

"Myles Johnson! You are such an asshole!" she shouts and slaps me on the chest. I continue to laugh uncontrollably. "What is your middle name?"

"I'm not telling you. You yelled at me." I point my finger in her face, and she bats it away. "I know you will use it against me. If you think I'll tell you my middle name, you must be crazier than I thought." I laugh when she glares at me. I don't think I've ever laughed as much as I have these past two days with her.

"Fine. I guess I'll have to ask your mama." She faces forward again with a huff.

"Oh, now you want to meet my mama?" I tease her. I pull into her driveway, and she immediately unbuckles. I think she's going to bolt out of the truck, but she surprises me and climbs into my lap straddling me with her legs. The memories of this morning come flooding back, sending a jolt of pleasure right to my groin. Her pupils are blown, and I know she's thinking about the same thing. I wrap my arms around her and my hands cup her ass.

"You drive me crazy, Myles Johnson."

Her hand flicks my hat off, and her fingers snake into my hair. I waste no time and press my lips to hers. I love the feeling of her moving against me. Nipping her bottom lip between my teeth, I can't help but get lost in our kiss. I haven't made out with anyone in my truck since high school, and it's the little things like this that I'm really enjoying with her.

"Alright, you two."

JT taps on our window, making Hunter jump in my lap. I sigh, leaning my head back against the headrest.

"You're making me lose my appetite. Let's go eat, and for the love of god, keep your tongues inside your mouths." JT's entire body shivers and walks inside the house.

"I guess we better get in there," I say, lightly rubbing my thumb against her cheek.

Her eyes flutter. "I guess so. Don't want him to come back out and drag us inside." Her teeth graze her lower lip.

"Well," I say, a little more huskily. "Maybe he would send us to your room as punishment." Her arms wind around my neck, crashing her lips into mine. *God, I can't get enough of this girl.* I don't want to break this kiss. I know JT and Jess are waiting, but I couldn't give a flying fuck. She places her hands on my chest and pushes me away when my fingers slide up the bottom of her thighs and under her jean shorts and find her wearing a thong. My dick springs to full hardness. She opens my truck door and practically jumps out like she won't be able to stop herself if she continues to touch me. I laugh, and she glares at me while walking inside her house. I breathe in deeply, attempting to calm myself before I get out of the truck. Grabbing my hat before closing my door, I feel JT staring at me from the entryway.

"The girls are doing a lot of squealing again. I can't make heads or tails of what they're talking about," he admits, rubbing the back of his neck.

I laugh because he seems so out of his element. He's used to flirting with girls but not hanging out with them. Actually, I'm not either, but I'm enjoying it. A lot.

"You seem happier. I'm guessing based on you practically mauling her in your truck that the trip was a success." JT wiggles his eyebrows, and I shove his shoulder as he laughs.

"Yeah. It actually went better than I hoped." I slide my hands into my pockets. "I mean, there were a few bumps, but it was great. Her dad's awesome too. You would like him."

"Dude! I'm jealous you got to meet Conrad Smith. Now that you're dating his daughter, you'll be an auctioneer in no time." He smiles.

Of course I still want the job, but I'm realizing it isn't the most important thing in my life anymore. I now have an amazing girl by my side, and I don't think life could get much better.

"You like her a lot, don't you?" he asks, but there isn't much question in his voice.

"Yeah. There was some shit that went down at the gala. She was hurting, and I hated it. It only made me want to protect her," I admit.

He smiles at me. "Okay, Moondoggie. Let's get inside to the women. Maybe you can help me figure out what the hell they are squeaking about." He claps me on the shoulder.

26

HUNTER

TOSSING the last of the decorative pillows on my bed, I can't wipe the smile off my face. Last night, Myles went home when JT did, reluctantly. Then Jess and I had a much-needed girls' night, watching movies and eating loads of ice cream. Although, we didn't actually watch much of the movies because we were too busy talking about all the events that took place while I was gone. She fanned herself at the steamy parts, and we laughed all night. She updated me on everything work-related. She also told me how much she and JT had hung out while I was gone.

When I walk out of my bedroom, Jess is already awake shuffling around in the kitchen, looking exhausted.

"Morning," I say through a yawn.

"Morning." Her voice sounds sleepy.

"I guess you're only a morning person when you don't stay up most of the night?" I giggle, and she glares at me. I put my hands up in surrender. "Well, Myles texted. He and JT are picking us up in thirty minutes. We need to bring bathing suits, jeans, and closed-toed shoes." Her eyebrows furrow when she looks at me. "Don't ask me. I don't know what's going on today. But we need to get going because we don't have much time to get ready."

With that, I turn around and head back into my room to take a quick shower. I wrap myself in a towel and do my hair, leaving it to air dry. I skip makeup and put on my purple bikini and jean shorts with a cropped T-shirt over top. After stuffing a towel, a change of clothes, my boots, and some other things I could possibly need into a bag, I'm ready. I walk out of my room and Jess is finishing up too. She has on her red bikini with beige shorts and a loose T-shirt. She stuffs the last of her things into a bag when a knock at the door, bringing us out of mindless packing. I dart to the door in anticipation. She rolls her eyes at me when I nearly crash into it before throwing it open.

My sexy man stands in the doorframe, looking like an absolute vision. He's in black swim shorts and a gray T-shirt. The shirt hugs his arms and shoulder muscles perfectly. He's wearing his worn hat backward, and he smiles at me. I jump into his arms and kiss him. He wraps his hands around me and grabs hold of my thighs, making sure I don't fall. I hear someone clearing their throat, and my eyes fly open. JT stands behind Myles. He looks a little embarrassed to be there, but we are blocking the doorway.

"Oh, hey JT," I say through a giggle, my cheeks heating in embarrassment. I wiggle and Myles gently puts me down.

"That's it, Fun-Size? Oh, hey JT." He mocks me in a high-pitched girly voice. "You launch into his arms and kiss him, but I get an, oh hey?"

I laugh at his teasing, walk over to him, and kiss him briefly on the cheek. I don't think he expected it because his face turns bright red. I turn back around to see Myles' arms crossed over his chest with his eyebrows lowered.

"What?" I walk past him before he can say anything. "You ready Jess?" I yell out. Nickelback comes barreling over to greet the guests. Both men sit on the floor to give him all the love he so desperately thinks he's lacking as if he's not spoiled rotten.

"Yup. Do you think we will need condoms?" she yells back.

Both of the guys stop giving any attention to Nickelback, and their heads whip up. The dog whines at the loss of attention.

Jess pokes her head out of her room. "Gotcha!" She looks at them, and we both laugh hysterically.

The guys look at each other and give small laughs. But they still both looked stunned and unsure. They don't know what they've gotten themselves into for the day.

"So where are we headed, boys?" I ask as we all pile into Myles' truck. The two of them climb up front while Jess and I make our way to the back together. Myles wanted me up front with him, but she tugged on my hand to follow her to the back. She didn't tell me much of what's going on between her and JT, but I get the inkling that she wants more. She isn't sure if he feels that way too, or if he's playing her. His reputation doesn't help. So I know she's trying to guard herself around him.

"We're going to my house," Myles says.

My eyebrows furrow. "We could have met you there. You didn't have to pick us up." Myles looks at me in the rearview mirror, making me smile. I am excited to see his house for the first time. I've imagined what it looks like, but I can't wait to see the real thing. He told me the view's amazing out the back of his house. It's nice we all live fairly close to one another, which is a miracle since we work all over the state. He reaches over the seat and hands me my favorite morning drink, a Mocha Frappuccino. JT also hands a drink to Jess. I don't miss the way her cheeks turned a little pink at the gesture.

"We wanted to make sure you were properly caffeinated, and I wanted to pick you up." Myles shrugs.

Jess leans over and nudges me with her elbow, and I can't help but feel a flutter in my stomach with how sweet he is.

When we pull into his neighborhood, I see the lake in between each house as we pass. We park in front of a small, white house with black trim. It's on the edge of a large lake with a wooden dock. We all walk inside, and Myles grips my hand tightly. I know he wants me to like it, and I already love it.

I spin around, and my eyes can't focus on one thing. There are so many details that make this place a peaceful haven. It's exactly what I imagined. In front of a huge flat-screen TV mounted on the wall is a large cream sectional couch. With an open floor plan, the kitchen is across the back of the house with a big island in the middle, and the kitchen windows look out over the gorgeous lake. The beauty of this place takes my breath away. All the details remind me of Myles. On the open shelves, his black dishes are on display. The picture above the couch is of a Texas Long-horn which adds a certain bachelor pad feel. I sense Myles' eyes watch me as I take everything in.

"Alright! Enough looking around. Let's get on the lake!" JT yells, and Jess claps her hands with excitement.

I smile and grab Myles so we can run after them. His boat is black with a large engine. There's a tube hanging off the back, along with a kneeboard and a wakeboard tucked inside. Jess and I jump onto the front and lounge on the padding while the guys untie the boat.

"Hm. Would be nice if I had another hand," JT says sarcastically, looking at us shamelessly suntanning.

"Thankfully, you have two of them." Jess peers over her shoulder and pulls down her glasses to look at him. "Unless one of them is too busy jerking yourself off."

Myles and I burst out laughing. Jess winks at JT, and he's giving her a little more heated look than before.

Myles starts the boat, and he takes us around the lake. I relax into the seat, wind whipping my hair. I feel free compared to the past two weeks I spent with my parents. After about fifteen minutes, Myles cuts the engine.

"Alright, ladies. You're up," he says to us.

Jess and I look over at him, confused. "What do you mean we are up? We're busy." I motion to our tanning bodies.

"Oh, believe me, I love the view." He laughs. "But you're going tubing."

I look at the tube and then give him a questioning look. He comes over to me and pulls me into his lap. Jess walks over and talks to JT while he's getting the tube in the water.

"What is it, Hershey?" he asks gently and tucks some of my wild hair behind my ear.

I bite my bottom lip nervously. "I dunno. I have never been on a tubey thing before." I look down at my hands in my lap. He gently tilts my face up, so I look at him and gives me a small kiss.

"I promise, you will love it. Just hold on tight." He pauses, seeing my uncertainty. "Do you trust me?"

My eyes flick right to his. "Yes," I say with no hesitation in my voice.

"Just try it." He kisses the tip of my nose.

"Okay."

I can't stop my hands from shaking. Myles zips up my life-jacket and starts on the buckles. I look all around. I know there are gators in basically every body of water in Florida. Why are Floridians stupid enough to get in the water with them? Why am I stupid enough to do it? I look over and Jess is just casually talking to JT. I can't seem to focus enough to know what she's saying. I jump when a hand goes to hold the side of my face.

"Hey." Myles gently strokes my cheek with the pad of his thumb. "You okay?"

I quickly nod my head a few times and continue looking around the body of water for any gators, but the water is too murky to tell. I would only be able to see one if it was swimming on the surface. One could easily take a bite of my leg off if I fall.

"Even I can see that you aren't." Myles gently tilts my face back to meet his. "Want to tell me why you're nervous?"

I can't see why this isn't something everyone is worried about. I look over at Jess again, and she's still as cool as a cucumber and has no signs of being nervous or terrified. Both feelings, I am currently overwhelmed by.

"Gators," I say flatly. When he doesn't say anything, I look at him and see a smile forming that he is trying hard to hide. "Hey!" I give him a shove. "They could eat me."

Myles belly laughs, bringing the attention of JT and Jess. "Sometimes I forget that other people aren't used to gators."

"I'm not crazy! You guys"—I point to each of them—"are the crazy ones. They could eat us out there!"

"Fun-Size." JT grabs my shoulders, forcing my eyes on his. "I've been stuck floating in the water on this lake more times than I can count. This asshole"—he points to Myles—"decides frequently to fling me off the tube or leave me when I fall off the wakeboard. He just takes off and leaves me floating in the water like a damn buoy."

"Well, that doesn't make me feel any better." I glare at Myles.

"Listen, I'll be in the boat. I'll take him out if he tries anything," JT says, winking at me.

Myles wraps his arms around my waist, making me feel safe in his embrace. "I will not leave you. Besides, gators leave people alone in the middle of the lake." He places a kiss on my favorite spot below my ear. He pulls back, meeting my gaze again. "Wait, can you swim?"

I nod before taking a deep breath.

"Come on. Let's have some fun." Jess grabs my arm, pulling me toward the tube.

Jess and I get on the tube, and I'm relieved we can go together. It makes me feel better knowing someone will be floating out there with me if we get flung from the tube. She shows me where to put my hands, and I grip tighter than a bow string on the handles. Myles explains the hand signals to give if we want him to go faster, slower, or stop. I listen as if my life depends on it. I'm nervous, but I tell myself, I can do this. JT helps untangle the rope as the boat gently trolls forward.

Once we are all the way out, JT yells for us to hold on tight. The boat roars to life and my stomach feels like it has left my body. I'm holding on for dear life. Thankfully, Myles goes straight for a while. I can feel the water pegging us lightly in the face, and I can't help but start to enjoy myself. Myles keeps peeking over his shoulder, and his face lights up when he sees me smiling.

He starts to maneuver the boat in small curves, which makes it a little harder to hold on. Then, after ensuring we can hold on after a few of those, he tries some sharper turns which makes us fly out to the sides. Somehow, Jess and I are able to hold on. Her laugh vibrates through my ears, as we focus on holding on for dear life. After a few minutes, we go over a wave that launches us high into the air. We both lose our grip and fly. The smack of my body against the water takes the breath out of me, and I choke a little on the cold water as I swim to the surface with the help of the life jacket. I hear JT cheering something while I see them whipping the boat back around to pick us up. Jess isn't too far away, and we start swimming toward each other. I focus on my breathing as I swim closer to her, and my eyes scan the lake just in case there is something swimming closeby.

"Well? Did you have fun?" she asks once we are close enough.

"Yes." I laugh. "The fall hurt like a bitch, though."

That was one of the most exhilarating things I have ever done.

THE REST OF THE DAY, the boys take turns on the wakeboard, and Jess even attempts a few turns on the kneeboard. I enjoy lounging while I watch all of them. Myles pulls me onto his lap now and then while he's driving. It's thrilling being out on the water like this with my friends. I feel so relaxed in his arms, and I can't help thinking how special this whole day is that he planned for all of us. As the day goes on, we start to see even more chemistry between Jess and JT, which only makes me happier. With a few playful shoves from Jess, JT finally says, "fuck it," grabs Jess, and jumps in the water with her over his shoulder, her screams almost shattering our eardrums.

Later, we float while we enjoy the sandwiches, chips, and sodas the guys packed for all of us. I can't remember the last time I had this much fun.

"Okay, Myles you have to tell me how the trip *really* was," Jess says after a little while. "I've heard all about Hunter's mom. How did things go from your perspective?" I groan, but Jess doesn't take her eyes off Myles.

"Honestly, Hunter's mom is pretty terrifying." He laughs, and my head snaps to him.

"Hey!" I yell.

"She is, and you know it." His shoulders shake with laughter. "I'm not used to moms like that," he admits and looks down like he said too much. I nod knowing what he means.

"Man, you girls will love Mama!" JT says, smacking his hand on his thigh. "She's the best, and her cooking. . ." He hums and rubs his stomach.

"In that case, I can't wait to meet her." I meet Myles' gaze, and I can't help but smile. I want to meet his mom. I don't know when that will be, but she sounds like someone I would love.

"Um. Actually." Myles rubs the back of his head, his gaze now fixed on the floor of the boat. "She asked if I would come by today. I haven't been over to check on her since before my trip." He takes a peek up at me. "I was hoping you would come with me?"

I have to stifle a nervous laugh. It took over twenty years for my mom to show me a glimpse of affection. I want his mom to like me, but what if she doesn't? She's extremely important to him and meeting her would be a big deal.

"Um," I stutter.

"We have more things planned for today, so it would just be a quick visit."

I nod and smile. I know he really wants this, and I can deal with my nerves, just like I did on the tube. After all, if he was willing to meet my mother under less than ideal circumstances, the least I can do is meet his.

"Okay. What are we doing later?" I ask, sipping my soda.

"You'll see. JT and Jess will meet us there." Myles winks, making butterflies swarm in my belly.

"Well, I can't wait to meet your mom!" I say cheerfully. JT cheers and Jess gives me a wink. She knows I'm not comfortable, but I can see she's glad I'm stepping out of my comfort zone. I've heard many amazing things about his mom, but I can't help but worry that she won't accept me like my mother doesn't. I lean over and kiss him on the lips.

"Ewww! Come on guys! I'm eating over here." JT groans, and we all laugh at his childish behavior.

27

MYLES

My hand is on Hunter's thigh while I drive us to my mama's house, and I'm nervous as fuck. But I suspect my nerves don't come close to hers with the way her thigh hasn't stopped bouncing since we got into the truck. I have never brought anyone over to meet her. I also didn't give her a heads-up that I was bringing anyone. I didn't want her to be ready with any baby photos or other embarrassing ammunition she might use against me. I also know she would have cooked a damn six course meal to keep us there all night. She had told me something needed to be fixed on her refrigerator. I'm going to try to take care of it as soon as possible and get us out of there, but I thought this would be the perfect opportunity to introduce her to Hunter. I already know Hunter will love her, but I'm praying mama stays on her best behavior.

We pull into the driveway, and Hunter looks around. Her hand reaches for the door handle, but she pauses when I don't make a move to get out.

"Are you okay?" She grabs my arm. "Crap. You have been so quiet on the ride over here." She lets go and tucks her hair behind her ear and starts fidgeting with her shorts. "This is a big step. Are you having second thoughts?" She rings her fingers together in her lap. "I want your mom to like me. What if she doesn't because I don't know your middle name? Or what you take in your coffee, or how old you were when you first learned to ride your bike?" Her knee bounces, and I can see she's panicking more by the second. "Maybe you can give me some cliff notes on how to get her to like me? I'm not good with moms, well at least not with my mom. I've never had experience with any others. Well, except Steve's mom, but I lump her in with my mom."

She's spiraling and talking way too fast. I can't catch everything she's saying or decipher what she means. I don't know how to get her to stop, I try to speak. But I don't think she has taken a breath since she started this whole speech. I grab her face and kiss her. She takes a minute, but I feel her relax into the kiss, leaning into me a little more. It feels good to be able to kiss her whenever I want. It's a high having her body respond to my every touch. I can't help but get a little carried away even though it was supposed to be a short kiss. She jerks herself back with such force, I almost fall forward.

"Myles!" She gasps and covers her mouth as she looks at the house. "What if she's looking out the window and sees us? Oh, my god, she's going to hate me!"

She covers her face with her hands, and I smile at how cute she's being. It means so much to me that she wants to make a good impression. I have no doubt she will, but it's cute watching Hunter freak out a little.

"Hershey, no one's going to hate you. She'll love you, and she actually doesn't know you're coming."

She looks confused and goes to speak, but I place a finger over her lips. If she keeps talking, we will never make it inside.

"I didn't want her to embarrass me with childhood stuff. She's the one I'm worried about. Okay?" I assure her, my finger still mushed into her lips so she nodded. "Okay then. Let's go." I get out of the truck and open her door. She hops out, and we head toward the door.

"Can I say one thing first?" Her steps falter. "What if I want her to show me all the embarrassing childhood stuff?" she asks, giving me big sad puppy dog eyes.

I shake my head, knowing I'm going to be in trouble with these two. *Fuck. . . this girl.* I laugh and put my arm around her waist to get her to start walking again.

"God, help me," I murmur, knocking on the door.

"What?"

But before I answer, my mom swings the door open, but she's not looking up as she messes with her dress.

"Miney! Call your mother first before showing up here an hour early. You never know if I'll be home or if I'm decent," she says, finally looking up at me, and her eyes bug out of her head. "Who's this gorgeous woman?" She smiles.

I lean forward and kiss her cheek then look at my phone for the time. "Mama, I'm not an hour early. You told me to come now, so how's that showing up here unannounced?" My eyebrows furrow, she's not making any sense.

Then Gus comes around the corner buttoning up his shirt. "Oh, hi Myles. Great to see you again." He clears his throat.

"Mama!" I know my face is turning every shade of red as my ears grow hot.

"Oh, hush." She waves me off. "Like you don't know that your mother has needs just like any other woman, and I guess we just lost track of time."

I rub my hands over my face. This is not how this was supposed to go. We just got here, and I already wish I would have stayed on the lake with Hunter.

"Um, hi. I'm Hunter."

I peek through my fingers to see Hunter waving at my mom. She seems so nervous even though this is already a shit storm. I sigh and do my best to not think about what was just happening.

"Mama." I sigh. "This is Hunter," I say, wishing I could pluck my eyes out. But Hunter doesn't deserve me losing my shit over this. Mama blinks at me because I've never mentioned Hunter to her before this. I put my arm around Hunter's waist to bring her tightly tucked up against my side. "She's my girlfriend, Mama." Her shocked face morphs into the most elated expression I've ever seen.

"What?" She screams, making Hunter, Gus, and I cringe from a pitch I didn't even know was possible. "She is…" She can't even form a complete sentence.

This might be worse than baby pictures. Hunter's going to think there's something genetically wrong with me. My mom's freaking out that I brought a girl over.

"Mama," I say again more firmly. This seems to make her snap out of it, and she launches at Hunter and squeezes her into a tight hug. Hunter laughs, her joyous laughter, making me relax a bit.

"Hi. I'm not sure of your actual name. He and JT always call you just Mama." Hunter laughs out.

I know she's nervous, but she's perfect. My embarrassment fades as I watch the two most important women in my life embrace in a hug. Mama finally pulls away but keeps a hold of Hunter's shoulders.

"Oh, sweetie. Please, call me Mama! It would make me the happiest woman alive. Oh, please, come with me. I want to hear all about you." Mama walks inside still holding Hunter close to her side.

"Okay. I'll shut this door for you, Mama," I call after her and shake my head.

"Thanks, Miney! Don't forget the fridge while you're at it," she says over her shoulder but focuses back on Hunter. "So how long have you been with Miney?" I shake my head.

"Mama. Please! Don't use the nickname. Can't you just call

me Myles for once?" This was a mistake. Why did I do this to myself?

"I believe it's actually Myles Alexander, Miney." Hunter winks.

THEY TALK the entire time I'm fixing the refrigerator. Of course, Mama pulls out a secret stash of photos she has easily accessible, as if she were waiting for a moment just like this to bust them out. When I finish the repair, it's impossible to pull them apart. Even though I act like I'm annoyed, I loved seeing how Mama embraced Hunter. I also saw the way Hunter got so comfortable with my mom. It made my heart swell. We stay a full hour, and they act like they are the best of friends. I hate tearing them apart, but when I see it's getting close to four, I know we have to leave. I don't want to miss out on what I planned for us tonight. They finally say goodbye, and I had to promise Mama that we will visit again soon. She even gives me a deadline, which make Hunter laugh.

Back in the truck, Hunter rolls her head against the seat to look at me. "I love your mom."

I reach over and squeeze her thigh. "I can tell she loved you too. Thank you for that."

"Are you kidding me? She's amazing. I can't wait to see her again."

I groan which makes her laugh.

"Come on, I didn't find anything out that makes me like you any less, Miney," she teases me by using my nickname. I fake a groan. "I mean, it honestly made me..." She trails off, but I snap my head over to look at her.

"Made you, what?" I'm white-knuckling the steering wheel with one hand, and I'm not sure if she still has feeling in her thigh with how hard I'm squeezing. She doesn't seem to notice. She keeps looking at my forearms, tracing my tattoos like she loves to do.

"It made me like you a lot more." Her voice is quiet.

I'm happier than I have been in a long time, and I can't stop the urge to want her in my arms. As I park the truck in JT's driveway, I unbuckle our seat belts and grab hold of her legs to bring her over to sit with me, moving my seat back so we have more room. I tuck some of her wild hair behind her ears. I want to commit every last detail of her face to memory. I gently rub her cheeks with the pads of my thumbs, and her eyes flutter closed. I lean in, making our lips ghost over each other.

"Oh, Hershey," I say, giving her a brief gentle kiss. "I'm so far gone for you, I don't even know which way is up or down anymore." She gasps, and I kiss her hard using her parted mouth as an advantage to kiss her deeply. Wrapping my hands around her back, I bring one hand into her hair to thread my fingers through. She melts into me, and I groan with how perfect she is. It makes me want to say fuck it and take her home so I can bury my face between her legs. It's been over 24 hours since we've had sex, and my craving is intensifying by the second. She's perfect in every way. Her toned legs are clutching mine while she's straddling me. I pop the button on her jeans and slide my hand inside so I can feel how wet she is. "Fuck me. You're soaking wet." I growl out.

"It's all because of you. I've never wanted anyone the way I want you."

She looks into my eyes. I slide my fingers inside of her which makes her gasp. I love pleasuring her. I kiss and nip at her neck. She's so beautiful. I pick up the pace, and she rides my hand trying to find her release. It doesn't take her long till I feel her spasming. She moans out my name, and it's the sexiest thing I've ever heard. Her body relaxes against me, and we hold each other for what seems like forever.

There's a banging on the window, making us jump and look to see JT wiggling his fingers at us in greeting.

"We have got to stop meeting like this." He smirks.

Hunter's like a statue in my arms not wanting to face him.

"Alright! We're coming." I wave my arm to shoo him away. She buries her hand-covered face into my neck and shakes her head as soon as he's gone. I laugh and try to pull her away to look at her. "Hey!" I continue laughing. She won't budge, and it's freaking cute.

"No!" she shouts, sounding like the little girl on Lilo and Stitch.

"Come on," I coax and gently scratch her back to get her to relax.

"No. I never want to see JT again." She groans, then pops her head up and gasps. "This is horrible!"

I bite my lip to hold in my laughter, and she shoves my shoulders.

"This is serious, Myles!" she screeches and shoves my shoulders.

"Come on. He doesn't care, he's messing with you," I say while opening the truck door and motioning for her to get out. She glares, but reluctantly steps down and walks toward the front door. I'm relieved until she spins around and bolts back to the truck. She looks at herself in the side mirror and tries to fix her hair. After all the wind on the boat this morning and then me running my fingers through it, there's no hope. She flips her head and ties it into a messy bun. She checks the button on her shorts again and then sighs, like she's hyping herself up to go inside. I try to hide my smile as she slowly walks back toward me. I grab her hand and kiss it before opening the front door.

"Finally!" JT yells from across the room and laughs. "I hope I didn't interrupt anything out there, Hunter." He walks toward her, giving her a wink.

"JT!" she screams and balls her hands up by her sides.

He laughs uncontrollably, and I eventually join in. She shoots me a death glare, making me hold my hands up in surrender. I slowly go out back to where Jess is taking in the view. I look over my shoulder and see JT fling his arm around Hunter's shoulder whispering something to her, and she looks mortified. But she shoves him and starts laughing.

They join us outside, and JT asks, "Seriously, how's Mama? And did she make me anything because I'm hungry!"

"JT, we literally just ate," Jess says and shakes her head.

"Eh, that was a snack. Besides, I'm a growing boy." He wiggles his eyebrows which makes me roll my eyes.

He's ridiculous sometimes.

"No, she did not. She was too busy embarrassing me," I complain.

"She was the sweetest! Jess, you would love her. I can't wait to see her again. She made him promise to bring me back. Right, Myles Alexander?" Hunter snickers.

JT covers his mouth with his hand to try to cover his amusement, and I give him a hard look.

"She middle-named you in front of your girlfriend? See what I mean? She's the best," JT exclaims.

"I love her, and I haven't even met her yet," Jess admits.

"Alright. Is everyone ready to go?" JT asks.

Hunter gives him a quizzical look. "Go where?" she asks.

I snake my arm around her waist and bring her right up against my chest.

"We're heading to my favorite place, where I go every Sunday evening," I say, giving her a hint. Her eyes light up.

"We're going horseback riding to the creek?" she asks in an awe-filled whisper. I nod my head and kiss her forehead. She squeezes me and takes off running to the barn, grabbing Jess' hand as she passes. JT and I slowly follow behind them.

"I'm glad to see you so happy, man. You deserve it," he says and puts his arm around my shoulders.

"Thanks. Anything you want to tell me about you and Jess?" I give him a knowing look.

He smiles and rubs his jaw. "Not yet. But I'm hoping maybe soon," he admits and looks down. I slap him in the stomach which makes him let go of my shoulders and give a little fake cough from the impact.

"Don't wait too long. Take it from me, it's way better to be happy with the girl than to be unhappy without the girl."

He nods his head. "Yeah. You lucked out," JT says.

"You're fucking right I did." I watch my girl kissing my favorite horse. She's standing on the bottom board of the fence. The brown horse looks like he's hugging her with his head draped over her back. Hunter looks over her shoulder at me and gives me the biggest and most beautiful smile, and I know I'm done for. I don't know when it happened. But somewhere along the way, I've fallen for this short, feisty, wild-haired woman with the most beautiful green eyes. I finally understand what it feels like to be the highest bidder.

EPILOGUE
HUNTER

"Cheers!" We clink our glasses, crowded around a pool table.

"Miney." Mama grabs Myles by his shoulders, yanking him to face her after taking her fourth shot of whiskey. "I'm just so damn proud of you, son." Tears well up in her eyes.

"Okay, Mama." JT gently unravels her white knuckles. "It's your turn to kick my ass." He gives her a pool stick. Her face morphs into glee.

Jess hunches over, putting her hands on the side of the pool table. "That woman has to be knocking back Coke or something, right?" Her glazed eyes meet mine.

It's true. Mama seems to have a very high alcohol tolerance. She just shot back her fourth shot, while the rest of us only knocked back our second, in the past two hours. Myles' eyes land on mine. He's told me about all his memories growing up, when he'd attemped to get her drunk. He was never able to get her wasted enough to have a hangover the next day. I giggle when Mama winks at me. She let me in on her secret, saying she had to keep them on their toes. She had told the bartender to make hers half coke and half rum, heavy on the coke.

Myles grabs my hips, planting a kiss on my lips. Even after

almost a year, his kisses still give me butterflies. It's hard to believe it's been a whole year since I moved here. I wasn't sure I would like it, or if I would make friends. Now, I look around the bar and watch most of our work friends all hanging out an enjoying a round of pool together. Looking back into Myles' eyes, a smile spreads across my face.

Myles tucks my hair behind my ear. "What?"

"You did it." My hands tangle in his shirt, and I nudge him. "You finally have your own lane. You're an auctioneer, Myles!" I can't help but beam up at him with pride.

The auctioneer, Aaron, decided to take his family and move across the country. Each GM called Myles separately, offering him the job. I'll never forget the look on his face. He's waited so long for this and worked so hard. We invited everyone out to celebrate.

"Can you guys move?" JT pokes Myles with the pool stick. "I'm trying my best not to let Mama embarrass me too badly."

Jess walks up, wrapping her arms around JT's neck, and sways a little. "You're so hot."

I cover my mouth to stifle my laughter. Jess is such a lightweight, but I've loved watching their new relationship blossom.

"Thanks, babe." He kisses her on the forehead. "Have you eaten the appetizers or had any water to drink?" JT stalks behind her to make sure she has something to soak up the alcohol rolling in her belly.

Jess giggles, grabs his biceps, and stumbles as he walks her backward. "You are so strong. What are you doing later?" Her attempt at wiggling her eyebrows nearly makes me lose it.

JT looks at her tenderly. "I think a sleepover on the bathroom floor is in *our* future."

"JT, are you going to keep this old lady waiting, or what?" Mama signals to the bartender to get her another drink.

Giving Myles one last peck on the lips, I pry Jess away from JT and take over getting her something to eat so JT can continue his game. He plants a kiss on Jess' temple and goes back to lining up his next shot.

"HERSHEY! ARE YOU READY TO GO?" Myles calls from the living room. I woke up late so I'm rushing to get ready.

"You kept me up late last night after getting home from the bar." I pull my bra on over my head. "Then, you didn't wake me up before you went to the gym this morning!" I yell from my bedroom, throwing a shirt on. His head peeks inside the room.

"You weren't complaining last night," he says, his voice gruff.

I roll my eyes.

"You could have woken me up before you left this morning. That's all I'm saying." I look in the mirror, trying different hairstyles. "What's the big deal anyway? We're going for a horseback ride. It's not like the horses have somewhere else to be," I shoot back with a sassy tone.

"Oh, believe me, I tried to wake you up before I left, but you sleep like the dead. I shook you, talked to you, kissed you. Surprisingly enough, you even responded to me a few times. But you never remember these things and always claim I didn't try to wake you up."

I shake my head. There's no way he did all those things.

"You must not try hard enough to make sure I'm awake. I'm almost ready, okay?" I flip my head over, settling for a messy bun since my hair won't cooperate for anything else. He sighs and walks into the living room. I pull on my boots and grab my Yankee baseball hat just in case. "Ready!" I walk out of the bedroom to see he already has the front door open. I roll my eyes at as I walk by. "Love you, weirdo," I say. He shuts the door and wraps his arms around my waist, walking wide-legged behind me.

He snuggles his face into my neck and kisses me right below my ear.

"I have to keep you on your toes. If I always acted the same, you would be bored." He playfully tickles my side, and I screech, trying to squirm away. He stops and kisses my neck again. "But last night was all about celebrating. Mama hasn't stopped texting me today. She seems more excited than I am."

We definitely celebrated. His mom's something else, and when we got back to my house, we celebrated in a more intimate way. I get butterflies just thinking about it.

"Of course, she's excited. We're all so proud of you. You have worked your ass off, and now you're finally the full-time auctioneer you've always dreamed of being. I'm going to miss you being my ringman though." I pout getting into his truck. He pecks me on the lips and shuts the door. I watch him rub the back of his neck as he climbs into the driver's seat.

"It feels surreal. I won't believe it until my voice feels worn out from announcing cars all week instead of just during the breaks," he admits.

We pull up to JT's house and walk inside. Jess is sitting at the kitchen island, covering her eyes and massaging her temples. She groans when we shut the door.

"Not too loudly," she whines. Nickelback barks and comes barreling over to greet me. Jess groans again. Myles and I kneel to greet him before walking toward Jess.

"Where's my perky morning friend?" I tease. She really does look like shit. Her hair is standing up all over the place, and she's wearing baggy, wrinkled clothes and somehow has on only one sock.

"This girl can't seem to keep up with how Mama parties." JT emerges from out of his bedroom and kisses Jess on top of her head.

The gesture makes me smile. They officially started dating six months after we did, and it has been the best thing. The four of us are always hanging out.

"Jess, I warned you." Myles shakes his head. "Mama's like another breed when it comes to partying. It's impossible for her to get drunk," Myles says, looking out the back windows toward the stable.

"She kept giving me drink after drink after drink..." Jess looks over at me, and I jump a little. Her makeup is smeared all around her eyes. She even has a smudge of something on her jaw. "It's not like I could tell a little old lady I couldn't handle it." She rubs her head again trying to ease the pain.

"Here, babe. This might help." JT sets some strange concoction in front of her.

I don't even want to know what is in it. It looks disgustingly orange with something floating in it. My stomach rolls just at the sight.

"What the fuck is this?" Jess's eyes look up to JT, pleading with him not to make her drink it.

He strokes her back and shakes his head. "You don't want to know."

"Okay. We're going to go for a ride," Myles states, grabbing my hand and basically dragging me out of the house.

"See you later, Fun-Size." JT waves.

Poor Jess looks like she's trying to convince herself to consume whatever JT has given her.

"Myles, I'm coming!" I say, a little frustrated.

"I'm sorry, Hershey." He pulls me into his chest and kisses the top of my head once we are outside. "I'm just excited to show you something."

"You have a surprise?" I squeal. His smile spreads across his face.

"Yeah." He rubs the back of his neck. "Can we go now?"

Instead of answering, I run to the barn and realize the horses are already saddled and waiting. I guess JT was in on the surprise is.

"Hey, Gizmo! Who's a good boy?" I nuzzle the brown horses's nose as I take carrots out of my purse and break off pieces to feed him, planting a kiss on his soft nose. Myles mounts his horse, so I take his cue and hang my purse in the tack room and get mounted too.

When we start riding, I lead my horse down to the creek where we always go.

"Hershey, we are going a different way today." Myles nods in another direction.

I give him a questioning look.

"Trust me. You're going to love it." He gives me a wink.

We ride for thirty minutes, but it's never boring on the back of a horse. The large oak tree leaves are rustling in the wind as the horses keep a steady pace along the dirt trails. Countless chirping birds flying overhead, and flighty wild bunnies zip by on our ride. These woods are one of our happy places. We could ride through here for hours. Myles leads us around another corner, and begin to hear a steady flow of water trickling. Myles turns to grin at me. I'm so excited to explore a new spot together.

We must be on one of JT's neighbor's land. I'm not surprised we have permission to explore it because all of the adjoining properties here have formed a tight-knit community, often riding together or helping each other out on their farms.

"Here we are!" He watches as I take it all in.

The bright sun peaks through the branches of the large oak trees surrounding the whole area. The grass and bushes are over-grown where there isn't a path to walk into the stream easily. Myles takes out a machete from his saddle bag and clears a little spot for us to sit and toward the water. The running water is clear, and I can see the pebbles scattered across the bottom.

Myles spreads a blanket close to the stream before we strip down to our bathing suits. It's still hot this time of year, even though it's technically fall. Fall is more of a state of mind here in Florida.

I wade into the water and let out a sigh. The water always feels good after a long horseback ride. The creek has a steady flow, and I go straight for the middle of the stream, where the water reaches my chest. Myles comes in after me and pulls me into his damp chest. I love feeling the cool water flow all around us. I admire the way the water bounces off the rocks along the edge. The oak leaves flutter in the breeze, like they are dancing for us. It's so peaceful here. I wish could stay in this moment forever.

"You know what day it is today?" Myles asks, pressing a kiss right below my ear.

I shake my head and tilt my head up to him. I love how tall he is. It makes me feel safe in his arms. He gently kisses my lips.

"It's the day that I first called you my girlfriend at that gala." He smirks. "Your mom looked like her eyes were going to pop out of her head, and that guy, Simon, was glaring at me." I swat at his chest and turn in his arms, so I can face him.

"His name is Steve." I laugh. "I remember you dropping the girlfriend label in front of everyone. I was in so much shock, I didn't think I heard you right." I sway. "Then we danced as if the world around us disappeared. It was amazing." That night holds some of my favorite memories. There were many unpleasant things about that night, but it was also one of my favorite times with Myles.

"Oh, don't forget the billiard room." He winks, and I laugh.

"Yes, I don't think either of us could forget what happened there." I kiss him on the cheek and snuggle back into his chest, feeling the water flow around us.

"It's also the day I realized I had deep feelings for you. I don't think I ever had a chance since the first day you walked into the auction. I've been yours ever since." He kisses my temple. "You mean everything to me, and I want to give you everything you could ever want." His eyes are full of such love and affection.

"Well, now that you are an auctioneer, I think you can afford me now." I laugh at my attempt at a joke. He continues to smile at me like I hung the damn moon.

"Do you like it here?" he asks, motioning to the nature that surrounds us.

"Here? I always love going on dates with you where we can enjoy the sun in the cool water."

"Would you like to live here?"

I look at him puzzled, not sure I'm understanding. "What?" I ask, giving him a "you can't be serious" look.

"I bought it—all twenty acres. There's a house, a barn, a chicken coop, a well…" he keeps listing things and my jaw drops.

"Myles! This is yours?" I gasp. "You bought this place? It's perfect!" I break out of his arms and spin around.

"Yeah?"

He wraps me in a hug before my hands push against his chest to look at him. "But you love your lake house."

He nods. "I do, and I'll keep it and rent it out."

I walk further down the stream to see everything because now it's not only some stranger's stream. It's *his*, and I want to know everything there is about it. He grabs my hand to stop me from getting out of the water. I turn around and look at him.

"Will you live here with me?" he asks, and I thought I couldn't be more shocked than I already was. "Hershey, I love you. I want to wake up every morning with your wild crazy hair trying to suffocate me."

I can't remember ever feeling this happy. I was hoping one day soon that we might live together. But to do it here, in the most peaceful area with friends right next door seems unfathomable.

"Myles!" I screech out. "Of course, I'll move in with you!" His face lights up, and he swings me around in circles, sending water splashing all around us. He stops and gives me the most passionate, perfect kiss. I love this man with every fiber of my being.

"Do you want to ride down and see the house? *Our* house?"

"Yes!"

His hands grab the sides of my face as his lips crash into mine.

I chuckle and place my hands on his chest, pushing him back. "What are we even still doing here?"

I spring out of the water toward the horses. I throw my reigns over the neck of my horse and mount, leaving behind my clothes. Myles quickly swings his leg over his horse and nudges his horse toward the trail again. The horses seem to sense our urgency and quickly make their way further down the trail until the woods open up into a clearing. About a half a mile in front of us, stands a large two story white house with a wrap around front porch. It looks older, in need of a little love, and absolutely perfect.

Myles reaches over and holds my hand, bringing my hand to his mouth for a brief kiss. My heart soars inside my chest looking at this man. This is the start of a new chapter together. Teasing, challenging, caring, and loving each other. Nothing could be better than that.

Bonus Chapter

Scan the QR code if
you want more steam.

ACKNOWLEDGMENTS

I honestly can't even believe I'm writing this. I never thought I would ever do something like this. Now, here I am, and I couldn't be more grateful for those who helped me get here.

My husband and best friend, I couldn't have done it without you. All the times you would be in the shower, and I would sit on the toilet or pace the bathroom trying to work out a scene that wasn't working. You always gave me the best ideas or planted a seed, and I would leave as quickly as I came to go write it down. You encouraged me always to keep going and never had a doubt I could do it.

My girls: Charley, Blake, Logan, and Lyric. You have been so excited during the whole process. I remember you all asking why I was going to an indie author boot camp because you thought I already knew what I was doing. I didn't/don't, but you've always had faith in me. My baby girls, you are my world.

My betas… honestly this book is legible because of all of you.

Sarah, you pushed me to write in the first place and volunteered to beta for me before I even had a sentence down. When I came to you saying I had an idea, you told me to sit down and write. Your faith in me meant more than I can ever portray. I'm eternally grateful for you! You had to read the first and worst draft of this book…thank you…and I'm so sorry!

Tisa, you're such a badass, and you brighten my day. I love your bluntness and value it so much. All the voice messages, helping me figure out scenes, pushing me to make the biggest plot changes, and being awake late at night because you're across the country and help me with any of my late-night writings. Also, you kept me motivated when I was discouraged and just told me to get it done. I needed you!

Heather, your knowledge and selflessness blows me away. I pretty much screenshot any information you tell me because I know it's gold. I remember buying your very first book (didn't even read it till your second came out because I used to hate to read), and I was blown away thinking that I know an author of a book. I am so thankful for you and your friendship. I've needed someone like you in my life, and I love having play dates to talk books and life with you.

Kort, I have loved learning all of this together. There is something about learning with someone else at the same time. I've had so much fun getting to know you and being able to talk plots, characters, and just wondering what the fuck we are actually supposed to be doing together.

Kali, you are so unbelievably smart. I thought you would be a proofreader, but you far exceeded my expectations. Your comments and suggestions helped me so much, and I really am thankful that you are willing to answer all my questions about punctuation, grammar, and sentence structure. You are always ready to give me suggestions while also being so encouraging.

Dad, thank you for believing in me. I know you also did it for Mom because she always wanted to write a book, and she loved to read.

Mom... thank you. You got me my first job at an auction. I remember driving to Tampa with you every Thursday for two hours, then going to St. Pete right after. We always would talk about what auctioneer we worked with. Being a block clerk was such an amazing job. You always calmed me when I had to work with an auctioneer that was a lot faster than what I was used to. You always told me I would be fine, then you were relieved when I said that I was after the sale. You were also the person that I would talk to during the long drives to and from all the auctions. Thank you… I miss you…

Finally to my readers, I've been blown away by the support I've gotten. So many people have said that they can't wait to read it, and it just is mind-blowing to me. You've inspired me to keep writing.

ABOUT THE AUTHOR

Dawn Anderson is a contemporary romance author who writes RomComs with open-door spice. She lives in central Florida with her husband and four daughters where most of her writing is done in her youngest daughter's bed as she sleeps with her little feet touching Dawn.

With an imagination that has run wild since she was a child, Dawn has found a love for writing and an outlet to make her ideas come to life.

A wearer of many hats—teacher, gardener, homemaker, DIYer, bookkeeper, and sports chauffeur—It's obvious her family is her life. Her hope is that by showing her girls that you can always learn something new and accomplish anything you put your mind to, they will see any dream is possible.

@dawn.anderson.books